Praise for *Pretend It's My Body*

"Luke Dani Blue defies every expectation in these ten ravish-
ing, razor-wired tales about transition. These characters hang
between genders, between stations, in the future of ten minutes
from now stuck in some essential way and struggling for a
way forward. In *Pretend It's My Body*, everything is possible,
and yet, life in the flesh proves maddeningly resistant to the
pressure of individual desire."
—**JANET FITCH**, author of *White Oleander*

"*Pretend It's My Body* is a wonderful collection, capable and
sure-footed as a pacesetter, and at once funny, jarring, disorienting, and bracing in turn, like trying to use a credit card at a
carnival. Unrushed, but with a real center; each story distinct
yet kind, afraid neither of ugliness nor loveliness. I liked it
marvelously well."
—**DANIEL M. LAVERY**, author of *The Merry Spinster:
Tales of Everyday Horror*

"These stories unsettle, secrete, vibrate with the incommensura-
ble tensions of being more than bodies, genders, consciousness.
In Luke Dani Blue's work, 'identity' gets ripped apart and recon-
structed into something marvelous, possibly dangerous. Blue
has put words to realities that I have known without ever being
able to articulate."
—**JOSS LAKE**, author of *Future Feeling: A Novel*

"Blending psychological realism and the supernatural, these
stories ooze queerness, horror, and a wild eeriness. This book,
an electrifying debut, will haunt you long after you've put it
down."
—**JULIÁN DELGADO LOPERA**, author of *Fiebre Tropical: A Novel*

"In *Pretend It's My Body*, Luke Dani Blue portrays each of their characters as having their very own (often sexy, always queer) logic—logic that is constantly d/evolving as they act, revealing compelling combinations of desire and determination, longing and intelligence, grief and (no small amount of) humor. In each paragraph of each story, Blue gives me what I want from fiction: intellectual surprise and thrilling, jagged mishmashes of intense emotion. An absolutely thrilling debut."

—**MATTHEW CLARK DAVISON**, author of
Doubting Thomas: A Novel

"Luke Dani Blue's debut short story collection is a twisted, tense triumph of a book that at once resists a cis gaze and insists that everyone, regardless of gender, has experienced moments of intense transition. The stories are imaginative, the characters idiosyncratic, and the sentences delicious."

—**A.E. OSWORTH**, author of *We Are Watching
Eliza Bright: A Novel*

PRETEND IT'S MY BODY

PRETEND IT'S MY BODY

STORIES

LUKE DANI BLUE

THE FEMINIST PRESS
AT THE CITY UNIVERSITY OF NEW YORK
NEW YORK CITY

Published in 2022 by the Feminist Press
at the City University of New York
The Graduate Center
365 Fifth Avenue, Suite 5406
New York, NY 10016

feministpress.org

First Feminist Press edition 2022

 This book was made possible thanks to a grant from the
New York State Council on the Arts with the support of
the Governor and the New York State Legislature.

First printing September 2022

Cover art by Luke Dani Blue
Cover design by Drew Stevens
Text design by Frances Ross

Library of Congress Cataloging-in-Publication Data
Names: Blue, Luke Dani, 1983- author.
Title: Pretend it's my body : stories / Luke Dani Blue.
Other titles: Pretend it is my body
Description: First Feminist Press edition. | New York, NY : The Feminist
  Press, 2022.
Identifiers: LCCN 2022022417 (print) | LCCN 2022022418 (ebook) | ISBN
  9781952177033 (paperback) | ISBN 9781952177781 (ebook)
Subjects: LCGFT: Short stories.
Classification: LCC PS3602.L838 P74 2022 (print) | LCC PS3602.L838
  (ebook) | DDC 813/.6--dc23/eng/20220510
LC record available at https://lccn.loc.gov/2022022417
LC ebook record available at https://lccn.loc.gov/2022022418

PRINTED IN THE UNITED STATES OF AMERICA

To Migueltzinta, for all of it

We have begun to walk again. We had stopped to watch it rain. It did not rain. Now, we are walking again. And it occurs to me that we have walked a greater distance than we have gone. That occurs to me. Had it rained perhaps other things would have occurred to me.

—Juan Rulfo, "Nos han dado la tierra," translation mine

Contents

Certain Disasters

Other kids always want to know about the tornado. They ask what it was like to be carried through the air, if that's why my little brother is such a nutjob, and did I see my life flash before my eyes? No one ever asks what happened after the tornado ended, what other disasters it made possible. That's because most kids don't know there is more than one kind of disaster. Disasters like the tornado happen in public, lit up for the whole world to see. Those disasters get broadcast on the evening news, and the next evening's news, turning a nothing like me temporarily famous. *That's the tornado kid*, people say. *That's that kid from TV.* But there are secret disasters too that happen in cars and shadowed corners, or in the dark of your own mind. Secret disasters are invisible. That's the hardest part. There's no proof, no witnesses. Half the time—at school, when I'm surrounded by people—what happened then doesn't even feel real. But if I close my eyes, I am right back in the moment after the tornado ended. Waiting, in the beams of those headlights, to fall or fly or be destroyed.

SINCE DAWN THAT morning the wind had been gusting gravel up against the siding. For a while it hailed, small stones of ice that pinged and clanged off the Oakleys' metal-roofed shed. Yellowish-green streaked the sky and the sirens went off. It should have been exciting except that every June there were almost-tornadoes that turned out to be nothing. The weather was holding me hostage, and I was stuck with Kyle and Deb, my younger brother and older sister, in me and Deb's tiny bedroom. Mom had another migraine, so no raised voices allowed or even TV with the volume on low. If the Nintendo still worked, I could have been finding new warp zones in Mario Brothers, but Kyle had spilled juice on it and Mom had said what did I need video games for anyway, didn't I want to go hang out at the mall like other girls? Deb stuck out her tongue at that. She had her own opinions about how I should be spending my free time. She thought I should be doing extra homework to get on honor roll. Like I wouldn't end up working at the Stop-n-Save, same as every other loser from our loser town.

Kyle and I hurtled from my bed to Deb's, seeing how high we could make the mattresses flop, how long it would take for Deb to go bitch to Mom. Deb must have memorized a tornado safety pamphlet because she just swatted our ankles and whispered for us to come down on the floor. "It's not safe up there. The windows could blow out."

"We're. Not. Scared." I punted a velvety, heart-shaped pillow into the light fixture.

"WE-ARE-WILD-MEN!" shouted Kyle, beating his baby Tarzan chest. I joined his chant, and we bounced across the room, kicking pillows, stripping the mattresses bare. From the other room, I could hear Mom groan.

Deb glared at me, proof she wasn't that worried about the weather. "You're copying a kindergartner, Leah."

"Lee," I corrected. I hated my full name.

"Yeah, well, when you get to junior high, there are different expectations . . ." This was Deb's usual lecture, only last year it had gone, *In the sixth grade . . .* and next year would be, *In the eighth grade . . .* She'd given this speech when I'd used my training bra as a slingshot, when I'd mooned the gas station guy, when I'd put gum inside her friend Cissy's jelly sandal and made her shriek like a gerbil. Smile more, went Debbie's basic argument, and the older girls won't dunk you in the faculty toilet.

"Like you're some popularity expert," I said.

"Poop-u-larity," Kyle said.

Sulking, Deb rubbed at her glasses' lens. "Real friendships don't even happen until college."

I punched the whiskered nose of Deb's stuffed cat and tossed it to Kyle. We threw it back and forth as the sky darkened and the hail returned, clattering against the window. I tossed the cat at the window. It bounced off. Kyle screamed. I screamed. In seconds, the icy chunks grew to the size of Kyle's fists. We screamed each time one hit. Deb covered her ears.

It was the sudden quiet that shut us up.

"Lee?" Kyle sank down onto the mattress. Deb scooted in next to him, their noses pressed to the glass. I made a joke about nuclear bombs but got down too. The sound had drained away like water from a tub. Nothing felt that funny anymore.

Deb pushed open the window. "Listen." All I heard was a hiss like radio static, the suck of our thighs unsticking from our calves. Then, faintly, from within the hiss: a train whistle as the twisted sky rushed in.

ACCORDING TO THE news footage, the tornado moved
our house half a block, setting us down between the faded
crosswalks, at the intersection where our street crossed
with a major road. All I knew then was that I needed to get
out. I shoved past Deb, past Mom's hoarse "Leah?", out
onto the front steps. Except of course the steps weren't
there. No truck tire knotted in morning glory or splin-
tered fenceposts that no one had got around to painting.
Instead: rain, and a string of traffic lights draped over
the edge of the roof; wet asphalt; glass shards pricking
my bare feet. The rain was so loud I didn't hear the car
coming. I was wiping the water out of my eyes when my
brain made sense of the headlights. *Move*, I thought, but
stood there frozen.

The car skidded to a stop just short of running me over,
its bumper panting hot air. I smacked the hood. My arm
did it automatically, like it, not me, was angry.

Through the windshield, the driver of the car gaped.
His shape lined up perfectly with my own reflection, his
shadowed chin in the shadow of my chin, his dark eyes
inside my eyes. If I'd have looked away, maybe the second
disaster would never have happened. But the rain on the
windshield warped the driver's face into mesmerizing
shapes, and we stared at each other for way longer than
you're supposed to look at anyone. His ordinary features
kept blurring into other men's—my dad's, Mel Gibson's, the
nasty Stop-n-Save cashier's, who winked at Deb and gave
us random discounts. I sank into those faces, my body
flickering with powerful feelings that disappeared before
I could name them. Pictures channel-flipped through me.
*A red and white cigarette box. A fist crunching cartilage.
Dust in denim. Metal chain taut.* Each one hurt like a stab

to the brain. When I closed my eyes, the pictures only got brighter and bigger.

"LEAH! WHERE HAVE you been?"

I spotted Deb's pink headband before I recognized her, drenched and wrung out as a load of laundry. Kyle was like a laundry sack, leaning crumpled against her. Random neighbors moved between ambulances and firefighters, picking through the household objects that scattered the road. A pair of kids were kicking around the shade from our living room lamp. A dented canister of Mr. Clean stood on a mailbox as if delivered by the mailman.

Deb peered at me. "Have you gotten checked by the EMTs?" Laundry-sack Kyle stared at the ground. I reached for his damp hood, but he flinched away.

"What's wrong with him?"

"He's fine," said Deb stiffly. Before she could say more, the news crew came over. I had always thought it would be cool to get interviewed, but when the reporter asked what it was like being inside a tornado, I just mumbled something because I couldn't remember.

My fifth grade teacher used to split these yellow apples with his bare hands. He'd walk around the room, holding the two halves parallel with a gap in between. The gap made a ghost shape that matched the break. "Negative space," he called it. That was how my brain felt. In one apple half was the scream of the approaching tornado. In the other, the driver of the car with his pictures and warping face. In between, a crack that was empty and full at the same time. The crack, which was only an idea or a feeling, nothing real, buzzed with weird energy. But that wasn't the sort of thing you could say aloud to the Fox 8 viewing audience.

"What's that, sweetie?" asked the reporter.

I glanced down at Kyle, glued to Deb's side. He scowled back like he didn't know me, his lips moving. I bent over. Breath damp in my ear, he grunted, "You man of paper."

"What?" I said, but Kyle's face pinched shut and he ducked inside his hood.

MOM WAS HAVING her arm wrapped by an ambulance guy. She gave me a watery once-over like just having to look at me tired her out. "You're okay."

I said I was though I really wasn't. The negative space feeling was getting worse, and I kept missing things inside the buzz. It was like having an idea on the tip of my tongue, except the idea was whole chunks of my life, like the name of my fifth grade teacher, and just, time. How long had the ambulance guy been waving a finger in front of my face?

"Good eye-motion," he said. He shined a penlight. I blinked. In the blackness, *running, the pound of dust-packed earth, whomp of a canvas base, a cluster of boys in striped uniforms cheering.* I'd never played on a base-ball team.

"Are you listening?" said the ambulance guy. Police were tying yellow tape around the house, which was lean-ing up on one side like a person struggling out of a pair of pants.

"Was it like that the whole time?" I asked.

"Was what like that?" said Mom.

"Shrug," ordered the ambulance guy. I shrugged. "Swal-low." I swallowed. "Blink."

His fingertips fluttered onto my eyelids and lifted away.

AT THE HOSPITAL there was too much light. Mom was having a cast put on, and Kyle was "getting tests." No one would say for what. I waited behind a curtain. Every time I moved, the paper-covered exam table crinkled under my hospital gown, setting off new pictures and sensations in my head. *The heavy paws of an orange dog, fall sun warming my skin. A teacher slapping a failed quiz onto my desk. Me, pissing on fresh snow.*

I'd always wanted a dog, not orange but black and wary like the mutts that prowled around the Stop-n-Save, and while I annoyed plenty of my teachers, the school desk in the picture was wooden and unfamiliar, its chair bolted on. But the peeing felt so real—the heat of my dick, the *sss* of snow melting where pee hit—that I had to pat my crotch to make sure all my usual parts were in place.

"It's normal to be confused after a bad scare," said the doctor. She'd given me a full exam, run the metal stethoscope across my chest, and banged the rubber mallet on my knee until I remembered to kick.

"It feels . . . un-normal." I tried to explain about the driver of the car, and how the pictures had spilled into me—something to do with negative space? Maybe a negative space that was already inside me, sucking the pictures up like a vacuum? I smiled to show I knew how bonkers that sounded.

"Hm," said the doctor, not listening. She carried her clipboard out through the curtain. I lay down and watched ghosts in the light, waiting for more pictures. I was afraid but wanted them to come. Even if it was bonkers, I liked being away from myself in those bodies of boys and men.

Deb pushed through the curtain and dropped a bundle of donated clothing on the bed. "Get dressed. We're going

to the Tans'.'" I could have listed a hundred reasons to spend
the night somewhere, anywhere besides our gross neighbors', but the fluorescent light cast green shadows down
Deb's cheeks that made her look too old to argue with. I
put on the clothes. They looked like what they were, other
people's garbage. The shirt, a lacy-collared thing, fit okay,
but the tapered jeans ballooned my hips and showed ankle.

"I'm not wearing these."

Deb cradled her bony elbows. "So go naked." She strode
out without looking back. I shuffled behind in the castoffs.
On the pay phone, Deb talked like a grown-up, telling the
cab company to get us from the loop out front.

"What about Mom and Kyle?"

Deb said they were keeping Kyle for observation and
that Mom had to stay with him, that they thought something might be internally wrong. She would come back
to the hospital after dropping me at the Tans'. She was
going to stay overnight to make sure Mom didn't mess
anything up.

"Let's both stay."

"No, Leah."

We stared into the parking lot, the red taillights of
cars, the women fumbling in purses for keys. I thought
about Kyle, drifting like paper in our levitated bedroom.
I hoped I'd grabbed him, tried to protect him, but probably I hadn't, or he wouldn't be screwed up now. The scene
was a blank. Had some version of my disaster happened
to him? At least I had the logic to sort out the negative
space pictures, but how could a little kid tell the difference between real and pretend? The last Halloween, Kyle
had bitten his teacher just because he was wearing a tiger
costume. He'd made her bleed.

"Is he going to be okay?"

Deb didn't answer.

MRS. TAN, neighborhood-famous for walking her schnauzer in only a bathrobe, opened on the first buzz. She was wearing that stringy robe over a pair of Dr. Scholl's. The dog yapped on the doormat.

"Thanks so much for letting Leah stay over," said Deb in her new parental tone.

"Yeah, sure." Mrs. Tan kicked at the schnauzer. I peeked past, looking for the Freak. The Freak, a seventh grader at my school, was also neighborhood-famous: for thick black eyeliner, carving band names into her arm, and reeking of cigarette butts. The Tans' house reeked worse than the Freak did.

"Pee-ew. Do you want me to get lung cancer?" I said, hoping to embarrass Deb into taking me with her. It didn't work. Deb apologized to Mrs. Tan about my rudeness, but Mrs. Tan was already wandering back to the sofa and the TV. I stood on the threshold in the warm dusk air, waving as Deb's cab drove off.

"Michelle's in her room," said Mrs. Tan, pointing to the staircase. "I told her to change the sheets."

Halfway up the stairs, the dizzying pictures returned and I had to sit. *Flexing skinny muscles in a rolled-up flannel shirt. A teenage guy dodging out of a liquor store, grinning. He uncaps a beer on the brick wall. It tastes like ocean minus the salt.*

"Hey." The Freak leaned against the banister. She wore underwear and a shirt with a skull on it. "You going to sleep there?"

With the feeling of beer sliding down my throat, I

entered the Freak's room. It had its own odor, spicy and sweet and funky. Drifts of fast-food wrappers and other junk covered her floor. "You smoke?" She waved a lit brown cigarette, releasing wafts of the spicy smell, and fell back onto the bed, throwing her legs across the sheets. "I got so wasted last night," she said, like we were in the middle of a conversation. "I got totaled. Trashed. People were talking to me and I was like, ya-ya-ya." She laughed and tilted her head, as if listening to the chatter of a party. "You ever get trashed?"

"I drink beer for the taste," I said, the sour-bitter flavor still in my mouth. "Not to get drunk."

"For the taste," the Freak repeated, like it was a riddle instead of a line I'd stolen from Mom's boyfriend. She patted the bed, inviting me to join her freaky, pajama-less pajama party. From downstairs, a commercial blared. "I've fallen and I can't get up!" cried one old person after another, their skinny butts thunking on the carpet. I'd seen the ad enough times to picture them lying like abandoned dolls, awaiting rescue.

"You can step on that stuff." The Freak crooked her big toe at the mess on the floor: grease-stained Domino's pizza cartons, wadded underpants, scissors, and shreds of *Playboy* and *Sassy* pasted together so the models had four heads and twenty eyes and boobs stuck all over like pustules. The pages were sticky underfoot, gooey. Avoiding the Freak's gaze, I climbed on the bed, lay down against the wall, and pulled the sheet over my head. As soon as I did, the pictures came back. *A beach highway at night. More ocean-bottom beer. I'm riding in a car with the top down, the guy next to me in the passenger seat. I'm pushing the pedal. Making us go faster and faster.*

"Ew, crotch rot," said the Freak. "Sleeping in pants will suffocate your beav." My crotch, which a second ago had been full and hard, packed into jeans, was back to being girl stuff and also, supposedly, on its way to going bad. It seemed believable. I wriggled out of the preppy clamdiggers and rolled over, determined to ignore whatever else the Freak said. Through the pillow, I heard another cigarette being lit. I was back inside the pictures. *He sucks in on the cigarette, flicking ash into the wind. Whoa there, cowboy, he hoots, meaning slow down and speed up and this feels good.* "Anyway, I'm still pretty hung over."

I pulled the pillow away. "I can't sleep with you talking."

"Lame," muttered the Freak, but she clicked off the lamp. Orange glow from the Stop-n-Save seeped around the blinds, dyeing the trail of smoke and spotlighting the Freak's semi-developed chest. She crossed her legs and sucked in on the cigarette. The tip glowed bright, that same parking lot orange. I saw how smoking could be pretty.

"I want to try," I said. She passed it over. The paper softened instantly in my mouth. I passed it back without sucking.

"Sick," said the Freak, when she felt the wet paper. She stabbed out the cigarette and arched, kind of, her nipples poking out the fabric of her shirt.

My dick started to swell.

I didn't have a dick.

The man/boy body had crept up from the back of my mind. I guessed how Kyle must have felt with his tiger costume on and how he must feel now in the hospital. Caught inside a tornado, even though from the outside he seemed to be on solid ground.

"I bet you have shell shock," said the Freak. "After wars, soldiers get these blackouts where they stab their own babies and shit. My cousin had that happen. He'd come downstairs in the middle of the night and eat everything in the fridge, then have amnesia about it." Like it was a normal thing to do, the Freak reached over and stuck her fingers in my hair. Every nerve in my body ignited. My ghost dick, my negative space, pressed into my underpants.

"What happened to him?" I whispered.

"Shot out his brains." The Freak slid down until she was lying across from me, our noses nearly touching. The thought came to me that she might really be crazy, but somehow I was okay with that. "So. What was it like?" Her voice hummed in the backs of my knees where the damp grass whispered, a memory my body had before it was mine.

"What was what like?"

She rained her fingers down my face and dragged at my lip, letting it spring back like a rubber band. "The tornado, dummy."

I wanted to do stuff to her. My body, my double-visioned body, was too much, had gone past the point where I could bring it back. I clenched my hands tight to stop them from grabbing where her shirt had ridden up, the piece of soft waist made for touching. I guessed I'd gone crazy too.

As if she could read my twisted, ungirl-like urges, the Freak rolled away and sat up, shaking out a cigarette from the pack. She had to be disgusted with me. I was. I willed the pictures back, wanting to be anywhere else, but they wouldn't come. The Freak flicked her lighter. "You have to tell me," she said sternly and then went into a moaning "tellme tellme tellme" that made me unsure of everything, the crazy, the disgust, the man-body. Which parts of this were normal, and if I'd even ever wanted normal. Deb was normal. Normal-ish. I didn't want to be Deb.

I pushed back into the wall, scooched upright. "It was like . . ." The wheel on the Freak's lighter wouldn't spark. She flicked it over and over, frowning at the metal. "It was like," I repeated, as if saying it again would bring back the disappeared memory, those minutes that the tornado had sucked away, opening a space in me that demanded to be filled. That's how it was with disasters. They broke you and put you back together in new, incomplete shapes.

I took the lighter. "It was like this," I said, not knowing what I meant. A tiny flame burst up and went out.

"C'mere," she said. "We're going to teach you to smoke." Obediently, I leaned in and let the Freak tuck her cigarette between my lips. This time I pinched tight around its end to keep it dry. "Good," she said. "That's really good." She repeated that while moving my hands under her shirt, to the wiggly roll of her belly, these hands that might have been mine, squeezing of their own accord, while she bent closer.

Later, this is the part I'll tell. Not the touch but the kiss of fire in my throat. How it hurt and how I wanted it, and how that's what made it so confusing. Except I wouldn't say that exactly. You can't say stuff like that, unless you're a grown-up on a sitcom shrink's couch. Instead, I'd tell anyone who asked about the tornado, "That's the day I learned to smoke." Then lean into my lighter, like Michelle the Freak taught me, giving into the body inside my body. Feeding it another inch.

Suzuki in Limbo

By the time boarding was announced, the suit Suz had gotten tailored for her visit home had crossed the line from excusably wrinkled to full-on rumpled. The pants, taut against her thighs that morning when she put them on, now sagged, giving the impression that she had gained weight rather than lost it. The state of their clothing did not matter to many cons in her position, but Suz knew it was important to look her best when she shared her news. She wanted her mother to see her at her most embodied and powerful. It was about making sure her family understood this was a choice. She hadn't failed at corporeality; she was surpassing it.

"THE SEATBOX SIGN is now on. Please return to your enclosure for landing."

Suz's seatmate, a middle-aged woman with chunky thighs, squeezed back into the row with an embarrassed smile. Once, Suz would have returned the smile. Several years in the con community, however, had broken her of such habits. As the woman struggled to fasten a belt across her ample waist, Suz double-checked that the antimicrobial seat divider was locked in place, an irrational gesture. Airplanes, with their routine sterilization and filtered air, were some of the safest parts of meatspace. Still, the proximity to fellow passengers seemed unhygienic, and there was no knowing how the next generation of viruses would spread.

I am in my body, not of my body. Suz mentally recited the mantra she'd spent thousands of dollars in therapy to learn. Her anxiety climbed. She was a five now. Or, no, a six. She'd taken a sedative in the Uber, but nothing worked, not really. She could drug herself into oblivion but the problem was her prehistoric nervous system.

I am in my body, not of my body. It was a terrible mantra, the sort a corp would find comforting. The therapist meant well but couldn't understand that being in a body was the *source* of Suz's anxiety. The closer she got to her upload date, the more the wound festered under these Band-Aid solutions. It was no wonder thirteen percent of pre-transitioned cons committed suicide.

"Going home or visiting?" her seatmate said through their divider. Suz gestured to her earbuds. Ignoring the hint, the woman bellowed, "DO-YOU-LIVE-IN-DETROIT?"

Suz removed the earbuds, her lovely white noise replaced by engine roar and the cant of flight attendants soliciting passengers' trash. Already the black bag was overflowing with in-flight ephemera, evidence of corporeal wastefulness.

"I am only visiting," Suz said, as if she were her phone's quasi-AI.

"From here?"

"Mm-hm." Suz did not understand the fetish of treating biographical detail as if it equated to identity. Better to ask what digital communities she participated in. Those at least reflected personal preference.

"I live out by the mall. The nice one, out by the Nordstrom's?"

"Cool." To signal the end of the conversation, Suz turned to the window, where Michigan's thumb dug into the black of Lake Huron. The view aroused no nostalgia. She could almost smell the swampy grass (soaked with chilly rain), the St. Clair River's open-sewer stench. Nor did she feel eager to see her mother, stepfather, and stepsister, or the town where they lived and she'd grown up. Arborville was identical to small cities everywhere, a grid of big-box stores and cafés whose punny names ("Up Latte"; "DiviniTea") distracted from the deforestation, land theft, and caffeine addiction at the bottom of each cup. Even the grassy quad and party houses of the university seemed mass-produced. Suz had discovered this her first week at school out-of-state, GPS leading her past familiar buildings that might as well have been branded Corporate-Owned Price-Gouge Bookstore, Phi-Kappa-Date-Rape, A-Restaurant-Except-It's-Cereal, same as Arborville, same as everywhere except BKLYN and maybe Prague.

"Excuse me," said the seatmate. "How long did your makeup take?"

Pointedly, Suz reinserted her earbuds. *How long did it take you to make* your *ugly face?* She would have responded but why bother when, in two weeks, it would all be over.

SUZ'S MOTHER AND stepfather idled outside baggage claim in a new SUV emblazoned with a hydrogen symbol, as if it mattered what fuel it burned. For its carbon-cost, they could have flown to New York and back a hundred times.

"Suzuki!" Lew jumped out and squashed Suz into a nonconsensual hug. In the driver's seat, Allison, her mom, tapped the horn.

"*I see you,*" Suz said from under her clear N99. With her makeup and freshly shaved scalp, she had anticipated a bigger reaction. Well, wait until they heard about her impending upload.

"What are you supposed to be?" asked Kyra, her normie stepsister, when Suz climbed in.

Suz buckled her seat belt and, because her mother would be hurt otherwise, put the mask away. "Nothing. Myself." Suz leaned against the door, lips tight against foreign aerosol droplets.

"Your self is nothing?" Kyra smiled gummily. "That's why your face is a big black hole?"

Suz rolled her eyes, relishing how creepy that must look, wide whites glistening from within the optical illusion makeup. Usually, she went for subtle—an inch-long crack, an extra nostril. For this trip, though, she'd used a tube of black foundation to make a gaping absence where eyes, nose, and mouth should be. "It's a thing in New York."

One-upped, Kyra hunched back into the seat. "I'm hungry."

"Good!" said Allison, sounding congested. "We're almost to the lunch place."

Suz fought the urge to grab her N99. "If you're sick, can you lower the window?"

She expected a comment about "interesting" East Coast communication styles, but Allison only exchanged an unsettled glance with Lew. "I'm not sick."

So plucky Allison *was* perturbed. Suz didn't want to scare her mother, she wasn't a sadist, but Allison had to learn to respect her. Change was healthy. It was about not having illusions about each other in either direction.

She could use that line in her coming-out speech.

She hoped they were eating somewhere plant-based. She wanted her organs to be top specimens when they deleted her used body, Suz's red heart upraised like Simba in *The Lion King* to surgeons exclaiming *Not an iota of fat!* "Where are we going?"

Allison said the name of a kitschy pizza arcade in the northeast suburbs. She was definitely congested. If Allison got Suz sick and caused her to miss her upload date, it would be unforgivable. "We made the reservation months ago."

"Seriously?"

"It's not far," Allison apologized.

"You don't mind, Suz? DTW was a long drive for this kiddo." Lew craned around to pat Kyra's knee. His hand lifted and froze, as if he meant to touch Suz too but had a muscle memory of how many times she'd jerked away. It must have been muscle memory, because he hadn't listened the many times she had requested to not be touched. Lew was nice but an antagonistically bad listener. Par exemple, posing this question in a way that she couldn't say no. She did mind the detour, and, even if she ate pizza, this place, with its oil-slick cheese, would have been her last choice. Even at Kyra's age, commercial food disgusted her. While other kids ate, she peeled up the flab of mozzarella to grimace at the horror-movie-red sauce beneath. Suz hadn't been spoiled. She'd only gone to the pizza arcade if it was a classmate's birthday and if another family drove her. Even then, the place had seemed overcrowded and babyish. She'd stood by, embarrassed, as her friends buried each other in the ball pit, while cool, older siblings played with their phones. Suz would have forgotten about the place had it not been the site of the fifth grade party where she'd received her first dick pic. She wished she still had the pic, not for pedo reasons but because it had unlocked something in her. Something about desire and distance and how it felt to see the body of a boy she liked pared by a screen to its sexual essence. Something about being the sole recipient of the image even as its existence annulled her. When she held her phone, careful not to reply, she'd felt invisible yet omnipotent. Across the arcade, a boy awaited her approval. The longer she kept him waiting, the larger she'd grow in his imagination and the more porous her identity, until she flooded the space around him. If she never responded, she'd expand to fill his future, his desire for her to see him lurking in the gaze of every other girl for whom his head swiveled.

There'd been other boys later, high school guys with whom she'd gone "all the way" (before grasping that that act, too, was more powerful unconsummated), but the prepubescent sext still crystallized a moment of peak selfhood, when she had held so much power beneath her thumb.

Lew grinned in the visor mirror. "Happy to be home?"

In answer, Suz smiled wider. People thought a facial expression revealed one's feelings, but it was just muscles.

"I bet they don't have Corporal Pepper's in NYC," said Kyra snidely.

"Thank god," Suz agreed. She relished the thought of

never speaking again to Kyra once she'd set her consciousness free.

"Then I feel sorry for you," said Kyra.

"I feel sorry for *you*."

Kyra stuck out a slimy tongue.

Suz mashed the "down" button on her window, hopefully blowing Kyra's aerosol particles back into her mouth.

"Dad! I'm going to freeze!"

"Okay, okay." Suz powered the window up again. She reached into her purse for the N99.

Lew saw. "Oh, live a little."

"What's going on back there?" asked Allison.

"Suz has her mask out."

"Honey, you're with *family*." Implied: that shared DNA (or a legal distinction) was antimicrobial.

"We don't live together."

Allison's shoulders fell, as if Suz having a separate life were an attack on her parenting. She said something too quiet to make out.

"I can't hear when you mumble."

Lew craned around. "Al asked if you quarantined before traveling."

Suz inhaled slowly. They knew she lived clean—solo-habitating, working remote, ordering what little she needed by contactless delivery—but bringing it up would trigger her mother's anxiety. Allison called the lifestyle dysfunctional. The deluge of forwarded news articles had only recently stopped and Suz had no interest in restarting it. "Of course."

Lew patted the console. "We're all in the same boat then."

Suz knew her family's "quarantines" included in-person

grocery runs and long chats with neighbors, but she wanted this weekend to go smoothly so she put the mask away.

Allison cleared her throat. "Girls, Lew and I were actually hoping we could have a talk over lunch."

"About what?" asked Kyra.

"About family stuff," said Lew, as Allison said, "Something I should have brought up sooner."

Allison was clearly nervous, but Suz couldn't read more than that. It would have been out of character for her to wait months to tell her daughter about a medical diagnosis, and there weren't any close relatives whose death would warrant a Talk. The other possibility, likelier the more Suz thought about it, was that Allison had guessed that Suz was a con. Not in those exact words, but Allison read the news; she might have a sense.

The idea made Suz uneasy. She did not want to discuss her fucking metamorphosis amid the odor of processed meat. The plan was to bring it up right before her return flight. It had to be like ripping off a Band-Aid, otherwise she'd get sucked into supporting Allison. It was hard enough to stay solid in her con identity and choice to upload without the burden of her mother's reaction.

Wanting commiseration, she flicked open her phone screen before remembering: she'd deleted her crutches, the social accounts where closeted cons traded gripes, in order to make the coming change feel real. Her therapist had suggested Suz wait until she'd crossed over before dismissing her support system. But Suz needed urgency. To go through with the upload—to delete her own meat-suit—would require the bravery only desperation could inspire. Besides, social was where her confused former self had tried on avatars and shared CRISPR results while swearing she was just "experimenting" with posthumanism, she would never really upload, gross. Recalling her own denial sickened her; she didn't want to go back to those self-important biohackers but forward to join the true cons. The ones who'd gone all the way.

Only the most skilled hackers had ever breached con-space. They swore it was beautiful. Pure code, replicating and editing itself at a speed they could barely grasp, much less explain. Suz's upload date was only a few weeks away, but she wanted to be there already. Wanted it so bad it hurt.

"Are you crying?" asked Kyra.

Suz blotted her face, leaving black smears on her jacket sleeve. "Allergies."

CORPORAL PEPPER'S HADN'T aged well. Cracks crazed the plastic letters of the business's name, and the cement ass of the mascot, a bear in a marching band uniform, was tagged with the initials of junior graffiti artists. Kyra, indifferent to the neglect, dragged her father by the arm while Lew attempted to wrestle a sparkly N99 over her head.

Suz could have used a moment, but Allison, misreading, slowed to keep pace. "Hope the ventilation system's in better shape."

Thus far, Suz had avoided Allison's gaze; as their eyes met, the old power imbalance asserted itself, her mother's craving for approval sucking at Suz like undertow. It had always been this way, Allison nursing a wound that Suz could not remember inflicting.

A group of kids in party masks in the entrance cut them off from Kyra and Lew. Through the tinted glass, small bodies shrouded in protective gear could be seen swarming the game floor; parents wore masks but clumped up in nonfamilial clusters that belied true safety concerns. *So loud,* mouthed Allison, raising her pale eyebrows. Suz, blasé, like *What did you expect?*

Neither of them moved to enter.

"How are things in New York?" asked Allison.

"Fine."

"Really? Because you've been so secretive."

"It's not like you tell *me* everything."

"That's true. I'm sorry."

Something about the apology reminded her of a night when she'd been sick and couldn't stop coughing. Allison had swaddled her in a blanket and they'd shuffled around the block. She remembered her mother's reassuring grip and the stars extra bright overhead. Her mother might not be perfect, but she did her best.

"I'm sorry too."

Allison smiled. "You go first."

Part of Suz wanted to resist, but another part was remembering how Allison could be easy to talk to. "I've discovered who I really am. Which should feel good, but—"

A woman balancing with a cake box held the door open. Allison waved her off. Gratitude gushed through Suz, and an impulse to lay it at her mother's feet—the specific suffering of knowing a cure existed yet remained, for now, beyond reach—and be soothed with sweet mom-nothings, *Shh* and *There, there, honey.* One last hit of oxytocin for the road.

"I think I'm *really* sad?" she said.

Her mother squeezed Suz's elbow. Suz didn't hate it.

"Like when you wake up from a dream of being punched

and understand that the punching was, um . . . your appendix. Bursting. It's good to know what's making you hurt, but it would be better not to hurt in the first place. I guess."

"I know what you mean."

Suz pulled away. Allison could not know how dissociated, disconnected Suz had always been. And if she had, how worthless. To be known and not helped.

"We should go in." She held the door without looking back.

CORPORAL PEPPER'S INTERIOR was actually in good shape. Since Suz's last visit, it had endured a bizarre renovation—Hieronymus Bosch's Limbo as interpreted by the Nintendo Corporation. "'This Area Reserved for KIDS!" read signs posted around the periphery of the strobe-lit, bass-pounding game area. Other signs bore pictographs of stick children surrounded by dotted lines of PPE. Real kids in ghoulish white playsuits fought for controls of flashing game machines and clung like wasp nests to every web, ladder, and tunnel of the disorienting climbing structure that vined along the ceiling, extending as far as the pizzeria area. The only part less appetizing than the apelike screeches echoing from the overhead ball pits were the disposable playsuits the kids wore, known for developing microtears and failing to protect against the common cold.

"That's . . . fun," said Allison, regaining composure first. Suz followed her past the jerky, animatronic "band" to a plexiglass-enclosed eating booth where Lew and Kyra were already seated.

"I ate on the plane," said Suz when her mother asked what she was having.

"You have to eat *something*," said Allison.

"How about chicken fingers?" said Lew.

To redirect, Suz said, "What did you guys want to talk about?"

Allison's eye twitched. "Ah."

"Honey, you don't—" said Lew.

"It's okay, hon," said Allison. "Girls, a while ago I started thinking that I, ah, wanted to be a man."

A combined laugh and whimper caught in Suz's throat. Her mother was trans?

"Over the summer," Allison's voice shook, "I began testosterone therapy. You've noticed I sound different?"

Suz no longer felt like laughing.

"The next step is a name and pronoun. And, um, I don't want to be called 'Mom.'"

It was a textbook midlife crisis. That was it. Someone—not Suz, but Lew, why not Lew?—needed to slap her. Metaphorically. Snap her out of it.

"Does that mean you're going to be gay?" Kyra asked Lew.

"If loving Al makes me gay, I guess I am."

"You'll be bi, honey." Allison touched Lew's stubble. He kissed her fingers.

Suz knew lots of trans people, had even identified as gender nonconforming at college, but her mother wasn't even political. She was square, practically second wave.

The sad, gray ocean of her mother's gaze sought hers. "You must have questions too."

"Nope." She was the one who was supposed to be coming out. Allison was *old*. Besides, gender was a construct. Everything except flesh was nothing but social norms. If Allison didn't like the norms she had obeyed for so long, she should disobey them. Switching teams wouldn't change anything.

Kyra seemed to share Suz's skepticism. "Do I have to call you Dad now?"

"You could call me Papa," said Allison hopefully. "Or Daddy Al?"

That was too much. "You want me to call you '*Daddy Al*'?" She drew it out with a sexual edge that made her mother flinch.

"I meant Kyra, not you."

She had never been cruel to Allison before. It had the same urgent feeling as the impulse to cut herself and provided similar relief: her hidden hatred gushing out into the light.

"I thought you could call me Al," pleaded Allison.

"Fine. It doesn't matter." Suz got up to pee. She didn't want to screw up her kidneys.

"Young lady," said Lew, "we're not done here."

But Suz was.

A LONG STRIP of toilet paper, one end dissolving in a mystery puddle, snaked across the floor of the stall. Thighs trembling in protest to their prolonged squat, a stream of dark pee finally trickled into the bowl. She was dehydrated, again. Tried to remember whether she'd drunk anything before the flight. It was so much fucking work maintaining this *thing* she didn't want and had never asked for. She wiped aggressively, relishing her body's protest. Let it hurt.

At the sinks, she pulled out her makeup kit, an array of cruelty-free colors that could be applied anywhere on the body. A pair of little girls watched as Suz placed the tip of the makeup brush at the spot where the black of the optical-illusion hole had smeared into the red of optical-illusion open flesh. She appreciated the girls' awe. It made her feel momentarily real. But it wasn't enough. Lately, body-mod had become another chore, the bare minimum required to retain a sense of self-recognition. Having so little time left made it feel inconsequential, even though part of her still couldn't believe she was going through with it. Stepping off a cliff into a total mystery. She hoped it wouldn't hurt. The doctor said the upload was painless, but no one really knew. Once a being became pure consciousness, they weren't motivated to stick around and explain. But any pain would be gone quick, along with guilt, love, and moral obligation. Untethered from flesh, a con was free to pursue pure existence.

The hackers who had penetrated con-space described it in conflicting terms, as "empty" and "teeming." They said the code "vibrated," that it was put together in a way they had never seen and couldn't make sense of, yet within it detected a singing kind of order. They said they knew they'd entered con-space when code ceased to be a logic-driven language and became more like extraterrestrial poetry. They said that after they looked away, they could not replicate a single character of con-space's code.

That was how con-space looked to an outsider. Con-space from its own perspective was, by definition, unthinkable. Still, Suz's brain kept generating clumsy analogies for the hypothetical post-upload experience. It would be like being a fish in a school of fish, the silent water flowing past. Or overlaid sheets of lace, like when she ate a bag of mushrooms and the world reorganized itself into patterns. Or it would be like containing a society's worth of dick pics, every person's internet searches and lonely nights. Their impoverished consciousnesses seeking hers, even as she became ever more dissolute, swarm farther away.

These suppositions used the body as reference point, but pure consciousness was beyond sensorial reach. Its unknowability was its beauty. *How can you be sure you will like it?* a friend from the otaku community had asked, but *liking* would be as irrelevant as running or jumping once the upload was complete. She had given the only answer she could think of, that anything would be better than being trapped in a body.

Momentarily, Suz considered that her mother might see her own female parts as a similar sort of cage, but it didn't hold up. "Female" was a social caprice. In a fetus, the proto-architecture of the clitoris and the penis were identical. In rural Romania, a "girl" had only to put on pants to become a "boy." Other places, sex was about who you lived with, or what community role you played, the caregiver, warrior, or whore. All of which were a more ornate set of prisons. Her mother believed she could change her sex by subtracting the *s* from "she," and she could. The difference between Suz's prison and Allison's was that Allison's was a figment made up of other figments. Allison could nudge her gender across the dividing line with a pronoun or could explode it altogether by ceasing to believe in it. That's why Suz had never needed different pronouns. Her self wasn't "she" or "Suzuki" any more than it had been "Bethany Ann." That was what her makeup did: reminded herself and everyone else that the body was nothing.

Suz should have been more sympathetic. After all, corps like her mother were less evolved than cons. Allison would take the deletion of Suz's physical self hard. She couldn't help that; she could, however, meet Allison halfway, by using gender as analogy. She would start by saying, *I know exactly what you mean.*

KYRA WAS HOPPING around on the nearest dancing simulator when Suz returned from the bathroom, but Allison and Lew were still huddled together in the booth. They jolted apart when she entered. Allison's face was all pink and very sad. Now that Suz had decided to be gentle, she could let herself feel sympathy for her poor, helpless mother.

"Sorry for being a jerk, Al."

"Sweetie," Allison croaked.

"I guess I was more attached to our roles than I realized, Al." She didn't believe this, but using the new name made it easy to pretend. Besides, it was like a block of code. The lines alone were inconsequential but as a whole produced a knowable outcome: Trust. Receptivity. She was modeling for her mother how to handle a loved one's change.

"Honestly, Al, you've always"—she thought of her own years of pain—"struggled. I became used to that and I shouldn't have. I should have wanted you to find your truth."

Allison pressed the back of Suz's hand into her moist face. "Oh, my Suzi."

Despite the touch, it was nice to have, for once, relieved her mother's anguish. It really was fine that Allison wanted to be a man. Knowing that she would soon be leaving made it easier, she discovered, to want for her family that coveted banality, happiness.

"So long as everyone's coming out . . ." She ignored

Lew's furious head shake, *Not now*. This was between her and her mother. "Mom, Lew, I am an unevolved consciousness. In two weeks I will have an affirmational procedure to upload into an evolved state."

Allison gaped. "Are you—are *you* trans?"

Calmly, she repeated herself in normie-friendly terms. "Like everyone, I am pure consciousness trapped in a corpus. Unlike most people, being in a body causes me daily suffering. Fortunately, there are treatments. My doctor has done the procedure hundreds of times."

"This is ridiculous!" said Lew, slapping the table.

She turned to her tantrumming stepfather. "Dr. Berryessa is going to transcribe my neural patterns into computer language. He will embed that code within what is called 'consciousness space' where it will join a growing neural network of other uploaded cons."

For a long, silent moment her parents beheld her without preconceptions. Their gaze, startled and open, washed over her like a bath of pure light.

"You're making a clone of yourself?" said Allison. "Online?"

Suz counseled herself to be patient. It wasn't her mother's fault she had been born pre-internet. "Technically, there is neural cloning involved. But the clone will be the new me. It's not as if my unevolved self will still be walking around or whatever." She swirled a hand to indicate the inexpressible absurdity of preserving the original only to keep it trapped inside the same, miserable container. If her mother could see continued embodiment from her perspective, as a form of torture, she would get over the deletion faster. At least Suz hoped so. She didn't like to think of her mother wailing over her dead meatsuit.

But Allison refused to understand. "It won't? Is there a long recovery period? Do you need someone to take care of you? I can drive out."

"No, Mom."

She and Allison looked at each other. Lew might as well have been a deleted corpus, the pizza arcade, a distant, white noise.

"What does con-land feel like?" said Allison in an almost-whisper.

"Like nothing."

"It must feel like something," said Allison desperately. "It must feel good—to be worth giving up all," her arm flailed against the plexiglass, "this."

Suz shook her head. "You need a body to feel."

"But what about pleasure? Kissing."

"I don't like kissing."

The tears that had been threatening like bad weather since the airport dripped down Allison's face. "Oh honey, that's awful."

Suz surprised herself by letting a warm, wet bead catch on her extended fingertip à la the anthropomorphic movie alien. "Ouch. Al-liot."

Allison smiled and was about to speak when Lew interrupted. "Where's Kyra?"

"I'm sure she's fine," said Allison, but she too turned to the dance game around which the moth-like shapes of kids in white playsuits, either too large or small to be Kyra, flitted. Still, she must have been fine. There were surveillance cameras everywhere.

"Guys, she's just playing some other game."

Lew stood. "She needs to eat first."

Arrested by the prospect of being left alone with her

mother (and the escalation of intimacy that entailed), Suz volunteered. "I can go."

"I'll come with you," said Allison, her voice full of a desperation that, Suz was certain, had nothing to do with Kyra.

She waved her off with a bright, "You boys eat your pizza."

A TEENAGER IN a walrus costume detained Suz at the entrance to the game floor. "Are-you-under-sixteen-or-the-chaperone-of-an-under-sixteen-year-old?"

"I'm checking on my sister."

"You need a playsuit." The walrus pointed to the health department sign: FULL BODY PROTECTIVE EQUIPMENT REQUIRED BEYOND THIS POINT. Bits of multicolored fuzz and lint clung to its tusks.

Suz waved her debit card over the PPE dispenser and plucked the playsuit from the slot. She hadn't worn one of these since high school and had forgotten how much they resembled hazmat suits made of dryer sheets.

Adult One-Size was, predictably, designed for an over-weight, extra-tall male. Surplus material hung from her in elephantine folds. In order to see where she was going, Suz had to hold the clear face window in front of her. Other-wise, it drooped uselessly. At least it provided the *feeling* of insulation between her and the juvenile hoards that swarmed the plastic race cars and wielded toy machine guns against VR enemies in "games" designed to accli-mate them to the violent, late-stage capitalism into which they'd been born. But Kyra was not there, nor was she shooting baskets, rolling skee-balls, or whacking alligators with a padded mallet. That left only the climbing structure.

Suz couldn't exactly blame her. The thing was a kid Arcadia, replete with nooks and hidey-holes that seemed private despite in actuality being surveilled from all angles by security cameras. Even she would have once loved to ascend to perch in one of its turrets, imagining herself the queen of all she saw. Kyra, though, a born herd animal, would be wading through one of the ball pits with the other germy kids.

It was tempting to go back to Lew and Allison and lie that Kyra had refused to quit playing. But there was the what if. What if, despite the cameras, Kyra had been lured off by a pedo? What if, at this very moment, some big boys had her cornered? Kyra might be a brat, but that didn't mean she deserved trauma. And anyway, going back to the booth *without* the kid would be as good as agreeing to endure the shitshow that was sure to hit once her mother absorbed what deletion really meant. This was why she should have waited until her last day. Let Lew be her mother's emotion-sponge. Wasn't that *supposed* to be his job?

Far above, she spotted a familiar orange sock with purple stars—hers, gone missing on her last trip home.

"Kyra!" she shouted, but her voice was lost in the cacophony.

It was her sock and she was going to go get it.

Struggling and puffing, Suz climbed a net wall, crawled through multiple humid tunnels, wobbled over a swinging bridge, and arrived soaked in sweat at the entrance of the deep ball pit. In the corner where she'd seen the sock, one medium-sized hooded head bobbled.

"KYRA, GET OVER HERE!"

The head popped under the balls. God, she was spoiled. When Suz was her age, Allison's idea of a treat was a trip to the grocery store. Suz's childhood wasn't "fun." It was winters shut up in a studio apartment and filling out online worksheets while incompetent teachers fumbled with their virtual classrooms' mute buttons. It was playgrounds she wasn't allowed to play on and other children seen only through car windows. It was worrying about money and worrying about her mother and ticking down the days until she'd be free.

Objectively, the world had only gotten worse since then. The planet was hotter, the governments more corrupt, the people meaner. Yet, somehow Kyra remained a happy innocent who now clambered underneath these disgusting balls as if her dumpy body were a glorious machine that would never let her down. One thing was for sure, she wasn't getting out to go eat unless someone made her.

Cursing silently, Suz squatted on the platform. Filled as it was, it was impossible to gauge the ball pit's depth, though logic said it couldn't be more than four feet. Nonetheless, her body tensed as it always had over water. What the mind knew made no difference to the dumb animal of the flesh.

It all happened fast. From the far end of the ball pit, a big kid took a flying leap at the same moment Kyra's head burst up. There was a muffled squeal as they collided, cut off as they both went down.

"Fuck," said Suz and jumped-fell through balls to the trampoline-taut bottom. Balls spilled over and around her in a chaos of primary colors as she groped forward, toward her sister whose neck might be broken. Kyra was so stupid. So careless.

Ahead of her, balls simmered with movement. She reached in and was thanked with an explosion of pain as a flailing limb connected with her nose. A reflex, she grabbed the nearest limb and wrenched upward. Kyra shrieked as they broke the surface, jerking away.

"Mo-om!" cried the little boy who wasn't Kyra.

The bigger kid surfaced, whirled to face her. "What did you do to my brother?"

Through the playsuit hood and her smashed N99, Suz clutched at her nose. Hot phlegm was trickling down the back of her throat. Had Kyra ever even been there? "Sorry," she tried to say, but couldn't get enough air. Someone slammed into her from behind and knocked her to her knees. Balls all around. She couldn't breathe. It was a panic attack. Or she was drowning. In desperation, she tore the fabric away from her face and jerked the mask away. In the bright, blinking light, she coughed out the fluid that was drowning her.

Confused, she blinked at the red makeup smeared over her hands.

"Blood! Blood!" cried a kid.

Suz touched her wounded nose. It was blood. And she had no mask.

"She's uncovered!" shrieked someone else. "Run!"

Beep beep beep, shrieked an alarm. Yellow lights flashed. Biohazard warning. Children scrambled from the ball pit, but Suz didn't move. Distantly, she was aware of them streaming from the nets and tunnels like ants from a flooded nest. She should leave too, she knew that, but she also knew they'd be gathering down below, the children and their parents, as she had so many times, to see which idiot had broken the rules. Waiting for the maskless sneezer to be ticketed or the careless custodian to be scolded for failure to properly sanitize. They would stare as, bleeding freely, she dragged herself across the bridge, through the tunnels, and, somehow, down the net to be escorted out of the building. Possibly arrested.

Unless she stayed here.

Not bothering to staunch her bloody nose, Suz sank once more into the enveloping cushion of the balls. They reminded her of her own childhood, something irrevocably over.

"We know you're in there," said a voice over the PA. "Please come out or we will send someone in to retrieve you."

It was not her body or their body. It was no one's. Let them drag her out. In two weeks, none of this would matter.

She thought again of Hieronymus Bosch. People said his work was surreal, but he merely painted life flayed of its skin. Amid the grotesque were intricate terrors and truths that anyone who was alive and paying attention would recognize. *Christ in Limbo*, not a true Bosch, was her favorite. She liked to think about the anonymous painter, credited in her college textbook as "Follower of Bosch," matching his hand to the shapes of his master's until not only was his own style erased but also his name. In the end, all that remained was the painting.

Crush Me

The boulder appears alone: a large, pale rock, stained by drizzle, half-sunk into the dry riverbed. I say *appears* because from my vantage point—glancing up from my phone through the streaky bus window—it has come out of nowhere. Screens do that. Make change seem sudden when it's been creeping up, bus ride after bus ride.

It is a funny coincidence, how much it looks like the limestone carving I made for Jillian. The boulder in the riverbed is a lot bigger, obviously, the size of a throne rather than a doorstop. The more I squint, though, the more similarities I see, certain angles and rough edges that I viscerally remember having to work the chisel around. I thought the dark patches on the boulder were water. The longer I peer through the streaked glass, though, the more they resolve themselves into the clumsy undulations that I so painstakingly worked into the stone over all these months.

It's my mind playing tricks. Could be that all limestone looks the same to a beginner like me. Stone-carving is like pointillism or Tetris, or any other repetitive activity where the brain insists on finding that pattern long after you've finished.

Even so, when I peek into the grocery bag at my feet, I am reassured to find my carving still there, complete in its awkward beauty. It's my first carving and I'm shyly proud. And nervous. I want Jillian to like it. It's for the sixteenth anniversary of our best friendship. Sixteen is the first number not included in the list of traditional anniversary gift materials. After fifteen, crystal, it skips to twenty, china. I've always felt a little superstitious about that gap. There's no explanation I can find for it. Is it that this is where time begins to blur and resentments replace affection? I don't want my and Jillian's time to blur, but we aren't a couple in the traditional sense, so hopefully it doesn't count.

I picked limestone because Jillian and I met in Earth Science, in the ninth grade, in a unit on bedrock. I want her to love it. I want it to be worthy of a friend like her.

"You are a wonder!" she exclaims when I present it to her on the roof of the Ellis building, a semisecret park owned by a pharmaceutical company but technically open to the public. The meeting spot was Brian's idea. I have to admit, it's perfect. It makes our humble, industrial city look majestic, spread below us like Grecian ruins.

"The design is supposed to represent time crystals," I say, unable to disguise my happiness.

Her mouth twists wryly. "You poet." This is a compliment wrapped in a jibe. Physicists think poets—or poets who write about physics—are ding-dongs who can't tell a Large Hadron Collider from a large hamburger. But I sense from the careful way Jillian fingers the grooves I spent so many hours smoothing that she genuinely wants it. That she'll keep it in her lab to gaze at while she and her team work on cracking the secrets of time itself.

"And for you . . ." Jill fumbles in her purse. Excitement hums through me as she searches for, I imagine, an envelope containing the details of the gift she promised last year: a week away at a luxurious resort, just us. That was meant to be how we spent our fifteenth Friendaversary, she told me, but then the MacArthur Fellowship happened and her wife, Nan, landed a major client, and life got too busy. Her life, that is. Mine was slowing to a halt around the same time. The web design business I had been trying to start finally tanked and Brian moved from teaching in a public middle school to a private college prep. My dad died too. Not that we were close, but I had been flying home a lot.

"Here it is!" says Jill triumphantly, coming up with an envelope. I should be eager to open it but something is off. Something about how closely she is watching my face, as if for signs of displeasure.

"Thanks," I murmur, as she puts it in my hand. It's all wrong. The envelope lacks the even thickness of a reservation confirmation for Cuba or Costa Rica. I already sense I will be disappointed, but Jillian is watching, so I make a small tear in the corner and spill the contents into my palm.

It's earrings. Gem studs the color of clotted blood. She is waiting for me to say something, but a small, resentful resistance, a splinter of ice in my heart, won't let me. My cheeks are too tense to smile. Our trip is still going to happen, I scold myself, unless you ruin it by hurting her feelings. I can't speak. I need her to say something. To reaffirm the promise, that we will go, just not this year, maybe next.

"They're garnet," she says. "They were my great-grandmother's."

I wait for the rest, but our silence only expands. I am beginning to sweat despite the cool air. It's like I'm a child in a school play who forgot her line; Jillian is prompting me, but my body refuses to speak. I understand how this goes. I am supposed to forget about the promised trip, chalk it up to wishful thinking. If I mention it, she will frown sympathetically, ask if I may have misunderstood. As if Jillian's words aren't my gospel, as if I haven't been committing her to memory like a religion since the first week of the second semester of high school. That is what love is, isn't it? The inability to forget?

An echo of Nan's voice is sharp in my mind: "Oh, Wendy is just Jill's 'straight' friend who won't admit she's in love with her." Overheard at a party that Nan thought I had left. The anger I felt then flows through me afresh as embarrassment, for the adolescent desperation implied, the cluelessness. As if friends can't be soulmates. As if I have not been Jillian's best friend all these years too.

"They're beautiful," I say, meeting Jill's gaze over the earrings.

Relief breaks across her face. "Here, let me put them in." With soft, deft fingertips, Jillian eases my old studs out and pokes the garnet ones in.

There are tears in her eyes, and in mine. We hug, the heat of her cheek radiating through my scalp. I probably was wrong about the trip. Not wrong that the conversation happened but for taking it literally, when she meant the promise as an expression of love. We will go somewhere beautiful together again soon, but it will be spontaneous, it will come because it wants to, not because I forced it or behaved like a lawyer waving a contract in her face.

"You're my sister," I whisper.

"And you're mine," she whispers back.

"And then she left you there?" asks Brian when I get home.

"She didn't *leave* me. We had a miscommunication. I thought we had dinner plans tonight, but she thought we were saying we were going to make them for another time. It was just a quick gift exchange. Look: these were her great-grandmother's."

Brian ignores the earrings. "*Did* you make plans for another time?" His maternal skepticism annoys me.

"It's not a big deal. We already have lunch every week." I hop around in the entryway, taking my boots off. I had dressed up expecting to eat someplace nice. Now I feel silly for wearing nude suede just to ride the bus. "Aren't you glad I'm home early?"

"Duh." He kisses me with tongue. We undress on the way to the bedroom, my nostrils full of his musky scent, and my head of stray thoughts, strands of my and Jillian's conversation, her expression when I gave her the carving, what she is doing right now, the clammy fear that she went out with other friends after I left. I push this insecurity away, bring my mind to Brian's thumbs stroking the sensitive place below my ribs. The boulder I saw on the way downtown pops into my head then, I don't know why. It gives me a feeling of dread.

"It's been too long," groans Brian as I rock on top of him. "Please thank Jillian for being such a *fucking*," he moans, "flake."

I lean forward until our lips meet, only part aware of my body, which is always aroused by him whether or not I notice. Sometimes I wonder if I would have married him, if it weren't for my and Jill's friendship. Brian is a great guy, but we don't understand each other in that unspoken way that she and I do. I couldn't live without it.

"I'm getting you pregnant," he mutters into my ear. "Say it, oh my god, say it."

"Ohhh, you're getting me pregnant," I say, though increasingly this line is less of a turn-on and more of a persistent worry. My mother's still waiting for us to have children, even though what brought us together was being the last two in our friend circle not to want any. I've told Mom Brian had a vasectomy, but she scoffs, "Accidents happen, Wen." Jill laughs at my mother's prediction, but it's wormed its way into my thoughts. If it happened, I'd get an abortion. But a part of me wonders, would I? If I was carrying a life-bomb in my uterus, would I so hastily defuse it? Would I not consider blowing the scaffold of my routine days sky high?

"Wen," Brian roars, quaking. I have a second to feel guilty before my body obediently responds with an unsatisfying spasm.

Brian rolls me under him, kisses my forehead. "I love you, hon."

"I love you too," I say. I do. I think I do.

THE NEXT TIME I ride the bus, I am on the lookout. It's sunny today and I want to reassure myself that the boulder doesn't look any more like my carving than any other similar rock. Again, though, it takes me by surprise. Because now there are two of them. Identical. Facing each other. It's a weird way to describe a relationship between two objects with no clear front or back, but that's what it looks like. Like they are in a standoff. They both exactly resemble my carving. Just bigger and farther away.

I have the thought that someone is trolling me, though that is neither likely, nor, in fact, possible. Only Brian saw the carving before I gave it to Jill. Besides, the boulders are giant. They had to be transported by truck or large machinery. Someone badly wanted them here. I'm just not sure why. I take a photo as the bus lurches forward. The image is a headlong-elephant blur of gray. I hashtag it #weirdrocks, comment, *Anyone know what's going on here?*

EVERY TUESDAY SINCE Jill moved to the northside to live with Nan, she and I have had a standing lunch date. We meet at the marina, where we can choose between the dark pub with the views, the Lebanese-run Chinese place, or the diner. The marina used to be our halfway point, but it's an extra bus ride for me since I got a nine-to-five. Brian thinks we should alternate, one Tuesday near Jill's work, the next near mine. I told him Jillian didn't want to, but I've actually never brought it up. A part of me is afraid that the only thing keeping our Tuesday lunches going is that they've become automatic, and it's the only time I seem to see Jill in person anymore.

"Public art?" she posits, when I tell her about the boulders. "It sounds performative. Reactions like yours could be the point. You made pieces like that in college."

"Out of papier-mâché. Anyway, there'd have been publicity around a big installation and I haven't heard anything."

"Erosion control?"

I shake my head. "I don't think so." I fiddle with a sugar packet, wanting to tell her about the likeness to my carving. I have a growing feeling that somehow those rocks

are meant for me, like a message. That sounds too para-
noid to say aloud. But Jill is vigilant. If there's a message
there, she will see it. I hand her my phone.

"Mm." She rotates the out-of-focus picture, holds it up
to the diner window. Past it, a bobbing line of boats. "It's
kind of hard to make out . . ."

"We could go in person."

"Oh," she says, surprised. "Definitely."

See, Brian? I think. It's not her, it's me. I just need to ask
for what I want. "This weekend?"

She crinkles her nose. "Shoot. Saturday, we're getting
the kitchen cabinets redone. Sunday, Nan has a dinner."

Nan is always dragging Jill to events for her clients
and her wide and shallow circle of arts industry friends,
and Jill is always rolling her eyes about them. I would
do worse than that if I were her. Nan's associates are the
scene-y types who made me go into graphic design instead
of trying for what Nan calls a "real" arts career. At least
I don't pretend my work is about more than money. At
least I'm honest that what I make means nothing. "You
could skip it." I try to sound mischievous, but the edge of
a whine sneaks in.

She frown-smiles, indulging me. "Another time, Wen."

"When?" I say, unintentionally echoing her. The sugar
packet tears. Grains sluice onto the table. "I need help
figuring this out." It comes out shrill.

"Are we still talking about the rocks?"

I nod, mortifyingly close to tears. The waitress returns
with coffee pitchers. She must have overheard, because
she is checking me out the way people do the mentally ill,
as if at any moment I might strip naked and start raving.
"Refill?"

"Thanks." Jill smiles conspiratorially at the waitress, who tops off hers and overfills my decaf so it puddles onto my saucer. The waitress doesn't apologize.

I grimace at Jill, wanting her to agree that our waitress is the unstable one, probably a drug addict, with her raccoon eyes and stringy hair. When I pick up my mug, coffee drips from the base onto the spilled sugar, turning it to brown syrup. "Good job," I say sarcastically. "Thanks so much."

"Wendy," scolds Jill, who can't stand complainers. I feel instantly shamed, even though it really was the waitress's fault.

"Sorry." I fumble for napkins.

"There." Jill points to a stain spreading on my cuff.

I dab it at with ice water. Too late. The brown settles into the cotton. "Fuck me."

"Fuck your shirt," suggests Jill. We both laugh. Like that, I see how dumb I'm acting. It's just coffee, just some rocks in a riverbed. Meanwhile, I haven't even asked Jill one real question. My self-absorption can be so extreme.

"How are things anyway? How's work?"

"Fascinating," she says and describes her research on time crystals and many-body systems. The sounds conjure images they surely weren't meant to: cloud giants, flickering patterns in the sky, the carving I made and its echo printed in shadow on the boulders.

She pauses. "Am I making sense?" I half-nod. She understands: yes, I feel it; no, I don't get it. She leans forward, lips pink with excitement. "Imagine an object that is different in each moment. Or . . ." she thinks. "Existing on a clock of your own, so that you are always a bit out of sync."

For a second, Jillian's work blinks into focus. It's like

me and the rocks, how I've seen them but no one else has, and so no one else can understand how wrong and strange they are. Or, I wonder, is it the rocks that are on their own clock? Or am I on the rocks' clock? Maybe I don't actually get it. My mind wanders as Jill's explanation grows more complicated. By the time we kiss goodbye, I'm back to trying to figure out who put those rocks in the riverbed and why.

"TEENAGE PRANK," declares Brian. "Has to be." I follow him into the shower. Water streams down his belly, carrying black curls of hair to the drain.

"I don't think so. They're giant."

"You'd be surprised what kids can accomplish when they work together."

Brian, unlike me, had multiple friends as a teenager. They were always getting into fun trouble. Marble statues were pulleyed onto school roofs, soap dispensers stocked with liquid cheese, and fountains dyed blue. As a result, whenever the inexplicable happens, he credits it to an anonymous cohort of thirteen- to eighteen-year-olds.

"Maybe."

"We should go down there together. I bet *dollahs* it's got 'Class of '22' spray-painted on the back."

For some reason, the idea of us going to the rocks together seems lonely and depressing. Far worse than going on my own. "Nah, you're probably right. It's kids being weird."

"Kids *are* weird." Brian grins like a TV dad. Like that, I see it: he wants to be a parent.

He smacks my butt with a wet washcloth. "You in the mood?"

I think about that vasectomy. When we were first dating he warned they weren't foolproof. They are also reversible. He wouldn't do it without telling me, though, would he?

"Not tonight, hon. I have to send some emails."

We get into bed and he curls his furry back against me, pulls a pillow over his head.

On the Who's Your Baby app, I mash up my face with Brian's, my face with Jill's, Jill's face with Brian's. I peer into the screen, contemplating our progeny. Jill and Brian make a firm-chinned infant, Brian and I produce a shrunken old man, me and Jill's baby is doleful and doubt-ful, its fat lower lip streaked with saliva. I refresh until Brian paws at the covers, muttering for lights out.

THROUGH THE DIRTY bus window, I scan the dry grass growing thick along the riverbank. So far as I can tell from up here, it is free of teenager tracks and clean of the scrapes and gouges a dragged boulder would leave. Boul-ders, plural. Four hunker in the riverbed now, three on bottom, one laid atop like a cat in the sun. "Excuse me," I address a young mother whose child and child-accessories take up a row of handicapped seats. "Do you know where those came from?" The bus jerks into motion.

She peels her headphones off. "Huh?"

"Never mind." We are already over the bridge. There's nothing to see but a grassy rise and a trash bag being tugged along the bushes by the wind.

I STAB A damp broccoli. "I'm going to report them to the city."

Jill chews and swallows the last bite of her steamed bun with a look of amusement. "Report the rocks?"

"They seem suspicious. And," I try for an angle that will convey how upsetting the boulders are becoming, "environmentally irresponsible."

"Oh?"

"Don't rock quarries destroy the topsoil? And the riverbed is the drainage for the whole city. We could have floods!"

She pats some crinkly bills onto the plastic tray. "Four boulders aren't going to tip the scales."

I remove her cash, replace it with mine. I want her to take this seriously. "But eventually there could be hundreds."

Jill searches my face. "Why do you do this to yourself?"

"I'm not doing anything." All I'm doing is what she always suggests, which is practicing mindfulness and paying attention to the natural world.

Jill turns her palm over. Automatically, I touch a finger to its center. Her skin is softer than babies. It contains years of my history. If anyone should be able to understand how significant these rocks feel, it's Jillian, who spends her days imagining particles too small to matter on their own but which, when clustered together, make up all of reality. Everything from a table leg to a mile-wide fog rising off the ocean. She squeezes my finger. "You have to let this go. You know I can't be okay unless you're okay."

"Okay," I say, but what I am thinking is that of course I'll let it go, I'll let it go as soon as I understand what it means.

SIGNS OF DAWN appear through our kitchen window. Light separates the layers of buildings, high-rises from brick walk-ups, schools and factories from high-rises. In their shadows, toilets flush. Probable exploited workers take smoke breaks outside probable sweatshops. Aging custodial personnel drag buckets across historic tiles. The white point of sun jabs my eye.

"Hey, early bird." Brian hands me an untoasted bagel. It tastes like the discount bin. "I have an idea. Let's go check out those rocks of yours."

I stiffen. "Now?"

"Why not? I'll drop you at work after."

Brian once said he loved me because I'm zany. It's the only time I've heard that word used unironically. I'm not zany. My favorite color is blue. My hair is styled however the woman on the magazine at the hairdresser has hers styled. At parties, I practice different ways of crossing my arms until enough time has passed that it's deemed acceptable to go home. When Brian called me zany, I asked what he meant and he said, "You know, fun. Fun to be around." I'm not fun to be around, but I stopped asking. If I hadn't, *fun* would have become *interesting*, and eventually *incomprehensible*. I wonder what Brian would do if I explained that there is no giggling, fun-loving woman trapped inside me. That you could peel back my layers and never find a decent wife, a decent mother for your future child. I'm less a woman and more a girl who got taller and heavier and had to get a job.

"Another time," I say, giving him a peck. Once he's gone, I text Jill. *I'm going to the boulders. Please come. I need you.*

JILL ARRIVES IN a new car, leather seats, gleaming shell. "MacArthur wheels," she explains, accepting an ice cream bar. My treat for her for playing hooky. We take the road that crosses the track of the river, pull off before the bridge.

"Run for it!" I yell. We dodge traffic holding hands and collide, laughing and breathless, with the guardrail. The rocks gaze back at us. They have multiplied again and been rearranged into squat, precarious towers. I count six towers, at least three or four boulders high. Each rock distinctly carved. The hair on the back of my neck rises.

I expect Jillian to be alarmed too, but she leans forward, taking them in appreciatively. "God, that's beautiful."

I look down, expecting the rocks to have changed into something else entirely: A sunset. Mother-of-pearl. They are still there, motionless and insinuating, still limestone. "You . . . like them?"

She exhale-laughs. "I mean, it's art, right? It's not a matter of liking or disliking. But, see, it takes us out of our skins. It makes us see things differently. That's wonder, Wen."

She has the same kind of reaction at art shows, drinking in the scene with pure, vivid emotion. I've always wanted to be like that, so susceptible, so open. But with these rocks, her emotion is wrong. There is a cruelty to these rocks. A relentlessness. Like how there keep being more of them. Will they stop multiplying? I don't think it is art, not unless a threat can be art. These rocks are someone, or something, holding a knife to my throat. It's as if I'm supposed to hold them back. As if only I can stop them.

"I guess so."

As we return to the car, Jill reaches for my hand. I can't look at her because, if I do, I'll cry. Out of anger. Helplessness. Of course she would see the rocks as objects of beauty, demanding nothing more than her momentary pleasure. It's like she's trying to prove that it's a choice to like or dislike them. Which it's not. Not for me. I've never been able to choose to think positive. I've never wanted to.

On the ride back, Jill goes on and on about the rocks. She sounds like Nan, all art-world theory. Affect this, and earthworks that. As usual when academic talk comes up, I feel myself devolve into a lower order of primate, attempting to translate sentences into my paltry vocabulary of hand signs: Milk, Mommy, Want, All done.

"I love that I can't tell if I, the viewer, am inside or outside the piece. It's Heizer's *Levitated Mass* but countering notions of the monument by proposing a collectivity, a body collectivity. But is it modern or postmodern? Does it resist its own form or is it trapped by it? What do you think?"

"I wouldn't know." My ice cream bar left a sour taste. I swallow, wishing to un-eat it, to never have invited Jill in the first place.

"But you understand what I mean. These effects the piece had on us. It's hitting us exactly where we diverge. Highlighting our differences. It's really intelligent work."

I want to spit. It's like she needs me to agree, to say how entirely unalike she and I are, when the important part is that, underneath all our superficial traits, we are the same. That's why we connect the way we do. It's why we love each other so fiercely. "It doesn't take Leonardo da Vinci to point out that two people might have different tastes. Anyway, if you weren't trying so hard to make a point, I think you'd find those rocks spooky too."

"What?"

"You're trying to get me to agree that it's a matter of perception. And it's not."

Jill shades her eyes and peers out the driver's window. I've upset her. I should back off, but I'm furious.

"You would have hated those rocks if you saw them on your own. You would have gone crying to Nan and then she would have done this exact thing to you."

"You're right," she says flatly. "Nan *would* have dropped everything to meet me in the middle of a workday. She would have thanked me for showing her something so unusual and interesting. Then she would have driven me where I wanted to go, even if it was on the opposite side of town from where she needed to be. And she wouldn't have even asked for a thank-you. Not that she'd have had to."

"Good for Nan," I grunt.

"Yeah." Jill's voice cracks. "Good for her."

There's nothing I can say to this that won't make me sound like an asshole. I cross my arms and stare out my own window. "Thanks for the ride," I make myself say when we get to my office. And then, because this all feels terrible, like whatever script I was meant to be reading got its pages mixed up with a farcical tragedy, I add, "Come in. I'll buy you a latte."

"I can't."

The anger has drained from me and I feel sick. Disoriented. I can't even remember exactly what I said, but I know it was mean. "Jill?"

She looks up. "What?"

"I'm sorry. It's these rocks. You're right. They affect me really differently than they do you. They upset me, a lot. But I shouldn't have taken that out on you."

She nods. "Don't worry about it."

"I really shouldn't have, Jill. I was a cunt."

"It's fine."

"Really?"

She shrugs. "It's not like I've never had to forgive you before."

I know I should ask what she means, but the fear is too great. The thousand possibilities of how I might have hurt her or let her down stick me like pins. I wish she could feel how much I hate myself for being this person. Then, maybe, she truly would forgive me. But before I can figure out what to say, she has rolled the window up and is turning the steering wheel away.

OVER THE NEXT few days, my vision becomes filmy like the world is coated in dust. Brian buys me allergy pills that don't work. I leave the office early, dabbing at free-flowing tears. I text Jill a picture of my inflamed sclera. Making fun of my own obsession, I add: *It's the boulders.* She responds with a cartoon face scratching its head.

She's still angry. I write her a long email, apologizing for what I said. It was childish and cruel. I didn't mean it. I add that whatever she's had to forgive me for, I'm sorry for that too. That I've taken her for granted. That I want to do better, because sixteen years is too many to lose fighting about rocks.

In the morning, she has written me back. She says she's sorry too, that we both said things we didn't mean. She admits that in her anger she moved her lunch breaks. She still wants us to have our Tuesdays, but it will have to wait while she fixes her schedule. I am so relieved we've made up that the temporary loss of our lunch dates almost doesn't bother me.

The itching in my eyes becomes a constant. I was joking about it being connected to the boulders, but it does feel like my eyes are full of sharp dust. I wonder if it's possible to be allergic to a mineral.

Fortunately, without the Tuesday lunches, I have no reason to get anywhere near the river. My office is close to home. I walk there, move objects around on the screen until the itching gets too bad, then walk home to drip useless steroid drops under my eyelids.

ONE NIGHT, LATE, Jill posts a picture of the moon, shiny as a tuna can lid. She is never up this late. Probably she can't sleep either.

Tell me about limestone, I message.

Three pregnant dots pulse on the screen to show she is typing. My fingers hover over the keyboard. The dots disappear, the fetus of Jillian's meaning—as large as a period, as loud as a politely cleared throat—unmaking itself.

?

Sorry, she messages. *Dinner guests won't go home*, winking emoji.

"Come to bed," calls Brian from the darkened bedroom. Wrapped in a yellow blanket, he resembles a bruised banana.

"Soon," I call back.

Gruffly, "It's just a few rocks, babe."

"Hah," I scoff, so pissed. A *few*. Staying away from them isn't working. It's like we have unfinished business and my eyes know it.

Lunch this Tuesday? I type.

Three dots and then, *Noon?*

TUESDAY I'M SO nervous I miss my bus and have to walk to the depot. I text Jill and she says she'll wait as long she can. The nervousness remains. I haven't seen the rocks in over two weeks. A part of me hopes they'll be gone, but another part wants there to be more of them. It's the longing I used to feel during a bad thunderstorm, afraid of the lightning and hoping desperately for it to strike close to home. I wanted to see the world changed.

There are more. A mountain of more, visible from the traffic light before the bridge. A heap of perhaps hundreds of stones looming above us. An artist or force has reverse-engineered a mountain from quarry rocks. If it's art, it's also a threat. One minor earthquake and it would come crashing down on the lane of cars. A few bus passengers look over with the glazed expression of children being marched through a museum. No one else seems to care.

At the pub's rear table, Jill is reading a natural history of invertebrates. She marks a line with her finger. "Sweetie, I'm glad you made it." Before her sits the plastic tray with its mint and signed receipt. She tells me she has to run. I tell her I do too. In truth, I'll likely sit in this booth all afternoon. There's no rush. I can tell the boss I'm working remotely. Proof layouts tonight while Brian sleeps, email them to clients by 5pm in Tokyo and 9am in London. I'm coming to understand: Time doesn't exist. It's just an ethos I can subscribe to or not.

"Next Tuesday though?"

"Of course," says Jill and squeezes my hand.

BUT THE NEXT Tuesday she cancels, and the one after that she's busy at work. Then, there are car problems. A dentist appointment. A trip to Texas for Nan's sister's wedding. Then, work is busy again. I ask if she's still mad at me, but she swears it's not that, it's just these lunches. She hasn't quite managed to get her schedule back on track.

"How about that dinner?" I suggest. Jillian can bring Nan. I'll have Brian.

"I really would love to . . ." Her ellipsis pops in my ear.

"Pop," I say aloud once we're disconnected, laying down the phone.

Brian, who has younger sisters, produces brownie mix and a hairbrush. "Want French braids?"

"Okay." I bow my head. The bristles crackle through knots. Each stroke snaps my neck back.

"Hon," says Brian, "talk to your huggy bear." He does the voice. "Huggy wuvs oo."

It's cute. Dumb, but comforting. I tell huggy bear I don't mind Jillian wanting space. In a friendship as old as ours, space is healthy. It's normal. I'm happy we're letting each other grow. I don't not mean this. I feel fine, a kind of numb coolness, like a building lit blue at night. "Really," I say, tucking my head under Brian's chin. "It's all good." Relieved, he kisses my head.

We work side by side on our laptops until the neon light of the skating rink goes off. When I reply to the last email, I see he is asleep with his face mashed into a couch cushion. I pick up one of his big, gentle paws and touch it to my cheek. His fingers clench as if zapped.

TUESDAYS COME AND go without a reason to ride the bus. My eyes stay bad. At work, I sink into trouble like it's bathwater, turn in projects late, miss staff meetings. I can't finish anything. I quit before they fire me.

"Freelancing is more my style," I tell Brian.

"Why don't you take some time off?" he says. "Let me take care of you."

This is precisely what men say before they ask for children. "You know I hate not working," I lie, scratching at the corners of my eyes. I stay up sending please-come-back emails to old clients, stopping only when Brian leaves, his briefcase jiggling against his slacks, his keys jingling on their ring.

Brian used to call me an insomniac. I'd argue it didn't count as pathology if the pathology was my preference. Clicking through fonts for a website design while drunks argued on the street below, I'd become optimistic, certain, for those brief, dark hours, that my life was on the right path. Before dawn, I'd crawl into the nest of Brian's limbs and share a little of his uncomplicated sleep. Now, night is just like day. It all stings.

I PLAY WITH the open windows on my phone, stretching and zooming, then swiping them out of frame to wherever the internet goes to fall apart. I search for people forgotten and lost and never known: a girl from freshman history, the stoner who sublet my first apartment, the preternaturally deep-voiced child star of a hit show. I locate them from fragments: a street address, an alma mater, half the hyphenated name of a fictional character. One by one, I roll stones off their graves and revisit other lost souls. I learn who has swelled, who has wizened; who went to prison, to rehab, to Honolulu on a cruise; who became Christian, gay, a woman; who time proved not as smart or talented or gorgeous as we all once thought.

I search myself. The internet is bedazzled with my

salient details. A graphic design website. A former
employer's website. A blog proclaiming that my brilliant
words are *Coming soon!* A white pages directory of other
women with my name. A pop-up ad that offers to reveal my
home address and records of up to three previous arrests.
There is a high school reunion event listing me absent,
and Brian's niece-in-law's graduation pictures, in which I
look sunburnt and happy, though I spent that whole day
crying. There are argumentative comments I left under
news articles and pathetic ones after beauty advice. There
is a question, unanswered, about substitutions for tofu
loaf. *does it work with almond milk,* I wrote, without punc-
tuation, in 2003.

I click through more results. I know all this happened
and yet the woman in question does not seem like me.

NIGHT. I SCROLL through my texts with Jill, a reverse
film of yellow cartoon meanings. Now happy, now sad,
now scratching a bald head, now tongue-stuck-out sarcastic. I touch the dial symbol and rest the device in my lap.
Jillian's phone is off, her voicemail a familiar whisper. It's
the sound of fifteen-year-old Jillian, the freckled sound
of a way out. *A way out of what?* I ask myself. It's one of
these late-night dialogues where I become the husband in
whom I confide. I tell my self-husband what he (I) already
knows. About Jillian and me as grown women, as college
students, as kids. A long-lost night we followed the train
bridge over the river, goading one another to jump into
the water below. How I howled with her before leaping,
but my teeth clenched as I fell. Her cry sounded so free. I
thought one day I'd grow into someone who could scream
or fuck or fall without worrying it would kill me. *Why can't*

I let go? I ask my self-husband. *Because you're bad at it,* he says. *I want to change,* I say, and the voice that answers is my mother's: *If wishes were horses, beggars would be a lot better off.*

MY YOUNGER SELF wouldn't like me very much. She would be furious with me for not finding a way to apologize to Jillian. She would be disappointed that I went so far away from my parents and cousins only for a city of office buildings and big-box stores, that I live in a neighborhood that's all cement and no glass. She would refuse to put her arms inside of Brian's old hockey sweatshirt, refuse to step outside. She would scream that I was crazy for my boulder fixation and how could I do this to her, in just exactly the voice she—I—used to scream at my mother about I-don't-remember-what. Which means only that I'm a traitor to that young girl, not that it wasn't important. As I creep through the night streets, bulked up in the pilfered hoodie, I hear my mother warning me about suitcases packed with severed arms and the serial rapist who attacked a woman *while she was walking her pit bull.*

The occasional car whizzes by on the otherwise quiet road and damp grass grows thick in the moonlit industrial park. Out of habit, I think, *Rape Central,* then feel a sudden, buoyant relief. I don't have to be scared of rapists anymore, or serial killers, cervical cancer, or antibiotic-resistant bugs. My heart hammers with strange exuberance as I pick my way through the scrub and gravel and broken glass, until the shape of the watchful stones, a sentient horizon, becomes visible. Awe grabs me by the throat. The boulder mountain has transformed into a river of stone, extending into the night glow as far as I can make out; in the other direction, it ends abruptly at the bridge, as if paused in its onrush. As if waiting.

I look up at the bridge, half-expecting to glimpse myself looking back down. There's no one. A car clatters over the metal seam and is gone. The light behind it turns red, signaling the empty road. If Jillian were up there, what would I look like to her? Like art, or like nothing, a useless traffic light, a message for a no one who matters? How would I rather she see me: As the person we both wish I was, or the one who I am?

The ground shivers. The boulders' brute faces glower down, their gaps, disapproving mouths. The gouges on their surfaces that I'd thought so like my carving now seem random, like scratches left by an animal trying to get out. Or in.

Several of the gaps between the rocks are wide enough to crawl into, and although I hadn't planned this, or anything in particular, I find I want to. I climb down into the riverbed, into the weeds where the boulders stop. I choose one in the middle, wriggle in headfirst. The boulders are ice-cold, dry to the touch. I twist and push deeper until freezing rock presses in on every side and the outside is a glimpse of blue beyond my feet. My phone vibrates against my stomach. "Jillian?" I answer, the stone making my voice resound. "Babe," I whisper, the name I've maybe always wanted to call her. Or maybe only since now, whatever now is.

"Where the heck are you, kiddo? I woke up and you were gone." It's Brian. I press the speaker against the college seal of his sweatshirt, swaddling his voice. Comforting it, as I would an infant hybrid of his and my faces, of his and Jillian's, of mine and hers. I feel them in my belly. The sheer weight of our doleful babes. These children with whom I am forever pregnant and never aborting. "Hello?" mumbles swaddled Brian. "Wen? Are you okay? It sounds like you're underwater."

"I'm not coming home."

"What? You're breaking up."

I say it again because it feels good. Or bad, but right. "I'm not coming home."

I unswaddle the phone, let it go. It skitters down a rock, light blinking out. From far, far in the distance comes a rumble like a giant faucet turning on. The river waking up?

My teeth clatter in my skull. "Crush me," I plead to the rocky current. Even before it happens, I feel how entirely I will be swept away. It's not good or bad or even right. It just is. I shut my eyes. Whatever *now* this is can have me. *I'm yours*, I think. That has always been true.

Other People's Points of View

Ted is pretty sure she was born with the power. Her earliest memory is of lying on the bed in a diaper while her mother stood by the closet debating what to wear, a soft violet dress or a clingy yellow sheath. Baby Ted, sensing how sticky the yellow would be, wanted her mom to pick the violet.

From the sink, Ted's mother snorts. "'Violet'? I've never owned anything that color." Without looking up from her trig, Ted describes the stitches on the skirt, the pleated bodice. *Bodice.* Do girls even use that word, or just Ren-Fest creeps? Ted's mother frowns into the rainy yard. "You can't remember all that."

This is typical Ted's mother. Typical Roberta. Fussing about the trivial to distract herself from the critical. Ted does remember the dress—she has the muggle talent of good memory—but the point is how she saw it in the first place. Baby Ted was lying on the bed while the yellow and violet dresses hung out of sight in the closet. They had flashed into her infant mind as bright and noisy as the racket of her mother's indecision. But Roberta doesn't want to hear this. She has long closed herself off from the supernatural.

Lately, Ted has been trolling witch reddit. She got the idea because of a girl at school. The girl was poking at her phone across from Ted's locker. Ted could feel her choosing what to listen to, Regina Spektor or a track by a reality star, one of those women whose face was such a heightened version of average that it functioned as disguise. That woman wasn't a true musician, in Ted's opinion, and it bothered her that a queer-looking girl would have her on a playlist. It would have been mansplainy to say so aloud. Maybe it was mansplainy to think it. But the girl's thoughts were loud, and the right choice so obvious that for once Ted couldn't resist the urge to try to change a mind. Shutting her locker, Ted sang aloud the Spektor line that was running through the girl's head. "Better, better, better . . . ?"

"Oh my fucking g, you *witch!*" said the girl with admiration—and promptly selected the reality star's song. Ted couldn't hear the actual decision—that was beyond the scope of her ability—but the generic beats leaked from the headphones and got stuck in her brain, along with the girl's exclamation. Annoyed and thrilled by the girl's bad music taste, Ted lurched home, her thumbs tapping into the search bar, *Are witches real?*

ON WITCH REDDIT, lots of people—girls—brag about extrasensory perceptions.

It starts with a tingling. Like my blood is carbonated.
i can cure bad breth + headahces
Visions of the future dance in my dreams, I get dejavu
ALL THE TIME.

Ted thinks they are lying or are on too high or low a dose of psychiatric meds. It's misogynistic to doubt women, though. If Ted is misogynistic does that make Ted a chauvinist or a victim of internalized oppression? Scrolling past her inner skeptic, Ted reads deep into the threads to no avail. None of the internet girls say they can read minds verbatim. Definitely no one claims to exclusively read indecisive minds.

If Ted *is* a witch, it's the useless kind. For as long as Ted can remember, Ted has perceived the thoughts of people trying to come to decisions. The choices can be life-altering but mostly are dumb, like whether to text someone back or which route home will avoid the traffic jam. The more banal the decision, the shoutier. Restaurants are a nightmare: BUT I HAD A BAGEL YESTERDAY; CHIPS ARE EMPTY CALORIES; WHAT CAN I GET FOR TEN BUCKS? Serious decisions, weirdly, are easy to miss. They are a white noise that Ted rarely notices unless Ted gets up close.

ONCE, WHEN TED was in the third grade—before Ted had thought about being "she," although wasn't the feeling always there?—Ted chased her dog, Yoda, into the neighbor's yard. The yard was full of rosebushes and sunflowers, stalks and snags in which a dog could hide for hours. Ted wished she could read dog minds, but dogs, it seemed, were born knowing what they wanted.

"Yoda?" whispered Ted. Ted tiptoed onto the neighbor's porch, listening for the jingle of a collar. That's how Ted discovered the neighbor was considering suicide. *I can't, if it hurts this much . . . But if it doesn't, if it would go away.* Ted had learned about teen suicide from the It Gets

Better campaign, which she would only later connect to herself and learn to tiptoe around the terrifying concept of her own dead self. That day, though, the thoughts were coming from an adult mind. Grown-up minds had a harder feel, grayer. Especially this one. The gray thoughts came from inside the house, the other side of the wall.

Ted had never heard of grown-up suicide. Until that moment, Ted had assumed growing up was safe. Boring, maybe, but protected. All the worst uncertainty washed away by trivialities, like what Ted's mother worried about, whether to get blue Tide in the clear bottle or white Tide in the blue one. But the adult thoughts that seeped through the wall were the opposite of safe. Their grown-up grayness only made them more frightening. When kids were upset, they thought in streaks and vivid colors, quick with feeling. The neighbor's gray thoughts were steady. Like a list she was reciting. One by one, the suicide options gif-ed in Ted's mind's eye: pills, bridge, car exhaust, oven, gun, razor, noose. Ted barely understood what they meant— what did a tailpipe have to do with killing yourself?—but the death wish was hard and sure as the clear-edged images themselves.

It was all happening too fast. In a flick, the, razor was gone, oven was gone. Pills gif-ed. A bridge gif-ed. A clothesline noose waggled like a charmed snake. Ted might have been in over her head, but she recognized the rush of a mind headed toward a decision. After that, it would go dark. And then nothing. You couldn't change a closed mind.

Ted smacked the sliding door, desperate, but also, if she was honest with herself, she'd been excited. Her powers were finally going to help someone. "Hello? Miss?" Ted could see herself—*himself* then—on the news. *Heroic Local Boy*, the banner at the bottom of the screen would read, followed by a shot of Ted leading the wan neighbor by the hand. Maybe over to some flowers? The woman, weak, but grateful, would say, "I don't know how he knew, but this child saved my life! He made me hope again!"

The door slid open, revealing an ordinary-looking woman in a tasteful pantsuit and blazer. The woman's expression was cooler than Ted had expected and her clothes were crisper. She looked like the type of person who hated waiting at a deli counter and honked her horn at red lights. Impatient, not crazy. The woman narrowed her eyes at Ted. "Why are you in my yard?" Ted doubted herself. This woman could have been the star of an action movie about a well-dressed assassin. The only person at risk of being murdered here was Ted.

"My dog got out . . ." Ted stammered.

"Your dog," the woman repeated, but she was thinking about whether her niece would miss her.

Ted's lip began to quiver. It hit her: this was real life, not some hero fantasy. "Do you want to borrow Yoda?" she croaked, thinking of her teacher's therapy dog. "Or I could watch *Star Wars* with you?"

Star Wars always made Ted feel better, but the neighbor said, "I have to get ready for work," her mind on pill labels and quantities.

Ted felt sick. She had to act. "I promise you'll feel better soon!" she blurted as the door slid shut.

The neighbor's mind jerked silent so fast Ted touched her own ears, thinking she'd gone deaf. But as the woman gazed at her through the glass, she curved her mouth up into a smile. Of gratitude, Ted thought. Of hope. Somehow

Ted had done it. They'd done it together, her and this stranger, they'd made It Get Better.

That day at school Ted prepared herself for fame, or at least a thank-you card, but when she got home there was an ambulance in the neighbor's driveway. Roberta, watching from their porch, explained about the accidental overdose.

"But it wasn't an accident," Ted sobbed into her mother's soft arms.

"Oh sweetie," said Roberta. "What could we have done?"

Even now, Ted feels guilty about the neighbor. Roberta couldn't have done anything, but Ted could. Otherwise what was a power for. It keeps Ted up nights, wondering. Wondering also, what Ted will do if the same urges come over Ted one day, the death wishes, and no one is in Ted's head to stop them.

"Hey, boy-witch."

Ted flinches at the *boy*. Or maybe the *hey*. She looks up through her eyelashes at a silhouette outlined by the sun. Regina Spektor–girl, whose position on the stairs above creates the glorious illusion that Ted is short. "Hi."

"Which way you going?"

Ted points across the green. "Chem."

The girl nods like she knew it. She descends until she and Ted are at eye level. She has fluffy hair and blue plastic earrings. Moles. She isn't the sort of girl boys like, Ted doesn't think, but if Ted is going to be a girl, maybe this will be the sort Ted likes. "I have Ancient Greece."

Normally, Ted would say *groovy* instead of *cool*, instead of embarrassing herself by misusing newer, trendier slang. But what comes out is a football-bro "That's lit."

The girl crinkles an awkward smile, like she thinks Ted is being sarcastic. "Greece is the original rape culture. But we gotta know where we come from if we want real change."

The girl is talking to her like another girl, as if on some level she detects their sameness. Ted nods quickly and lowers her chin. For a girl, Ted's neck is grotesquely long, the Adam's apple a patriarchal rock hurled through feminism's front window. She is taking up way too much space. She would die—no, kill—no, die—to be five inches shorter. Six.

"See you," says the girl. She pounds down the steps until Ted spots dandruff in the fluffy hair. Dandruff schmandruff, the girl's confident stride seems to say. Only later does Ted realize why the girl seemed so confident: Ted couldn't read her mind. There was no flicker of doubt there to be read.

TED MAKES PRACTICE coming-out videos. Hormone-blocker videos. Transition videos. Ted—she—turns on the tub and records and deletes and records and deletes until Roberta taps on the door. "Honey, the drought." Roberta is concerned about climate change. Roberta can't decide if she should stockpile canned meats or chill out because Ted's generation will probably perfect carbon-capture technology and water desalinization. Roberta's thoughts are bland and constant. She has trouble deciding about many things: outfits, routes, whether to insist that Ted go to community college before a four-year or if that would be shooting Ted in the foot since studies show that men pay off their loans more successfully than women. Ted has to listen to Roberta agonize about swiping on her dating app but has yet to hear Roberta entertain the possibility that her son is really a daughter. A mom would intuit that, right? Would go back and forth, trying to decide which version of her child was true. If so, Ted, having a literal sixth sense for inner conflict, should have heard some stirring. Unless Roberta has known all along that Ted was a girl and is waiting for her daughter to catch on.

When Ted was little—when she was a little *girl*—she asked Roberta, "Can I have a vagina?" as if female genitalia were sold at toy stores in pink cardboard packages. Roberta repeated this story every Thanksgiving and Christmas, even though it made Ted's dad, Allen, uncomfortable. Allen finally divorced Roberta and moved to California, a decision he questioned but not so much to make him call or come to visit. Ted knows for a fact that Allen didn't divorce Roberta because of Ted wanting a vagina—if Ted *does* want a vagina—but Allen not liking Ted was a factor. Ted is glad her father moved away. It was depressing hearing Allen debate whether to invite Ted to play *Super Mario Kart* when Allen really wanted to do single-player behind a locked basement door. Ted doesn't like Allen either. On the "gendercritical" net, lack of male connection is listed as a prime cause of trans identity in "bio-males." People, or bots, who knows?, on those sites also say that "boys" with "gender identity disorder" dress up in lipstick and pumps, have lisps, like barbies, hate sports, and might try to saw off their penises with plastic knives.

Ted's pale chest puckers above the bathwater, nipples pricked red. She doesn't love her penis, it's gross and needy, who could love that, but she has never felt compelled to

maim it with picnic cutlery, and not even Roberta, who
is against Barbie on principle, wears lipstick and heels,
except to divorce court. Ted pulls the plug with a toe.
Water glugs down the drain.

"Hi, my name is . . . My name is whatever. Today was
my first day living mentally as a girl. I am already more in
touch with my anima. I've decided to give her, my anima,
a name. Like a spirit guide? But not really, because, you
know, appropriation? Anyway, her name is, um, Leia."

Ted hits stop, then trash. Not everything can be named
after *Star Wars*. Ted replugs the tub and runs more hot
water. *My clit*, she—*she*—thinks as she rubs it. *My clit is
hard*.

"YOU INTO HEALING crystals?"

Ted pictures the structure of rock salt: a cube, the ordi-
nariest shape. "Yeah. I mean, I'm interested."

"My coven eats lunch above the theater. You should
come."

Regina Spektor–girl says she has to run, then does, her
backpack slapping like a wild, free animal kicking up dust.

TED IS DISAPPOINTED. She thought a coven would be
female. In fact, it's two girls, two boys, and an enby who
Ted, because of internalized gender normativity, couldn't
help mentally categorizing as female and, aloud, like an
idiot, called "she."

The coven asks Ted's pronouns. Ted chickens out.
"Whatever," she says. "He. Or them. Or whatever."

One of the boys, a Tom or Tim, makes a disgusted
sound in the back of his throat. "Not caring is a privilege."
Tom-Tim debates whether to say something to Aline, the

Regina Spektor–girl, about Ted being one of those guys who fakes pansexuality to earn feminist trust.

The rest of the coven is nice. The enby, Dash, is deciding whose Brit Lit homework to copy, the other boy, Kiran, whether he thinks Ted is cute. Petite Mary wonders if she should go on a cleanse. "Do you want my fries?" Mary asks. "Sure," says Ted. If Mary is right, the fries are loaded with trans fats. Ted prays they go to her thighs.

A coven turns out to be a group of friends who throw mellow parties that Roberta dubs, cringingly, "adorable." These gatherings fit cross-legged on one of their beds, involve quantities of herbal tea, chalked pentagrams, and the overwriting of Ted's *Star Wars* knowledge with dialogue from *The Craft*. Supported by her coven, Ted grows her hair less short, buys high-waisted jeans and tucked tops ("they're shirts," said Aline, "unless you work at the Gap"), and transitions from awkward "he/they" to embodied "she." *She* tells her new friends about her power and *her* friends share stories of their own empathic sensitivities: Mary's ability to smell pregnancy; Kiran, whose poltergeist once shattered a bulb in the language lab; Timo's tarot cards; Dash's gift for anti-hexing. Only Aline leaves paranormal territory unstaked.

One night, when the boys have gone to make out on the pull-out sofa, after the girls plus Dash have battled for and won Ted's woman-born right to slumber upstairs, Aline and Ted squat on the wet balcony vaping mullein. According to Ted's phone, mullein should get her a little high, but if so, high feels a lot like the usual anxiety of being near Aline.

"Do you want this aragonite? It came with my quartz." Their fingers touch as Aline passes her the crystal, its facets cratered like a magnified wart. "Aragonite's for making decisions." Aline kisses her. Ted drops the vape, which clatters loudly on the metal balcony. Ted and Aline freeze. They must have woken up the parents. But the only noise is literal crickets, the buzz of the bulb above the garage. Aline kisses her again. Ted smalls her lips to match Aline's, stills to not disturb Aline's mouthy-tasting tongue. No false moves, thinks Ted. It's what Roberta says around cats, though Aline is more like bird of prey.

"How did you do that?" Ted means how did Aline kiss her without agonizing. Ted has worried for months about whether to kiss Aline, if this is true desire or a crush of convenience. Does she want to *be* Aline or *do* her? It is lucky Aline isn't psychic or Ted's indecisiveness would have chased her away. Aline is the poster girl of certainty. Aline's few inner battles relate to music, and that's because Aline doesn't care much about music, which she considers pure soundtrack. Ted should tell Aline that she's pretty. Ted clears her throat. "You're so confident."

Aline drags a bitten nail across Ted's palm. The sensation is uncomfortable but erotic. Ted wonders where Aline learned it. Ted pulls her knees to her chest to hide her clit's needy outburst. Aline whispers, "Deep down we all know what we want."

Aline leans in and Ted obediently slouches lower. Aline gropes under Ted's shirt. It's more painful than sexy, a relief, since the pain shrinks her clit. The night air fills with their mingled stink. A second relief: Aline's sweat, leaking through her salt crystal deodorant, smells worse than hers.

Does Ted know what she wants? Her hand hurts where she has been squeezing the aragonite. She endures Aline's energetic kissing until her chin burns from saliva and

Aline proclaims that "that was hot." In the morning, Ted's stubble hurts and the leftover flavor of Aline's mouth is stronger than her own morning breath. She feels invaded. Claimed. She can't tell if this feels good. She wonders, watching Aline wolf down cereal, if Aline is tasting Ted, or just Quinoa Puffs and peanut butter. Ted can't quite imagine her own flavor lingering. There is nothing as strong inside her as the spit inside Aline.

ROBERTA CLEARS HER throat. "I notice you are giving away your clothes?"

Ted should have an answer ready. Roberta has been considering bringing this up for weeks. She should, as Dash advised, have written Roberta a letter like Dash and their parents did as homework for Dash's family therapist. Then, a letter had seemed impossible. Now it's a missed opportunity. It would be much nicer to never have to say it aloud. "You said I should scale down before college."

"That's months away. And I meant your old toys. The plushies and Lego."

"I'll do those too."

Roberta actually sticks her foot in the closing door.

"Mom."

"Honey. They're your boy-ey clothes. If there's something you want to talk about . . ."

Ted presses her face against the gap, her body safely hidden. "*Boy-ey* isn't a word."

"Anything can be a word." Roberta's voice high and tight, her eyes a guilt-inducing pink. Why is Ted doing this to her mother? But also: Why is her mother doing this to her?

She channels Aline. Forces herself full of confidence, of Aline's quotes from Judith Butler and Rain Dove and Vivek

Shraya. "Mm, that's not really true? Language happens organically. *Boy-ey* would never be organic. *Girly* exists because of negative biases about girls. Even if you say *boy-ey*, it still isn't the opposite of *girly* because the opposite doesn't exist. Like with reverse discrimination." Ted is lit up with herself, this articulation of ideas she barely grasps. She should do this, always. Wrap her mind around a steadier one. She can find herself by becoming someone else. "You know what I mean?" She waits for Roberta to be impressed, to say, like she used to, when Ted would really wow her, *I almost can't believe you're my kid.* But Roberta only says, "I guess you aren't ready to talk," and recedes, her features shrinking, her undecided thoughts silenced into impenetrable certainty. About what, Ted isn't sure.

IS HE—? He can't be—because. Should I say they? *It's so awkward, though!* Thoughts Roberta abandons midway, not that Ted needs to be a mind reader. Mornings, they slink around the kitchen, Roberta going for creamer to avoid Ted at the cereal cabinet. Ted crouching for nettle tea to keep from brushing into Roberta at the coffee maker. At school, Aline pulls Ted onto her narrow lap. "Homo!" boys shout from cars speeding out of the lot. "Lesbo!" screams back Aline. Ted knows Aline means it as an editorial suggestion but wishes in this case she would be quiet. It's riskier for me, she wants to tell Aline, but isn't sure that's true. Ted is larger than Aline. Whiter. Ted has never been beat up. The worst threats she gets are when she's with Aline. Maybe if she grows boobs it will be worse. She has heard that, that change can be worse than denial. But if she's not in denial anymore, if the change has already begun, if she's on a trajectory of want that won't quit till she gets, is staying the same any safer? Each direction she looks is dark and full of danger.

Ted considers hormone blockers. Online, she finds a magazine article about "desistors," ex-trans kids whose gender dysphoria turned out to be a passing delusion. Adult women, former FTMs with testosterone-bristled chins, stare out from the screen, telegraphing across space and time: Don't Make Our Mistake.

Ted divides a sheet of paper into PROS and CONS. On the PROS side, she doodles tits of various shapes and sizes. Pointy tits, melon tits, small, square tits like deflated pecs. On the CONS side, she copies out a phrase, "deep vein thrombosis," from the website Roberta calls hypo-chondria-dot-com. She thinks of these de-transitioned ex-transmen pouring out their body-sorrow to a magazine reporter. Their voices will never un-deep. Their beards will keep needing to be shaved. Ted strokes her own concealer-dusted jaw in confused kinship. Estrogen, she knows, will soften her only subtly. She is stuck with her overgrown skeleton. On Tumblr, trans girls write about wanting to rewind themselves so the cells that veered boy can turn girl instead. They talk about always knowing they were female. But Ted isn't sure about herself. Is she a real girl or just an ill-fitting person? She imagines being born into the Right body, an XX body, growing up girl. In her mind, though, that road dead-ends at this same confusion. She imagines her XX girl-self asking for a penis. What if gender dysphoria *is* Ted's true gender? What if she's doomed to always be lost? She watches a playlist of reac-tions to those old, bullying videos. It Doesn't Get Better, these ones are called. She wonders when she will begin to want to kill herself.

"YOU'VE REALLY SWALLOWED the binary, T.D.!" Aline roars. Ted's heart fluttering in anxiety, Aline, furious, Wonder Woman hands on hips. "Gender's fluid. You can be anything you want. You think I'm a 'normal girl'? I go by 'they' sometimes, I have genderless days."

Ted insists that no, she wants to take Aline's birth control pills, to start today. Ted is a girl. She's sure, deep down. She knows who she is.

Ted gives Aline head. It is sloppy, her nose streaked with vaginal secretions. Aline tells her, "Don't stop, don't stop," and then, "not *there*." Aline debates whether to let her keep going. Ted's tentative jabs turn her off, but Aline doesn't want to make her insecure. Too late, Aline, Ted thinks. Seeing herself from her girlfriend's point of view, Ted is so ashamed, she drips tears in Aline's pubic hair. "Let me." Aline jams her knuckles against Ted's nose, groping herself manually. She arches in pleasure, blocking Ted's mouth from a repeat attack. Ted's lips bob uselessly against the knot of Aline's fist. Ted might as well be on a lonely moon of Saturn. She might as well be the moon. Cold and shut-off, in outer space.

On the front stoop, Ted finds a pube crusted to her cheek. "How long has that been there?"

Aline pokes the spot. "A while."

Ted pictures herself again from Aline's perspective, lapping away like an untrained pup. Boy-ey. "You could have said something."

"You're always messy. It's cute."

Ted, who spent several frustrating pre-date hours sponging on and cold-creaming off bronzer in a failed effort to create feminine contours, feels betrayed. Confident—narcissistic?—Aline puckers for a kiss. Ted offers the corner of her mouth. *You two witches are soooo cute,* the coven would say if they were here. Aline pinches Ted and tells her she loves her.

"Love you," echoes Ted, erasing her own pronoun. *No one ever says their pronouns are "I"/"me,"* she thinks. Is that weird? It feels like a "gendercritical" thought. Ted tiny-walks along the curb, her lower back cramping. Left-over leaves from before winter lie limp in the gutters. Most of the trees flaunt green buds but a few remain bare. Ted identifies with these late trees and maybe-dead trees, bony naked against the sky. Maybe she is a plant. Maybe she was never supposed to be human.

"I SUPPORT TRANS women, Ted. You know that. But you've never been . . . binary. When you were little, you played dolls and trucks. Have you thought about a more flexible label? Agender? Isn't that a thing now?" Roberta pronounces this between rabbit nibbles of her Impossible Burger. Around them, diners mentally shout about sweet potato fries versus olive oil coleslaw, chickpea bake versus seitan enchiladas, sharing appetizers versus solo entrees, we split versus I pay. The restaurant was Ted's idea. Plantopia is the coven's favorite and Ted thought the noise of so many strangers thinking would help distract her from Roberta's inner monologue. Hubris, Ted recalls from Aline's flashcards, is when a heroine's misplaced confidence causes her to defy the gods. Had Ted not been pummeled by eaters' this-or-thats, she would have noticed her mother's thoughts and fled to the single stall bathrooms long before Roberta spoke up.

Ted fake-laughs. "Funny."

Roberta lowers her bun. "Sweetie, no, um, person is an island. You need to communicate."

"I communicate with my *friends*," she says scathingly. *You are not my friend, she thinks at Roberta. You are my enemy.*

Roberta inhales, holds for three, exhales. She is offensively calm. "I've been reading. There are some kids who change their minds later. They say it was traumatic. Having done that to themselves. And, ending up . . ."

"Ending up like *this*?" Standing to show Roberta her monster body, Ted bangs her head into the lamp and trips on the carpet. Everyone, the old-school lesbians, the beardos, the hippie students on dates, stares. Humiliated, crying, Ted, shrill giantess, flaps out of the restaurant, brushing nonexistent hairs from her contoured cheeks, screaming, "Don't you fucking follow me!"

Aline agrees to meet at the elementary school. Mary and Dash come too. They stand on the swings, yelling across to each other. Ted exaggerates what happened so they'll understand why Roberta made her feel so terrible. "And she said maybe I should go to one of those camps!"

Mary leans into the plastic-coated chains. "A conversion camp?" Ted actually meant one of those LGBTQ2IA bonding camps for queer kids too awkward to make their own friends, but a conversion camp sounds more right. That's what it felt like. "You know Roberta. She's a liberal. She'd never say it directly. But . . . yeah. That's what she wants."

"Ohhh, messed up," exclaims Dash, who wants to tell about when their grandmother tried to get them exorcised but worries it will come across as insensitive since Dash has always had the loving support of their parents and family therapist.

"Maybe she's right," says Aline. "About you regretting it. You're always saying you wish you were FTM . . ." Aline trails off suggestively, as Roberta had, a gesture toward the elephant on the swing set, the fact that no one believes Ted is a girl.

Ted thrusts herself against the air, the chains buckling, the swing barely dipping forward. She might as well be on the ground. "I *meant* I wished being MTF was like being FTM. Being MTF, you're like everyone's whipping girl, and girl hormones don't fix anything important. Trans guys inject themselves and, whammo, sound like Barry whatshisface."

"Manilow?" says Dash.

"Ew. Nooo." It comes out whiny. Barry whatever, rumbling deep, an underwater river she could get washed away on. Barry the other singer, the Black one. Aline sails neatly back and forth, a straight line. Aline is made for swings. She can go anywhere, stay the same if she wants. The world will make way. Ted stumbles down to kick at the hollow metal pole. It *dongs* like swing sets everywhere. Mary is not sure what to do, she wants to make everyone feel better and can't and this makes her feel worse. Dash has a Latin test tomorrow and wonders what Aline would think if Dash peaced out.

"I'm fine," Ted announces. "You witches should go." But they don't. They all four walk together to the liquor store where a former super-senior sells Aline tallboys of Colt and drink behind Big Ben's QuikMart, sitting on a curb that smells mildly of pee. Mary gives Ted a fringe of spiky braids, declaring her hair to be "like a baby's." Aline and Dash wrestle in a patch of dead grass. Aline pins Dash, who shrieks. Neither struggles internally about flaunting mutual crushes in front of Ted. They should bone right there. Have fun. See if Ted cares.

ROBERTA TEARS OPEN the plastic cereal bag and hands over the box. "Everly."

"Huh?"

Marshmallow horseshoes tinkle against the bowl. A previous morning's cereal, sterile from the dishwasher, is caked on the ceramic. Ted scratches at it with the blade of her spoon.

"It's what I would name you if I had you now." Roberta doesn't add the "if" Ted's brain fills in: *if you were a girl.* Roberta crinkles around the eyes, but her mind reveals nothing. Maybe Ted has been too hard on her. Everly, though. It sounds like the kind of girl who wears a pony-tail and sings piano ballads. A horse-girl too shy to raise her hand in class.

"It's nice." It's okay. The leprechaun on the box, tumbled by *3 NEW rainbows!*, grins filthily. Roberta considers hugging Ted. Instead, she lightly brushes Ted's neck and trundles out of the kitchen.

That's it. Even her mother is labeling her now. Ted's got to learn to commit.

I LOVE YOU. Ted folds the note, then unfolds it to check her handwriting is legible. It is, but the folds have smudged the letters. Aline might not know who it's from. *I could be anyone.* Ted signs a heart and letter T. Refolds. Is it weird to say love then use a heart? Unfolds. *Love,* she pens redundantly inside the heart. She adds an *E-D* after the *T.*

Aline gave Ted her locker com weeks ago. This is Ted's first time turning the black knob and being alone with the taped-up Instax of them kissing. At first glance, like always, the Ted and Aline in the picture look like boyfriend-girlfriend. Then, as if a switch has turned in her brain, Ted sees two girls kissing. One girl is tall, yes, and angular, like architecture interpreting the female body, and the other is curvy, but both seem like girls.

Ted, knowing deep down what she wants, pushes the folded note into the *Odyssey*. Hopefully near the part where Penelope decides to believe Odysseus, even though it's bullshit that Penelope had to wait so long. Ted vows to identify more with Penelope from now on. She will unstick her foot from the doorway of manhood. She could always have opened that door if she wanted to. But she didn't want to. That's the point. She didn't want to. Now she does. She's doing it.

"THANKS FOR THE note."

They are under the vaping tree, their meeting place during Friday free periods. They both believe in having good lungs but appreciate the smell of e-juice. Tobacco, Aline points out, has been healing people for centuries. Ted mostly likes how nicotine makes people focused: smokers rarely broadcast their thoughts. Today, though, the peace is interrupted by a whisper of indecision. Too quiet to tell who the thought is coming from, the emos or the scene goths or the out-of-place, normcore guy-person lurking by the fence.

Ted sproings Aline's curl. "Thank *you*."

The whispered thought gets louder. *If she* and *am I* and the seep of guilt. It's Ted's least-favorite kind of indecision—where the person wants to do what will hurt someone else and is only calculating when.

"Are you expecting someone?" asks Aline.

Ted turns back around. "Just my witch radar going off."

"A-ha." Aline wears an unfamiliar expression. One side of her lip drawn up, skeptical.

Could come across as TERF-ish, says the whisper. *Everyone will think* Do it already! Ted wants to scream at whichever brain is being so annoying. Aline has straight-up challenged Ted's witchcraft; trans-exclusionary radical feminism is the last thing Ted needs to be thinking about. To Aline, she says, "You don't believe me."

"What do you mean?"

Ted lowers her voice, not wanting the scene kids to overhear. "You don't think my power is real."

Aline smiles in a way Ted will have to tell her comes across as condescending. "Truth isn't a binary, T-T."

Ted's chest feels tight. She is probably overreacting. She wants to be overreacting. "What does that even mean?"

"If it's real for *you,* it's real."

Ted has been around this block but never with a sister witch. The point is, witches work with forces others ignore. She toes her boot into the mud. "What about Regina Spektor? How did I know which song it was, if I'm not psychic?"

I could wait until graduation. It's expected to break up before college. Everyone else will understand. But she's already so needy . . . Aline's vague expression, the too-familiar look of a person lost in thought, tells Ted what she must have already known. Her girlfriend wants to break up with her.

"Dump me then," Ted whispers. "I'll tell the coven it's not because you're transmisogynist." She throws out her arms like MTF Jesus. He—she—probably was one. That pretty hair and befriending sex workers, and doomed to misgendering until the end of time.

"Baby." Aline engulfs Ted in her ample, taken-for-granted softness. Fickle estrogen, thinks Ted, gently mauling cis-girls into womanhood while hormonized transgirls barely get butt-chub to cushion their fall. "I'm not going to dump you. Don't cry, sweet Ted." Then: "What's so funny?"

Ted against the vaping tree, crumpling with laughter. Hysteria, actually. Seventeen years old and she finally understands the secret to changing a mind. People decide the *opposite* of whatever they are told. *Commit suicide this afternoon!* she should have ordered the neighbor. *Force me to come out in a vegan restaurant,* she should have instructed her mom.

"Uh, T, the bell's ringing." Aline's sideways face through the veil of Ted's hair. "Should I text Roberta? You're acting kind of . . . bananas."

Ted breathes one, two, three. Giggles through her nose. "Ev . . ." She gets it out. "Everly."

"What?" says Aline.

"I'm Everly," chokes Ted—chokes Everly. Aline rubs her back in slow circles. Today is the first day of the rest of Everly's life. Wait. *Not* Everly, not a horse-girl, not blue puff–haired Aline. Today is the first day of this witch's life. *Call me Power*, thinks the witch. *Call me Anima.*

Call me Leia.

Yes: Leia. For this moment at least, it is exactly what she wants.

Pig in a Poke

The kid was Dara's idea. This was back when Dov and her were still together, grifting as South American shamans under the aliases Ana del Mundo Irreal y el Perro Hundido. They were undressing in the EcoVillage guest yurt after a real crap-ride of an ayahuasca ceremony when Dara brought it up. She'd been especially quiet that evening, but Dov assumed she was brooding over the weekend's paltry take. A third of the turnout promised and the attendees the wrong kind of hippies, either too broke or too cheap to buy anything. After the hippies finished vomiting and came down from their last high, they loaded into VW buses, battered minivans, and puttering electric cars. No time for Dov to snake oil them about the carcinogenic molecules in drinking water, let alone demo the plastic water filters he'd cleverly repackaged as Hippocratic Sieves. On the way out, he heard a woman say that, of her ten ayahuasca experiences, Ana and el Perro's had been the least spiritually uplifting. "The leaders seemed awfully tethered to the material realm if you ask me."

Dov trampled a ring inside the yurt, fuming to Dara. Material realm his ass. They hadn't even brought out the merch that packed their van: nicotine chakra patches, VA(so)LI(ne) HAI fertility balm, mystic room spritz, vibrational soaps, reed mats woven by Ana y el Perro's tribe (or so Dov dubbed the poor saps employed in Taiwan's factory district), CDs that cured headaches, illuminated salt lumps that cured cancer, latex mittens that cured impotence. But the philistines only wanted to get high and go home.

"Why shouldn't they?" said Dara, shedding her vole headdress. "The high is the only thing we're selling that's not garbage."

"These are quality wares," protested Dov.

"Oh Dov," Dara sighed. She scratched her scalp vigorously. Dov rolled the shell bracelet down his arm trying not to rip out any hairs. "They buy that stuff because they want the tribal mojo, which lately we're in short supply of, in case you haven't noticed. Olive skin and ethnic looks don't cut it anymore. I swear, we're getting paler by the day."

The hairs ripped anyway. "So it's a race thing."

"It's a *perception* thing . . ."

Dov tuned her out. As if in masculine solidarity, the yellow teeth of his vole headdress shone at Dara's perfect rear. Traditional shamans, those pious jerks who refused to brand themselves, wore wolves or cougars. Anyone looked powerful with a predator on their head, but it took real artistry to make rodents terrifying. Toothpaste applied weekly for a spiky ruff was the magic ingredient. That and supergluing their lips to their gums.

"When the competition was blondies with one Native American great-great-great-great-grandmother between them, we looked authentic. But the field has changed. The competition has gone global. Multicultural. The human race has diversified. We have to keep up."

Dov was bored to tears by these reverse pep talks. Dara loved to pronounce their doom, not that she ever proposed a real solution. Brainy or no, she could be a real downer, a trait made bearable only by sex appeal. Even after ten years, her bead-draped legs, oiled and sinewy, still made Dov shiver. The best practice was to expedite these little talks. "How 'bout we do a visualization?" It was the kind of hokey exercise marks ate up. "Let's picture ourselves climbing a mountain, about to plant our flag—"

"I want to adopt," said Dara.

Dov stopped. "Huh?"

"Let's adopt a kid."

"A kid?" He had to have misheard. "A *kid* kid?"

Dara unwrapped the leather thongs of her sandals from her legs. It seemed to take a very long time. "A smart, foreign kid, light-skinned enough to pass as our own, dark enough so we're taken seriously. We teach it the ropes and get some extra help out of the deal too."

He resisted the urge to bang on his ear. "You want us to have a kid."

"Not *have*. Adopt." Dara peeled off her rabbit fur tunic. "Consider it a new product line: Same 'tribal mojo,' now with overtones of better futures and unconditional love."

Normally it was Dov who dreamed up the crazy plots then waited for Dara to stab holes in them. If his idea leaked, she'd scold, *You have to play nine moves ahead, Dov.* If it held water or only dripped, Dara would disappear on a long walk and return hours later, notebook crammed with diagrams and figures. *Here's how we'll do it*, she'd say and he'd nod, stunned to find his wispy vision transmuted into muscular reality. Brains as well as hots. Who got that lucky?

In their decade of partnership, this was the first time Dara had come to him with a pitch, the first that he found himself in a position to do the approving. He couldn't imagine saying no, but neither could he picture them as parents. For example, where would they put it? Dov liked his legroom. If they had a kid there tonight, it would have to sleep on the ground. And what if it complained to someone? Was Dara having some menopausal hysteria, an urge to symbolically procreate before the last of her eggs spoiled? Even a logic-minded woman was a woman after all.

Dara undid her embroidered skirt and stood before him, impassive, in a pair of heart-patterned panties. The hearts were made of lace. The lace had little holes in it. Through the holes, her shaved pubes seemed to wave.

All through the ayahuasca ceremony she'd had the panties under her furs, the coarse animal skin rubbing against the tatting, the tatting against her mons, the irritable, erotic fur arousing her juices . . . Dov brought his mind back manfully to attention. "Aren't kids kind of . . . tricky?"

Dara crossed her arms. "Tricky how?"

"You know." His examples fled. "They spill things. They, uh, put stuff in their mouths. You trip over them. Um, fleas?"

Dara bent over her duffel bag. Dov visualized the panties slithering to the dirt floor, exposing Dara's wet lust. That was what this conversation needed: a turn. But the visualization didn't take. Dara pulled on her jeans, and handed him a notebook.

"Here."

"What's this?"

"Open it."

Dov flipped through the gridded pages. Dates, place-names, and dollar amounts appeared in Dara's tight cursive, some in black, some in red. She clearly wanted him to ask what it meant.

"Black stands for income. Red, for losses."

The open page was mostly red. The others too. "No, wrong. Way off. You forgot to carry something. Check your numbers."

Dara flipped the book to the very back. Here she'd listed every shaman they'd ever met, from the obvious fakes to the true believers, plus a bunch Dov hadn't heard of, each with earnings and family size. "Carlos Cielo Montaña, white Mexican with three sons, brought in 250K last year. The de San Jacintos, a Peruvian couple, they're about as shamanic as the crap I took this morning—I know for a fact the woman has a PhD in astrophysics—childless but morenos, earned half a million. Eye of God Sacred Heal-ing—white as bleached teeth—six adopted kids and a net worth equal to a pharmaceutical company. The Tonalpohu-allis, billionaire Swedes who actually think they're Aztec warriors. They adopted Quechua triplets. We, on the other hand, spent this fiscal year sixty grand in the hole."

Dov resisted the urge to burrow under Dara's T-shirt. Those guys' online warehouses sold *generics*. Cloying sage, stinky copal, salmonella-carrying eagle feathers, tiger teeth—riddled with cavities, he bet.

"But they're chumps!"

"Successful chumps."

"What do they have that we—" but he'd seen the link. Children were worth their weight in Indigenous great-grandparents. If those Stone Age twig-burners could keep a barrel of kids alive, he and Dara could handle one measly stinker.

"I already made an appointment. We fly out tomorrow. It's obligation-free. If you don't like the orphans, we'll go to the beach. What do you say?"

Dov *had* wanted to tour an orphanage ever since that movie about the pickpocketing British urchins. The film's rousing musical numbers raised big questions. Did the kids know how to dance when they arrived, or did the orphan keeper provide lessons? Were orphans universally nimble? What happened to the rhythmless duds?

"I guess a look-see couldn't hurt."

"Think of it as browsing. If a Dov Junior shows up, that's icing on the cake."

Even he could admit, *Dov Junior* had a nice ring.

THEY SHOWED THE orphan keeper a video from Spirit-Guide.com, a small boy spinning in a feathered skirt.

"One like him but with either my chin or nose, ideally both," said Dov.

The keeper rubbed the back of his neck. "Solo hay niñas y ya están grandes. A lo mejor la semana que viene. Es un mercado inestable."

Dara negotiated with the guy in Spanish, flashed the cash. From a back room, the guy retrieved a grotesque female infant. Dead-eyed, its mouth was stamped in a frown, and coils of mucous arced from the nostrils.

"Aquí tienen," he announced with as little enthusiasm as Dov felt. As if the baby guessed what they were thinking, it opened its black hole of a mouth and clamped a lone tooth onto the guy's finger.

"Puta madre," he swore, thrusting the baby away from his body with both hands.

Suspended and wriggling, the baby looked even worse, gargoylish and weirdly eager. With uncanny precision for a baby—not that Dov was an expert—it straightened one leg and strained a wrinkly foot toward the key ring on the desk. "What a freak show," he whispered. But Dara was transfixed. As if this little performance meant anything, she watched the baby's toes flick and grab and dangle the keys for a moment before the orphan keeper plucked them away.

The orphan keeper winked admiringly at the baby. "We have a live one," he announced in the stiff, proud voice of a TV host, before muttering to Dara, "Es una ganga, señora. No se lo pierda."

"Let me see her," said Dara.

Dov rolled his eyes. Crows collected shiny objects too. Didn't make them geniuses. "C'mon. This one's too young."

Dara ignored him. With an effortless, feminine gesture, she scooped up the infant, murmuring, "You're trouble, aren't you?" Same line she'd used on Dov the first time they fucked.

"That's not a boy," he hissed.

"True," Dara said as though the thought had just occurred to her. She balanced the thing against her shoulder while counting bills into the orphan keeper's palm. The baby cried and twisted, but Dara, unfazed, held tight.

IF IT HADN'T been for the noise, Dov could have gotten used to even a girl baby. On the flight back to the US, the thing went off in his lap like a car alarm. Its cries diminished to smoke-detector-at-low-battery volume when Dara held it, but Dara didn't like to, she said it felt moist, and handed it back to him.

The second they landed, Dov left the howler on the seat and strode alone into the terminal. Dara caught up with him outside the ladies' room.

"Gotta pee," she said, dumping the baby into his arms.

It did feel moist. Swampy almost. Its damp, close heat made Dov sweat. Its cheeks reddened and its lips pursed. "That's right," urged Dov, though it was ridiculous, talking to a baby. "Hold it in." The lip trembled. "It's like holding in a fart. You gotta clench up your butt muscles." Talking to a baby was not only ridiculous but pointless. The mouth stretched for a wail so piercing that other travelers dropped bag handles to cover their ears. The blare was like a freaking siren.

A group of well-coiffed mothers rotated in unison to take in the frail, miserable infant. They chattered loudly among themselves.

"How awful."

"That diaper needs changing."

The last scoffed, "Some people should be sterilized," looking pointedly at Dov.

Dara emerged from the women's room, dabbing on fresh lipstick.

He gestured after the ladies huffing retreat. "Those bitches wanted to cut off my balls."

Dara lit up. "Oh?"

"'Oh?'" he mimicked. "What is this, female conspiracy?"

She leaned in and darted a tongue in his ear. "Don't be silly."

He shivered, relieved and a little annoyed to feel his anger turning to want. "Then what?"

"You *passed*," she whispered hot against his neck. "They believed you were the father. The real kind. A baby *maker*."

He straightened. "Baby maker." He could get used to that idea. Puffing with pride, he barely felt the loud, wet, smelly weight in his arms. "Your man's still got it, eh?"

Dara squeezed his ass. "Hon, you are slick as an oil spill."

DARA WAS RIGHT about everything. They put up a few family pics on the website and voila. Constant email pings, bids and out-bids for Ana y el Perro's services, booked straight through the summer. Them and their secret weapon.

One hitch: their secret weapon wasn't fit for public appearances, not with those lungs. They could take turns babysitting at events for a while, but word traveled. If people figured out the baby hated its parents, adoptive or otherwise, Ana and el Perro's keisters would be cooked.

Dara collapsed onto the motel bedspread and kicked off her shoes. "Let her cry it out."

So Dov tossed and turned through nights of wailing. Days. Nearly a week. Meanwhile, the kid frowned, eyes full of vitriol and blame. It didn't look at Dara like that, just him. And why? Did he stink? Was he failing to support its neck properly? Did he have bad vibes? Dara dismissed his concerns. "That's her resting face, babe. It's not personal." Dov wasn't so sure.

He googled. He had the neck support thing right but the feeding wrong. One night he watched YouTube videos of fathers burping babies until his brain was crammed with hairy knuckles and spit-up, splattered bibs. Wired,

Dov paced the grimy carpet. The baby—a-snooze at last—lolled in its cardboard box, slippery gums working tongue, the milk curve of belly rising, falling. *Infanticide* was such a judgmental term. Nature left to its own devices snuffed out the defenseless faster than you could say "coochie-coo." Any predator would regard the kid as a tasty side dish, its powder-soft arms a finger-lickin' delicacy. Dov could sneak the box out to the curb while Dara slept, let rats and raccoons feast.

Worry lines creased the baby's forehead, then relaxed. Slowly, quietly, for no good reason, Dov poked his index finger into the whorl of its fist. Like a Chinese fingertrap, the hand snapped closed. Dov jerked away.

"Waaaaaaaaaaaa!" screeched the baby, clawing at its box.

Chest pounding, Dov backed toward Dara's side of the bed. He could still feel the ring of pressure where the baby had gripped. Something was wrong with that thing. It had engorged his finger like a snake eating a mouse. It cried like a deposed dictator.

"Dara," he whispered. Legs splayed across the mattress, hair frizzing from under her pillow, Dara snored lightly. She did not so much as murmur when he took shelter inside her arms, but her heart thundered like a missile strike and he dreamed a skyful of baby-bombs dropping from split-bellied planes.

Dov woke to quiet. Blinds atomized the sun into a thin, sick light. It took a moment to register that Dara and the baby were gone. So was his luggage.

On a stack of takeout menus, a note was scrawled. It said Dara had packed the car and taken the baby for diapers and milkshakes, would swing back after.

Uneasily, he switched on the television. Pitches for Avon membership and home refinancing. A shammy that sucked cola out of carpet pile like a vacuum. On a life insurance ad, a bearded man lifted a toddler onto his shoulders as the image faded into text: *I Love You, Daddy. Little snot-eater*, thought Dov. In real life, Daddy would fake his own death and move to Borneo with the insurance money, but you couldn't put that in a commercial.

It bugged him, Dara and the baby going off together. Not that it was out of character, Dara often left him asleep to go "walk," claiming to enjoy the morning air—a.k.a. the car exhaust of rural highways, stench of manure, eye-watering pollen. Dov had never gotten what was so great about "alone time." The buzz of the could-be-anywhere hotel room, the droning voices on the TV, the chatter of his own thoughts all bleated like a dial tone, a demand to hang up or call someone, anyone. Still, Dara, rare creature, lied only by omission; if she said she'd gone to buy milk, she had. If she said she wanted to let him rest, she did. But she'd taken the baby. It bothered him, her and the baby jollying around like a couple of Thelma and Louises, Dara confessing secrets while the baby, communicating via facial contortions, eviscerated Dov in absentia. The baby gesturing at the wide Dov-less horizon as if to say, "Plenty of fish in the sea, gurl!"

DOUBTS ASIDE, business continued to improve. He and Dara followed the trail of new work up the coast and down again. Communes, health spas, nonprofit organizations, a Tahoe mountain resort. After all the drama about infantile moistness, he had expected Dara to stick him with babysitting duties at showtime, but in fact she insisted he lead the various healing sessions and cleansing rituals while she and the baby stayed behind. "People love you," she said. He couldn't argue with that. In two weeks, he sold off backstock they'd been dragging around for years. He signed new contracts, brought in substantial donations, and negotiated a week-long Soul-Spiration session with a men's fire walking group in Kauai that provided a deluxe suite at the base of a volcano. He would have told Dara, but when the message came she was outside their chalet coaching the baby to escape from a snow tunnel.

He'd seen them play this "game" before. In Oregon, Dara set out a rabbit snare and clapped as the baby wobbled and rolled sideways, dodging the trap. In Yreka, she dumped the baby in a gunnysack. Through the burlap, its tiny, eerily dexterous fingers coaxed the knot loose. Yesterday, Dara had bought it gag handcuffs, size extra small. Just that morning, Dov was sure he'd heard her tutoring it on the basics of lock-picking.

He leaned into the windy cold. "Seems like you two are getting along."

Dara straightened, brushing off her gloves. "It keeps her quiet."

Dov forced himself not to argue. With a determined scowl, the baby wriggled from the mouth of the snow tunnel and slid on its belly down the short slope to their feet. It was like a miniature American Gladiator, steroidal and too young, Dov knew from googling, to propel itself so powerfully.

"Clever girl!" said Dara, hugging the baby around its snowsuited middle.

"We made two grand today on blank CDs."

"Wow."

Dara wasn't even listening. She was hoisting the baby into an awkward victory dance that was a bad match for her serious, angular features, and for the baby's. They really did look related, Dara and the baby. Her tawny, tan skin and its, chestnut brown, their pairs of shrewd, dark eyes, blending into something intense and ancestrally slippery. A pair of chameleons. The shaman fad would eventually fade and when it did, Dara and the kid would morph into Arab heiresses, Israeli diplomats, Greek sheikesses. Whereas Dov, sallow, too thin, pocked by the long-lingering zit scars of adolescence, had only ever transformed by association with Dara.

He knew the score. A shark needed but one shill. The best con artist movies had costars, not ensemble casts. Screw the family story Dara had sold him: an extra comrade made him expendable. It would happen in a month or five years, but it would happen. One day the women would shrug their brooding shoulders and be gone. He'd be left with nothing but the clothes on his back and the creep of a humiliation he could already feel.

THAT NIGHT, Dov took control, riding Dara's muscled back like a wild mare. "Giddyap! Get along now, dogie!"

Afterward, Dara rolled from under him. "That was weird."

"More like weird *sexy*." He traced the curve of her muzzle, patted her flank. "We should have tried this ages ago."

"Mm."

The nonsound made him bristle. He yanked her mane. Instead of leaning in, she brushed him away. Went and opened the windows, blasting frigid air.

Dov's sweat chilled and dried. They'd shut the baby up in the bathroom to muffle its sobs. If Dara didn't care about his dying boner, she'd at least want to protect her new protégé. "Come on, sweets. The kid will catch cold."

"If that's what it takes her to learn, so be it."

Dara must have meant the crying, which aside from the baby's sporadic naps and Dara's Houdini games showed no sign of improvement. So, the human noise pollution *was* getting to her. It was a chink in the baby's armor Dov intended to exploit. "I heard something funny," he said, "about excessive crying. It can mean big mental problems down the line. Like, damage that keeps the kid from learning to talk. Some of them can't walk either. There's this video of a four-year-old whose parents still have to carry him. And he drools. Tons. He was adopted too, come to think of it."

Dara's mouth twisted in something like amusement but more unsettling. "The baby's fine, Dov."

"We'd have a decent chance of getting a refund," he persisted.

Dara's expression shifted from maybe-amusement to clear outrage. "A *refund*?"

He put up his hands as if calming a horse. "Or we can resell—sorry, re-home it. For a small re-homing fee?"

"Dov! She's not a coffee maker."

How had Dov never noticed: Dara did look like a horse, and not in a sexy way. The flaring nostrils, the oversized teeth and overarticulated joints, her manic trampling of obstacles, including her visionary-of-a-boyfriend-slash-business-partner. Physically and emotionally, the lady was a freak.

"Listen, woman. If you really want a baby, we can make

it happen." He gyrated suggestively, ignoring Dara's look of repulsion. She'd liked his moves well enough a minute ago. There was nothing wrong with reminding her what that mating dance was for. "*Our* baby. The best of you plus the best of me."

"It is *so* too late to have this conversation," said Dara.

Because the cold was shrinking his balls, Dov manfully threw the bedspread around himself. "And it's only getting later." He flung open the bathroom door. The baby's wails exploded. Dov shouted, "This might be a Mayan curse situation. I know how that sounds, but there are phenomena beyond our understanding. You should have seen how it grabbed me the other night—"

Dara shut him up with a single touch to his cheek. He didn't stop her when she gently closed the bathroom door. Her breath smelled like sugar cubes. Ever so softly, he tweaked her nipple.

Dara took the hand away and grasped it in her own. "I'm sorry."

He nodded because she was nodding. He stopped nodding because now she was shaking her head.

"Buddy. I'm keeping this baby."

Dov registered the plastic object she had put in his hand. It was the fob to the rental car. She beheld him with pity, as if he were a bug she had mashed with the bottom of her water bottle.

It was that image that poured gasoline on the fire of devotion, turning it to white-hot rage. Fuck the horsey bitch and her foal of the damned.

Fob in hand, he slammed out of the chalet and, not having stopped for boots, sank into freezing, wet snow. In the car, he revved the engine to a roar before easing it down the mountain road. The moon was smugly full. Another night, he'd have had to turn back or risk driving off the cliff; tonight, the vista might as well have been floodlit. He could be at the train station in under an hour, free of Dara for good.

His foot lowered onto the brakes, as the recent events aligned behind him, domino-esque: a plot. Dara's. If he drove away now, Dara would keep a decade's worth of spoils—the safe deposit box jammed with cash, passports, gifted jewelry; the storage unit full of his genius inventions; their shaman costumes; his pants. The baby.

The baby swirled at the center of Dara's whole miserable scheme. Five minutes ago he'd despised the baby but now could hardly remember why. Sure, the crying annoyed him, and yeah, the baby was kind of . . . precocious, but that was less a sign of possession than of, say, a future on the arm-wrestling circuit. Or maybe the baby did have a disorder, and that was why Dara had chosen that baby—to drive Dov away. Hell, Dara might be planning to return the baby to the orphanage tomorrow, indifferent to its fate. In a sense, Dov mused, the baby was a victim too. How sad was that? A *baby victim*.

It made Dov think of this old-timey scam where a peasant is given a great bargain, or so he thinks, on a sack of squealing piglets. Only to discover later that the sack is actually full of worthless, mewling kittens. What *did* happen to the kittens in that scam? Dov had never before considered the question. Drowned?! And cats hated to be wet.

Whether it was the thought of sodden felines or the growing discomfort of his goosepimpled butt skin, Dov resolved that for once the Daras of the world would lose.

With that, Dov threw the car in reverse, crunched and skidded back up the hill.

THEY DIDN'T TALK about what happened. Went to sleep with the bathroom fan on. The rage faded with sleep, or its lack, replaced in the morning with a hangover-like disconnect from the previous night's clarity and determination. It was as if that rage had caused Dov's muscles to swell and height to increase until he felt as invincible and ginormous as the sportos who'd pummeled him regularly in his youth. Only to realize, after his deflation, that it had all been a lot of hot air. Where, anyway, was he going to go? He was made for the two-man job. If he was honest with himself—and like all good hangovers, this one shoved Dov's nose into the offal of his truth—he and Dara fit together *because* she was, kind of, a guy. El Perro would say she had a dominant rainbow serpent; Dov, out of uniform, just knew she had balls. Balls didn't mean she'd be capable of concealing subversive intentions from one as expert in the con as himself. What sort of low-self-esteem issue was it, anyway, for Dov to think she would actually want to replace him with a baby? He needed to get real, and pull their dynamic duo together. Occam's freaking razor: the sleep deprivation was going to kill them. They'd been kidding themselves, no pun intended, thinking being parents—even pretend ones—would fix anything. The solution was to dump the lump. He just needed to figure out how.

Maybe there was a god, or maybe Dov was an intuitive, or maybe, just maybe, babies were easy to kill. So went Dov's first thought upon awakening not a week later, one humid Hawaii predawn morn, to infantile wails of unfamiliar tenor.

He'd become enough accustomed to the baby's cries to recognize the change. The texture had thickened like it couldn't catch its breath.

So that he couldn't later be blamed for inaction, Dov prodded Dara until she moaned from underneath the pillow. "D. Something's wrong with the baby."

"Sh'll sleep it off," slurred Dara and proceeded to do so herself.

"You're more right than you know," he murmured to the ceiling and listened to the little lungs struggle.

The brain would go next. The walnut-sized heart would pump a last burst of blood and the baby would stiffen into a glassy-eyed doll. Dov and Dara would bury the creature in its box and drive away into the sunset. United again, by folly. By love. By need.

He would wrap his arm around her, strong and silent. She would admire him like a man, finally. She would have to.

Dov waited for a sense of peace to arrive, the anticipation of restored normalcy. Instead, he felt disappointment, like a kid whose silver dollar has rolled into the storm drain. He knew how it would be once the baby was out of the picture, Dara and him alone again together, planning, working. Dara, saying, *You're wrong, babe*. Dara, scrawling in secret books. Dara, going out alone while he slept. Dara, standing back to him, blocking the light, hoarding the power, binding him in invisible ropes. Quicker than you could say "three card monte," she'd have him back on his leash.

A small, violent cough broke through his earplugs. The crying had started again. It was weaker now, a forlorn mewling.

Dov carried his pillow to the box. Radiant with fever, the baby stared up. Two dark eyes beheld him fearfully. From the baby's perspective, he loomed like a titan whereas it—*she*—was puny. He could cover her and with one pillow cure a lifetime of illness. It would be a mighty act of mercy, such as gods performed.

He rested the pillow on her experimentally. She quieted. A meek baby, conceding to his judgment. It was remarkable how she responded and marvelous how it filled him with vigor. He removed the pillow. The baby paused as if asking permission before taking a tentative breath. Her swollen eyelids threatened to close but she fought them open. Dov's finger found her fist. The grip this time, soft and burning hot. *Please sir*, the hand seemed to say, *please help.*

"YOU WERE SMART to bring her in," said the nurse. "The flu's dangerous in a little one. What a lucky girl to have you as her superhero."

Dov flipped magazine pages outside the pediatric ICU, buzzed from having saved a life. Dara had ignored the baby's distress, while Dov, born baby whisperer, spotted the danger and rushed to the rescue.

He checked the clock and asked at the nurse's station, but visitors were barred from the patients' cribside until vitals were stable. It was torture. He was ravenous to hold that pint-sized human. He'd never felt as large as with her in his hands.

The low quality of the lobby magazines made waiting that much more challenging. *Motherhood, Rad Mom*, and *Baby Bump* had headlines about losing pregnancy weight, the challenges of being a working mother, and glossy photos of smiling women in track pants. Where was the magazine called *Fatherhood*? Where were the pictures of celebrity dads effortlessly carrying a baby in each hand like a pair of grocery bags? In nature, the alpha male warred with predators and brought home food for his cubs. The male's superior energy put him at a parenting advantage that the human race had so far failed to exploit. Dov, for example, could be an expert parent, if he set his rational mind to it. He already knew what he'd buy: a travel crib, a rattle, cotton blankets, and a sock monkey in case the baby got lonely. He'd feed her mashed peas, mashed carrots, and crackers he pre-chewed himself. A baby couldn't get luckier than to have him for a dad. Dov whispered this to the baby when the pediatrician finally reunited them.

"That was a close shave, wasn't it, little girl?" said the doctor.

The baby lay docile against Dov, tugging gently at his arm hairs. She smelled like salted caramel, melted into him like butter. "Bah bah bah-bah," she said adoringly.

"Will getting too cold make her sick?" Dov asked. "Like if someone let her roll around in snow?"

"Mm, could weaken her immune response, but the bigger risk is hypothermia," said the doctor. "You'll want to be more careful."

"Oh, we will be," said Dov, squinting out at the parking lot. There was a new sheriff in town.

DOV'S EYES HAD been opened. He started to notice things about the vulnerable child and, more importantly, about Dara's deficient instincts. How she'd turn over snoring while terrified sobs foghorned through the darkness and couldn't remember the simplest of doctor's instructions, when and how much medicine to give the baby or to tie on a hat before taking her outside.

Once, Dov caught Dara putting her to bed facedown.

"That's how they get SIDS," he scolded.

"I'd love her to understand Secure ID System hacks, but it's hard to teach her with your coddling."

Dov could not believe Dara had never heard of Sudden Infant Death Syndrome. What kind of woman—what kind of *mother*—didn't worry about or at least consider the thousands of ways a child could die before her first birthday? Drowning in a bathtub, crawling out a second story window, baked in a car's backseat like so much bread dough, frozen in a car's backseat like so much fish filet, dropped headfirst on cement, smothered in bedclothes, succumbing to a common cold, to swine flu, to parasites transmitted through pigeon droppings, to leukemia and on and on.

The next day, Dov had an infant sling express shipped. He took to wearing the cotton band everywhere. Orphanage kids had all sorts of emotional problems from getting too few hugs. Though the place they'd gotten her from hadn't seemed that bad compared to those Russian horror houses, he wasn't taking any chances.

"*In the shower, Dov?*" said Dara from the other side of the beveled glass.

"It's called attachment parenting," said Dov, soaping the baby's fine shoulder blades. Her eyes regarded him through the warm drizzle like inside-out moons, black and dense and tide-making. Growing up, he'd watched the night sky for hours straight. Better than television or music, it made the bigness of the universe pulse at him.

He'd forgotten about that until now. "It prevents eating disorders, anxiety, suicidal depression, peer pressure. Think how confident I'd have turned out if my parents raised me this way."

Outside the shower stall, a wiggly shadow-version of Dara paced back and forth. He heard the rustle of the miniature soaps being unwrapped. Dara was pissed. A siege, she'd called it. All because he refused to take the baby on any jobs until full recovery. While the baby's fever had dissipated weeks ago, she showed subtle signs of developmental delay. When pulling herself to a seated position, for example, her spine arched in a way that could eventually compress the vertebrae, causing slipped discs and hidden fractures. If allowed to scoot freely, she would put any available object in her mouth, even toxic things like mousetraps and remote controls. So what if they dipped into their savings. If Dara wanted their child to thrive, she'd have to be patient.

Dara was waiting when they emerged from the shower.

"C'mere, lover." She tapped the mattress but didn't sit herself. Dov perched, dripping, on its edge to towel off the baby. The baby coughed but didn't cry. Instead of complaining, Dara should have been praising him: the sling worked. No more middle-of-the-night awakenings. No more hard-to-soothe tears. The baby cooed and smiled often. She'd grown a thick cap of curly, black hair and yesterday she'd made a drawn out *daaaaaaa* that Dov was trying to not overreact about, but at six months was it impossible she'd tried to say Daddy?

"What did you want to talk about?" he said.

Dara was glaring at the baby, who laughed hysterically as Dov pumped his legs, making her fly.

"Put her down for a minute?" There was a shrill anxiety in Dara's voice. Exciting.

"No problemo." He lifted the squirming child back into her sling. She relaxed instantly.

"I mean *down* down? As in, not stuck to your body."

Dov paused. The baby's heat seeped through the cotton. He'd grown so used to her physical closeness that he had to force himself to undo the clip at his shoulder and ease the fabric away.

Dara was talking about money, and pragmatics, and long-term prospectuses. A whole lot of sounds that refused to sink in. Without the baby, there suddenly was not enough of Dov for them to sink in *to*. "You've made your point. You win, but please drop the performance already. I'll cut you fifty percent of what we've got and you don't have to change another diaper ever again." Dara'd actually come out and said it. She wanted him to leave.

Behind Dov, the baby—who must also have felt incomplete—began to sob.

"It's sick, how you're using her to get to me," said Dara.

The baby screamed. Dov felt it in his very cells. He turned and took her and pressed her cheek to his. Dara reached to grab her, but the baby nestled into Dov's neck, a seal pup cowering before a vicious harpoonist. "Please go," he said. "You're upsetting my daughter."

The light in Dara's face flickered. "Don't play me, Dov. I will fuck you so hard you'll cough up last year's breakfast."

Calmly, Dov replied, "Take thirty percent. But I want you gone by tonight."

Dara packed her suitcase one item at a time, her shoulders jutting against the fabric of her shirt. Dov had always

been the stronger of them. He only wished he'd understood sooner.

AS SOON AS the coast was clear, Dov and the baby left by
cab. He booked them a flight to British Columbia, then
onto Newfoundland, the farthest point on the continent,
where the wind tasted like salt and the Robin Hood Inn
offered a cable station geared to children under two.

"I'll call you Dovina," he murmured, tucking the safe
deposit key into his daughter's diaper. They fell asleep
clinging to one another before the pleasant glow of the
screen.

Dov woke to a draft. He'd dreamed he was a mother
sea turtle paddling through chilly swells with his baby
on his back. He hooked an arm to retrieve her from wherever she'd migrated in sleep, warm her against his chest.

The blankets were empty.

On the carpet lay one of the red socks he'd put on
her after her bath. Dov hugged his robe around himself
and, full of dread, followed the draft into the bathroom.
The window was wide open. A cloth knotted to the towel
rack draped over the sill, out toward what Dov knew
to be a two-story drop. Afraid to look, Dov tugged on
the makeshift rope. It came up easily despite the wind.
Hand-over-hand, section by section, he pulled through
the window: a fitted bedsheet, a flat bedsheet, his favorite blue tie (ruined), his favorite orange tie (also ruined),
his second-best brown shirt, bath towel, bath towel, bath
sheet, hand towel, bath mat, his third-best gray slacks,
his wool pants, his jacket, a second fitted bedsheet. With
a skip and a hop, the last section, a used diaper, skittered
over the toilet and splatted at his feet. The stink of baby

shit, *his* baby's shit, filled Dov's nostrils. He leaned out
the window, fearing the gory worst. "Sweetheart?" The
shabby brick of the hotel extended straight down, the bluff
beneath tumbling precipitously into the sea. There was
no baby.

A darker darkness than he'd ever known spread inside
Dov. He thought again of those childhood nights staring
up at the sky. Yes, first came the universe hum, but that
wonder never lasted. Always it was followed by the pick-
axe of loneliness, chiseling him down to pathetic pebbles.

Waves crashed against the rocks below. He pictured
that tiny body borne upon them, red blood mixing with
the sea's black. Had she run away from him on purpose,
or been stolen by Dara? Bracing himself on the makeshift
rope, he leaned farther out. "Baby!" he screamed into the
wind's groan and whistle. Against his adult weight, the
towel rack creaked in protest. Momentarily he felt what
it would be to fall, and wondered—should he? Would the
baby want him to follow her into death? Unless she had,
somehow, survived.

Or—it was *possible*, nutso, but still—had the baby never
existed at all? He knew about the pit that was the human
mind. Anything you wanted could fit inside.

He tied himself to the tracks and let this train of thought
run. All this time he could still be twelve years old, stuck
on his old man's roof, waiting for the wonder that would
never come back, inventing stories like this one.

What a fucking mark he was.

Like a fool, he opened the coin purse of his stupid hope
and spilled the last gold piece he'd been saving, for if there
was a child, she was his. She was his forever.

He called her name. "Dovina!"

He held his breath, twisted the sheet around his fist until it was numb. It could have been blood pounding in his ears or the scream of the wind, but it was possible— it *was*—that the high-pitched wail, the hard *D*, the drawn out *aaaaaaa,* the *dee*—his girl was out there, summoning him with his one true name.

My Mother's Bottomless Hole

"It showed up out of nowhere," my mother said. I stood beside her over the neat opening of the hole in her back lawn. It was large enough for an adult to tumble into, vertigo-inducing, and unsettlingly dark. I fixed my gaze on her eager face. She seemed happy about it. "I saw it right after the TV said we were in a pandemic. That upset me, so I stepped outside for some fresh air and *there it was.*"

The hole, my mother said, had appeared by sheer coincidence in the shady spot where she did crossword puzzles summer mornings. "Now I sit and watch it!" She said the hole was bottomless, which apparently meant it extended deeper than the length of her broomstick handle, and too far for her to hear the various household objects she had dropped in hit bottom. I had driven up from Florida, was still holding my duffel bag, a kink in my lower back throbbing. Except for gas stations, I'd gone fifteen hours without stopping because the rest areas were crowded and the motels shone like germ beacons.

"Holes have bottoms. By definition."

"Not black holes. Not button holes." My mother argued like a child.

"Those are different kinds of holes."

She made a scornful sound, bent down to pick up a good-sized rock and dropped it in. She pointed down. "Hear anything?"

"The soil must be absorbing the sound."

"Uh-uh. If there were a bottom, it would be all trash, and you would hear it hit."

I couldn't resist a jab. "Didn't realize you threw anything away."

"Well, I don't *waste*. But if something's not useful, I throw it out. And now I throw it in here!"

"So," I parsed my mother's squirrel-on-amphetamines logic, "the hole that manifested in your yard is your personal garbage dump."

"It's a little bonus."

It didn't matter to my mother where her garbage went or when it surfaced, as it inevitably would.

"Fine, you win. It's an infinite hole that also makes a convenient trash receptacle. Can I use your bathroom?"

"I didn't say 'infinite.' I said 'bottomless.'"

"Okay, Mom."

"*Okay*, Daughter."

I went inside, knowing if I looked back she'd have her hands on her hips, impatient to continue fighting. Our disagreement about the hole would end when I admitted she was right.

BECAUSE OF THE pandemic, lots of my friends were moving in with their parents too. They, however, had good excuses. They'd been laid off or evicted, gotten divorced, or their sickly parents needed someone around to get cat food. One friend moved back to Oklahoma because she said she was losing her mind from lack of physical contact. "I haven't been hugged in weeks!" This friend was known to order sex off Tinder like pizza, any time she had a hankering. When she said the thing about the hug, I made sympathetic noises into the phone, even though I'd given up touch cold turkey when I moved south. My last human contact was the ER doctor back in the fall. I'd gone in screaming and come out with fresh stitches on my abdomen, thinking, petrified and strangely excited, *I have cancer.*

In April, the Tampa school district where I taught English moved classes online. Trapped in my home, the accidental nature of my life choices was laid bare. I hadn't ever wanted to be a teacher, problem one. Problem two, I was realizing that I maybe hadn't ever wanted to be an adult woman. And yet here I was, six months post-removal of an ovary, back in the bedroom where I'd once proudly called my best friend with news of my first period. The closet door was still covered in pictures of a nineties sitcom idol, whose yellowed magazine clippings bore kiss-shaped smears of ancient lip gloss. Maybe that's why I had come back. This was the last place I'd been excited to have a female body.

ACCORDING TO A receipt I discovered while trying to plug in the coffee maker, my mother's bottomless hole had "appeared" by the most mundane of means: retail. She bought it from a local discounter of novelty products for over a thousand dollars. A thousand dollars, so a woman who saved everything could have an illegal dump. I found the receipt in a pile of sticky recipe cards on top of the fridge. My mother believed especially in saving receipts and packaging in case an item had to be returned. Not that anything ever got returned. Once an object came through the front door, it was there to stay. In the nineties, a new toaster had malfunctioned, burning bread on one side and leaving it white on the other. My mother insisted it was a "bagel toaster" and made my father and I switch to eating bread in bun form. "I love this thing," she'd say, displaying a crumpet's toasted inside against its pale, soft top.

That sort of thing used to drive my dad nuts. He would corral the mess by heaping it against the walls. Since his death, the piles had crept inward. On my previous visit, there was still an open rectangle of carpet in the living room; now, a mom-sized path snaked through the avalanching clutter, and the counters in the kitchen were stacked high. The coffee maker lived on the kitchen table, but I'd had to relocate a cache of sticky notes and brand-new mugs from the range in order to reach the filters. Wiped clean, the vulvar pink Formica produced a kick of nostalgia. It only made sense at that point to keep going.

My mother came down in her bathrobe while I was excavating expired salad dressing bottles from the fridge.

"What are you doing?" Her head was wrapped in a silk scarf that emphasized the curve of her skull. Yesterday's curly bob had been a wig. Without it, she looked scrunched, a piece of fruit forgotten on a windowsill.

She caught me staring. "I was balding like an old man."

Her directness took me aback. We never talked about our bodies like television mothers and daughters. "I like the," I searched, "scarf. Silk?"

"Oh, who cares." She reached down to the garbage bag

at my feet and began removing objects. "This is my stuff."
She held a pint of cottage cheese in one hand, a sticky pair
of scissors in the other. Before she could complain, I held
up the receipt.

"This is yours too."

"It's my money."

"Eleven hundred dollars for a *hole*?"

She tucked the receipt into her bathrobe. "Most of that
was installation."

"I thought it 'appeared.'"

"It was *like* it appeared. They didn't even bring digging
equipment! It was a—a *kit*. I went inside to get the men
refreshments and when I came out, they were already
done." She lowered herself into a chair. "Did you make
any joe?"

I slid my mug over. The grounds had come from a half-
empty, industrial-sized bag; the coffee tasted like licking
a café floor.

"It would have been nice to have that money for my
cancer surgery."

"Mm." The wrinkles around her mouth deepened as
she sipped. Her birthday was in a few weeks and I couldn't
remember if she was turning eighty-two or eighty-three.
Which wasn't that old. Eighty was like sixty had been for
her mother's generation.

"I could have died." I flashed back to the orange curtain
of the ER flapping open the first of the three times they
sent me home. They'd diagnosed me with a muscle cramp,
a stomach bug, and, finally, a cyst on my right ovary, which
they scheduled for removal the following month. No need
to worry, the earnest young doctor said. If it was an emergency, you'd be screaming. An hour later, I returned

screaming in an ambulance. I wasn't sure if I was screaming because I had to or because the doctor had suggested
it, but I couldn't seem to stop. While they were running
the IV for surgery, I thought about the phrase *no need to
worry*, as if worrying were ever necessary, as if bad things
needed any help to unfold.

It turned out no one was too young to die.

"Do people die from stage one?" my mother said. "I
thought they didn't."

I wished she'd heard me screaming, that anyone had
besides the nurses and EMTs. If not my mother, then a
partner or friend. Someone who cared if I died. I'd been
alone when they told me the cyst was a tumor. It was so
small, they said I could keep the left ovary in case I wanted
to get pregnant.

"I'm over forty," I protested, but the gynecologist, an
infant in a lab coat, claimed I'd be surprised.

I didn't want the left ovary, or the uterus. I realized that
the moment it seemed they might get removed. Those
organs weren't mine; they just happened to be there.
Having this brought to my attention, I wanted them gone.
But insurance wouldn't cover it and my mother claimed
not to have the money. It's stage one, she'd said. You'll be
fine.

"Tell you what," she said from over my shoulder as I let
the fridge's fan cool my rage. "You put everything back
where it goes and I'll make us omelets. You can even throw
the eggshells in the hole!"

I met my mother's small, black eyes. "I have work."

From the upstairs landing, I heard the trash bag being
unpacked, all the clutter returning to the counter, as if it
had never been moved. As if by magic.

EVEN IN MY pre-pandemic teaching life, classes tended to blur. From year to year, I taught the same, few English courses, and the students were interchangeable. Like plastic dolls on an assembly line, spring semester's Jason Trogan merged into the fall's Troy Jensen; the clique of Billie Eilish fans in the back row replaced the giggling K-pop girls. Online, these transitions were so seamless that teaching was like dreaming, half-aware and ephemeral. Class time drifted from roll call to lecture, to small group discussions in breakout rooms. Invariably, I'd catch the groups sharing memes and gifs inappropriate for school. I scolded, but they knew my power was fictitious. It was no longer teachers over students, grown-ups over children. The planet was in chaos. Evidently, bats at a Chinese wildlife market had pulled one over on the human race. In the face of disaster, their president, parents, and, by extension, I, flailed. It was my ninth grade English students who would lead us through this mess, if only by understanding that things falling apart was normal now, was how life would be. They were fifteen years old, mostly virgins; they wore ugly jumpsuits that looked like pajamas, scrutinized makeup tutorials, and cheated on their homework, but somehow understood the world better than I. They knew it didn't matter if they'd read chapters 4 through 6 of *The Grapes of Wrath* or in what context they used the word "literally."

Years ago I'd made the mistake of agreeing to be the Gay-Straight Alliance's faculty advisor. The principal had promised it would only be an hour every Monday but hadn't mentioned that that hour would feel longer than an entire school week. When classes went virtual, I'd figured the GSA would realize it could convene online whenever it wanted without me. What kid wouldn't prefer to talk about sexuality without an adult present? But I'd under-estimated their nerdiness. Today, they'd even signed on early. One by one, their earnest faces popped into view, hair dyed unbecoming colors, expressions full of yearn-ing to belong.

The GSA advisorship was my punishment for being out at work. Straight people assumed all queers loved gay children. On social media, my friends were always sharing inspiring articles about LGBTQ kids: preschoolers transi-tioning to the opposite gender, queer teens crowned prom royalty, and rainbow-themed summer camps. I'd click the links, overcome, as I scrolled through, by a resentment so strong I thought I might pass out. This generation's kids had it so easy, it was obscene. With their support-ive parents and gender-neutral bathrooms, peers who didn't blink an eye at a pronoun change, pansexual movie characters, lesbian Barbies. Fuck these kids. I sometimes wished a small hate crime on my GSA students. Noth-ing major—*faggot* shouted from a moving car, an isolated locker defacement.

When I came out to my mother, she said, *You will have to get used to being alone*. Time proved that good advice. With low expectations came less disappointment. I only wanted to impart the same to my students. Or at least make them consider for an instant that I might know more than they did about this gay life that so obsessed them.

"TikTok is, like, the worst offender," one of them, a self-styled activist, was saying. "They censor LGBTQ2AI content all around the world, even though their biggest accounts are queer."

"That's why I'm off social," said the arty one. She sat

back far enough from her computer that we could see the
sketchpad in her lap. She was drawing everyone's faces
without looking at the paper. She did this every meeting
and was, in fact, talented. The portraits were cartoonish
but captured some essential quality of their subjects. She
had gifted me a picture of myself looking splenetic.

"What if we organize a school boycott? Is that allowed,
Ms. Becher?"

An enby said, "I don't think we should be part of call-
out culture." That kicked off an argument between factions
I could not be bothered to categorize, as their loyalties
veered wildly from meeting to meeting. I was getting a
headache.

"Listen." They didn't, so I hit mute all (a beautiful
button). "This is an important conversation, but I think
we need to do some research before further discussion.
Last week, the group voted to spend more time on identity. Let's discuss pansexuality. What is it?"

i want to talk about my GENDER, appeared in the group
chat.

mee 2222222!!!

I gritted my teeth, then stopped, fearing I'd be the
subject of Angelique's next portrait. "Okay, then. Gender."
I unmuted them, releasing a flood of statements in favor of
and against breasts and penises. They bandied about the
cost of surgery as if any of them knew what debt felt like,
or how humiliating crowdfunding actually would be, like
prostrating before your friends with a tin cup.

My main advisor responsibility, as I understood it,
was to prevent the outbreak of sexual activity on school
grounds. Other than occasionally interjecting to stop an
argument or get conversation going, I tended to busy

myself with grading or scrolling through social media. Today, though, my irritation compelled me to speak.

"People," I said. Eight excited voices trailed off. I felt like I'd walked in on a private conversation though I'd been up on their screens the whole time. "Those of you who had me for American Lit, remember *Ethan Frome*?" *Frome* tells the story of a farmer who attempts to escape his unhappy marriage via suicide pact only to paralyze his young lover and leave himself alive. This year's class had been particularly upset by the notion that Wharton's deterministic masterpiece better reflected the human experience than the *Leaves of Grass*'s manic euphoria. Whenever I needed to quell my own fantasies of self-transformation, I recalled the novel's tragic epilogue: poor Ethan still at the beck and call of his nasty, invalid wife but now with an embittered and bed-bound ex-lover to care for too. Free will was an indulgence that we on this far end of the human timeline could scarce afford. "Remember what happened when Ethan tried to change his life?"

"Ugh, that novel is so misogynistic," said the enby. "Like what about his *wife's* perspective?"

"I don't get why they were suicidal."

"They could have run away together instead."

"Yeah, or been poly."

"It's so unrealistic."

I held up my hands in a *T*. "Morally, Ethan didn't have a choice. He was boxed in by social rules."

"So what? *We* break social rules every day," said a kid whose name had been Taylor and was now Teelor. "We're not queer or trans because we're supposed to be."

"My point is," I said, exasperated, "when you're older this penis-breast stuff won't matter. Bodies are like . . .

tattoos. Yours mean a lot to you now because they're perfect, but eventually they'll be worn out and falling apart. You'll get," it was important for them to think about this, "prostate cancer, breast tumors, low libido. It won't matter what parts you have because you'll want to keep your clothes on." I was overcome with the passion that accompanies speaking the truth. "*Every* adult has dysphoria. It's called aging."

Eight pairs of eyes were cast down, indicating they were watching me, not the camera or the feed of themselves at the top of the screen. They looked . . . I wasn't sure. Scared? Angelique had put down her pencil, brow wrinkled, as if what she saw was too sorry to commit to her sketchbook.

"Ms. Becher," there was uncharacteristic caution in Cale's voice, "you know that adults can be trans, right? And, like, transition."

"It's nothing to be ashamed of," said Tiff.

I flushed. "I didn't mean *me*." I changed the subject to Pride plans, but it was too late. Kids were like bear traps. Having latched onto a theory, they'd only continue bringing it up week after week. They'd make me into their personal project. It was a horrifying prospect. At the end of the hour, I closed the chat window and wrote the email I should have years ago. *Dear Principal Lamb, Due to circumstances beyond my control, I am unable to continue advising the GSA.* Well, it wasn't a lie.

"THERE'S MY SALTY girl," my mother said, coming in from the yard. She'd been hole-watching all afternoon but at least was put together. She had on the curly wig and one of the more casual outfits she used to show houses in when she was a real estate agent. She looked like herself, young for her age, vivacious.

"You're not using 'salty' right."

"I'm saying you look fresh! Like you stepped out of the ocean."

This would have been accurate if she'd meant that I looked shipwrecked. "Salty," as in "annoyed" was, however, close to how I felt. I was beginning to see I'd made a mistake coming here. Fortunately, my mother was scarily social by habit, so I anticipated getting some alone-time that evening. I wondered which of her many groups would be convening after dinner: tai chi, stitch & bitch, book club, or a get-together for some newly acquired hobby. Somewhere in the labyrinth of the garage were buried roller-blades, skis, an inflatable kayak, tap shoes, even stilts, all used a handful of times then put away for a future season that would never arrive, because there were always new activities to commit to and new accessories to buy. Last winter she'd texted me about an upcoming snowmobile trip. I'd pictured her parka-encased body pinned underneath the heavy vehicle or crashing through a frozen lake. If she were killed or even badly injured, I had not wanted to know, hadn't wanted to sit vigil at her bedside as her mind and finally breath slipped away. I'd avoided her calls so that if something happened, life could at least continue unchanged. From Florida, the logic had seemed reasonable. Now, I saw how cold it was, and how foolish. My mother was the last person left who'd seen me grow up. If she died, it would be as if I had no past.

My mouth opened to ask about her plans for the evening before I remembered there were no plans, not for anyone in this brave new world. I blinked, remembering that and remembering myself. Forty-two, single, standing in the living room of my childhood home with my descending boobs and expanding hips and one, useless ovary. I might still have cancer. All it would take was a misbehaving cell. The doctor said she could order a CAT scan whenever I wanted, but even if my insurance covered it, I'd seen the videos of pandemic corpses stacked like meat in refrigerator trucks. I would not be going near a hospital any time soon.

I was sweating. I reached for the tissue box on the arm of the couch and knocked over a bin of crafting supplies. Pins spilled across the cushions and rolled between stacks of magazines. When I squatted to retrieve them, a piece of plastic dug into my heel. It appeared to have fallen off one of several unplugged lamps on the coffee-table. Standing, I bumped one and they fell like dominoes. I had to get some space.

"I'm going out."

"Where?"

"Nowhere." I sounded like one of my snotty students. "I thought I'd catch up with some friends."

"You shouldn't be *gathering in groups.*" She made it sound like code for sinister behavior.

"I'll be careful. See?" From my bag I unearthed a cloth mask with a sports team logo. The school receptionist had made them for the teachers as a counterintuitive going-virtual gift, but had apologized when she handed me mine. *I ran out of girl fabric. Do you mind? I thought you might be a football fan.* I wondered whether "football fan" was Southerner for "lesbian."

I had worn the mask once to go into a gas station. With only my stubby-lashed eyes and short hair showing, the clerk assumed I was male. "Will that be all, sir?" he asked. "That's it," I said. "So sorry, ma'am," he said. "I just thought . . ." I backed through the door, stammering my own apologies, horrified not by his mistake but by how I hadn't noticed. I'd responded to *sir* as if it were correct.

My mother wrinkled her nose. "That's a hoax."

I was lost. "What is?"

"Those face-things."

"Masks?" This, I wasn't expecting. My mother was staunchly left-wing. She'd kept her "I'm With Her" yard sign up until the blue faded to pale yellow. "Have you been reading memes?"

"They're articles from reputable whistleblowers. Masks don't work. And"—she waggled a finger—"some people who sell them *cough* on them with covid to make you sick."

Even for a conspiracy theory, this was convoluted. "Why would anyone do that?"

"Because if people think sticking a shirt over their faces will keep them from getting sick, the president and his cronies can open their businesses again."

"That doesn't make any sense."

She threw up her hands. "Some things don't make sense but they're still true. Besides, I thought you and I could have a nice dinner by the hole."

I wished she'd have that thing filled in. "Can you explain why you're obsessed with a glorified garbage can?"

"Excuse me?"

"You just invited me to have dinner out there. It's not a duck pond."

"Of course it's not a duck pond." She shook her head bemusedly.

I sighed, hoping I didn't sound as annoyed as I felt. "Don't wait up." I kissed her dry cheek.

She pulled away. "I'm a vulnerable population!"

Member of a, I corrected, but only in my head.

FROM THE LOT of the neighborhood strip mall, I messaged every former high school classmate I could find online. It was a desperate tactic, made more embarrassing by how few seemed to remember me. By the time Cindy Lundy replied, it was getting dark. Cindy and I had been in the same classes, but never friends. On social media, she thumbed-up my reposts of news articles about banned books and I thumbed-up pictures of her posing in hiking gear on scenic footbridges. Cindy had three kids and was passionate about her job working for the state's Green Party. I hated my job, didn't understand the fuss about NAFTA, and often forgot to vote. We had nothing in common.

Want to go for a walk? I texted.

She responded a second later. *Six feet apart? Sure!*

"OVER HERE!" Cindy Lundy waved from the arboretum entrance. In high school, she had been on crew, a sport that required round-the-clock commitment. Those girls had been compact with muscle, their bodies honed for the sole purpose of rowing in perfect unison. She still took care of herself, was slim in her expensive-looking yoga pants, track jacket, and name-brand sneakers. Only then did I consider my own outfit: a pilled, fleece pullover borrowed from my mother's laundry room and cut-off sweatpants with dangling threads. I wished I had stayed in.

Cindy waved again. "Over here!"

"Sorry, I—"

"It's so—"

We both laughed. Her, naturally. Me, awkwardly.

"You first," she said.

"I was just going to ask if the park is even open." I pointed at the sign: *8 AM to sunset*.

She shrugged. "Everything's sort of a free-for-all these days."

Cindy led us down wooden steps descending through a grove of elms. By the time we reached the native prairie, the outlines of shrubs and wildflowers black and spooky in the dusk, I had learned she found fundraising rewarding but exhausting, she was training for a marathon that might get cancelled, and her youngest son had recently lost his last baby molar, a fact I found unnecessary and gross, picturing the bloody roots of the milk tooth, its enamel tacky with dried saliva. "The tooth fairy brought him plastic pirate coins and he bit one because he thought they were chocolate!" She had an odd laugh, a quack, high up in her nose, that brought me straight back to the echoing halls of Whitmore High. I remembered an exchange in which she'd asked if I was a druggie. When I'd said no, she seemed startled, *It's just, you always wear that hoodie.* She meant it innocently, but I was so ashamed I threw the sweatshirt in a dumpster, lying to my mother that it had been stolen.

"What about you?" she said. "You seem so smart! All those posts about books. And the fun pictures from Mexico!"

"It was Puerto Rico, actually. I go every summer."

"Oh, wow, the Caribbean. So *sunny*. Too bad you can't go this year."

"Well, I can wait one more."

"*If* there's a dang vaccine," said Cindy.

"Right. Who knows?"

"Who knows!"

I couldn't tell which of us was so boring, or if it was a two-to-tango situation, but I was reminded of how much I disliked Midwesterners and their conflation of predictability with virtue. At least the antics of "Florida Man" gave people things to talk about. My landlord couldn't have found a new tenant yet. If I set out early tomorrow morning, I'd be back to Tampa by midnight.

"It's so peaceful here," Cindy said.

I looked around. "Oh. Yeah." We'd made our way down to the river, a dark tongue lapping between grassy banks. A gold charm glinted against the fabric of Cindy's high-necked tank top, against the soft curve of a breast. She turned her head and smiled. I felt a kind of shiver and had a premonition of us kissing: the approach of mouths, the warmth of a tongue. The last person I'd kissed had been a man. We were drunk. It was a surprise how much I liked the feeling of him, rough-chinned and animal-smelling, and how much I disliked the feeling of me *with* him, my softness, my small body. Against his heft, I had felt infantile.

Cindy tightened her ponytail. "Let's do something bananas."

Did Cindy Lundy want to fuck? No, she was straight; she'd want to *be* fucked. Which was good. I could keep my clothes on.

"How polluted do you think it is?" She kicked off a shoe.

My R-rated thoughts screeched to a halt. Was swimming in the river her "bananas" idea? "Pretty polluted."

"Well, can't give me more cancer than I already have!"

Despite the quiet, I was sure I'd misheard. There was not a polite way to double-check. *Excuse me, Cindy, did you say you had* cancer? *What kind? Has it metastasized to a major organ?* In my fantasy, she said it was stage four, and I pretended to be embarrassed for asking, and she said, *No, no, it's a relief to talk about* and that she had only a year left, tops.

I felt a flicker of excited envy—what freedom to have one's life pared to a discrete span—then shut it off. I did not want to die. I did not want Cindy to die.

She shucked off her shirt and pants, revealing toned legs bluish in moonlight, an unidentifiable splotch—melanoma?—on her ankle. "Coming in?"

"Oh, no. I don't think so." She was lean, but not sick-skinny. Her shoulders were rounded with small muscles that flicked as she lowered herself into the mucky water. "Oh heck. Do you mind if I—?" She mimed undoing her bra. I said I didn't, and Cindy's breasts peeled away.

I must have looked startled because she crossed her arms over her chest and began apologizing. "I thought I mentioned? I had a mastectomy. These are my falsies. That's what the drag queens call them." She moved to refasten her bra.

"You don't have to."

"Are you sure?"

I wanted, badly, to see her de-breasted chest. To know what it felt like to have her boobs suddenly gone. "I don't mind."

She paused, then shrugged. "Oka-ay." The bra and falsies came off. Automatically, I held out a hand to take them. She smiled her appreciation and deposited the wad of cloth and silicone in my palm.

I fingered the jelly-weight of the artificial breasts, prodded my own boob through my shirt. Mine was heavier and
somehow looser than the falsies. Somehow less believable.
For an instant I thought, *Why do I still have these?* As if
they too were an artificial appendage I could deposit in a
waiting hand and never have to see again.

Cindy let out a long sigh and stretched into a back
float. Her boyish chest glistened. Even if she had loved her
breasts, it must have felt a little beautiful to be so light.

"Do you miss them?"

She raised her head. "My breasts?" I thought I had
offended her, but when she spoke again, she sounded like
she didn't care either way. "I miss everything."

The way she said it, so matter-of-fact, filled me with
dread. I took a backward step up the hillside. If I hadn't
been holding her fake breasts, I might have left her there.
I had a terrible feeling she was going to tell me she was
dying, and I did not want that. Before I had wanted Cindy
to not die on principle, because death was bad; now, I
wanted her, this woman half-naked before me in the water
and so alive, to continue living. "We should probably get
back."

Cindy either didn't hear or ignored my plea. "Come
over here."

"Why?"

"I want you to."

There was a heft to how she said "want" that made
it impossible to argue. Reluctantly, I approached the
riverbank and stripped to my underwear. The water was
breathtakingly cold. I sank to my thigh in the smelly ooze
and wade-paddled toward her.

"Wait," she said. "I'm immune-compromised."

"Okay." I still wasn't sure if she wanted to kiss, or something else.

"You have to hold your breath. Or if you need to breathe, turn your head away."

She lay back again, took my palm, and ran it over the bony ridge of her nippleless chest, the mottling of swollen tissue around ragged scars. She had been ravaged. That was the only word for it. I imagined I was touching my own chest. Asked myself, would I want this? It wasn't like a man's at all.

"Does it hurt?" I asked.

"Nope. It's all numb."

I understood then that she had not yet let her husband touch her like this. She had saved it for me. Not me specifically, of course, but someone like me. A woman, or maybe just someone who didn't matter.

I had saved something for someone like her too. Because she didn't matter. And because we would never see each other again. "I might be a man."

Her breath rolled across the river's surface.

"What I mean is that I feel like a man inside myself sometimes."

She was quiet. I wanted her to ask, *Only sometimes?* so I could say, *Yeah,* and we could both wonder what that meant. What she actually said was, "You're a beautiful woman." The water made her voice hollow, ghostly. "No matter how you feel."

"Thanks," I replied, because I could tell she thought we were having a different conversation. She was the kind of person who thought all women are beautiful. My mother without her wig would have been beautiful to Cindy. A dead body made up to resemble its previous inhabitant would have been beautiful. She was giving a compliment even if I didn't want it.

"You're welcome."

We stayed like that a while longer, her sick body lapping back and forth in the toxic water, mine, tight-muscled from driving, sitting at a computer, and years of accumulated self-hatred, slowly retreating toward dry land. My body which was healthy, not dying, only wanted to be. When Cindy's smartwatch told her it was 1:00 a.m., she got out and dressed.

She caught me looking at the splotch on her ankle. "It's Earth. With a dove carrying an olive branch."

I murmured a compliment as she tied her shoes. We headed back to our cars, a careful six feet apart, her falsies in her hand. It was a relief and a disappointment when neither of us said we'd see each other later.

AT LUNCH THE next day, my mother was back in the yard. The window was open and she heard me rattling around in the pantry. "Is that you?" Through the screen, I saw her adjust her headscarf. "Come outside."

Too sleep-deprived to invent an excuse, I carried my canned minestrone out to the sleek, black edge of the hole, where a second chair awaited.

"What a beautiful day."

"Mm." The air was muggy and, thanks to the french fry plant one town over, smelled like saturated fats. It was impossible to tell where my sweat ended and the ambient moisture began.

My mother was eating pistachios and flicking the

shells into the hole. As each flew from her hand, she said, "Goodbye, goodbye," in the voice of the baby spiders from *Charlotte's Web*.

"Stop being eccentric."

"You stop being avoidant."

I snorted. She was so childish. It was true, though, that I couldn't get myself to look directly at the hole. My eyes tracked the shells through the air and then slid sideways to a bare patch in the grass where some ants were fighting over a dead wasp.

"Scaredy cat," my mother taunted. "Scared of a hole."

"I am not." What I felt was vaguer, a sense of unease.

"Then look at it." Her lips peeled back to show receding gums, the bony outcrop of her teeth.

I wanted to go inside, but when my mother bid farewell to the next pistachio shell, I forced myself to watch it penetrate the hole's opaque blackness. My stomach lurched as the shell crossed its horizon and was absorbed. After that, pure black. It reminded me of a viral article a student had shared about a new paint that absorbed all visible light. In photos, the paint, smeared across concrete, looked like the holes from Saturday morning cartoons that good guys zipped through while bad guys bounced off. This hole was like that ultra-black paint in reverse. Looked flat but went on seemingly forever.

"Stick your hand in," urged my mother. She loved proving I was uptight.

"Fine."

Careful not to end up like the pistachio shells, I knelt at the its edge. Cold air seeped out, spreading goosebumps over my legs. "Are you sure it's safe?"

"It's from a store!" scoffed my mother, the anti-capitalist conspiracy theorist.

Gripping a clump of weeds for ballast, I hovered a hand over the hole. "It's freezing."

"I know," she crowed. "It's nature's refrigerator."

Adrenaline raced through my body. The hole did not seem remotely natural. That it had been purchased from a store where most products sported bright red, "As Seen On TV" stickers provided little comfort. It should have been recalled, was certainly made in Mexico or Taiwan, some country with notable lapses in consumer safety. My mother was watching. I tensed every muscle and lowered my hand until it disappeared.

"Ack!" I shrieked, falling back onto the lawn, arm clutched to my chest. My mother chortled while I shook my hand to get the feeling back in. "I could have frostbite!"

"You're being dramatic. Wiggle your fingers."

I ignored her and pressed them to my neck. They were warm again but tingly. I got up to google frostbite symptoms. "Whoever installed this, I'm having it filled in."

"You can't fill it in. It's bottomless," my mother called as I walk toward the house.

"Whatever." Everything had a bottom. One just had to find it.

THE NEXT DAY, I texted my landlord in Florida to see if I could get my place back. Then I called the discount store. The clerk only remembered selling one style of outdoor hole, which he said went in large, well-developed trees. "You know," he said. "For sitting."

"I'll take store credit. I just need to get the thing uninstalled."

"We can't do returns because of the virus? It lives on surfaces up to three days."

I asked myself how it made sense that the state was reopening universities in the fall and this store was worried about a virus being transmitted via *hole*, the literal opposite of a high-touch surface. When I hung up, there was a text from my landlord, saying I could have the place back if I paid for this month.

I imagined driving south, all the red states to pass through, only to arrive in a swampland populated by explosives hobbyists and lizards. I hated Florida. The thought rose up as if it had been there all along. I hated Florida, and I hated my name. I wanted to be called Darren, or Michael. I, a middle-aged woman, wanted to be called Mr. Darren Becher.

The GSA students were technically correct. I knew a few women who had become men, meaning they'd changed their names and gone on hormones. People obediently called them "he," but you could hear the quotation marks. It was like when children insisted they were Batman and, until they moved on to being an Avenger, or a cat, adults would humor them, saying, "What's that, Bruce Wayne? Did you hear the Bat Signal?" It was cute when a four-year-old did it; with a forty-year-old, it was pathetic.

So, yes, I could have had my breasts removed, but that would bring me no closer to being Mr. Becher. I preferred to accept reality and my own limitations. I was born a woman and would die one, no matter how I felt about it. At least I'd keep my dignity.

"WHEN I DIE," my mother said one evening, leaving her dinner plate on the counter, "I want you to throw me in the hole."

"You want your ashes in that thing?"

"No, my body."

I rinsed her dish and jammed it in the overcrowded dishwasher. "You want to be buried in your backyard? I hope you're okay with me going to prison then, because that's illegal." I couldn't take this conversation seriously. My mother was in better shape than I was. She'd live another fifty years just to drive me crazy.

"It doesn't count as burying if I remain in motion." She threw her arms in the air and mouthed an *O* like a girl on a rollercoaster. I thought she was having a heart attack, but then realized she was playacting her corpse in infinite free fall. Not infinite, I told myself. It's not bottomless. Just very deep.

I turned the dishwasher on. Water whooshed through the hidden machinery. "Thanks for the image."

"Say you'll do it."

"We're done talking about this."

"I'm adding it to my will. If you don't do it, your aunties will know, and they'll be very disappointed in you."

"I'm sure they will," I said, thinking that if my cancer came back, my mother and her sisters would all outlive me.

I STARTED DREAMING about the hole. At first, it was like the real-life hole, except in the floor of the living room. Once, my mother was dropping pieces of bread in it. When I asked why, she said she was feeding the ducks. In another dream, she was dead and I was trying to push her body into it, but it was just a circle of very black paint. Later, I dreamed I killed myself by jumping in. The mechanics of this, whether I died hitting bottom or starved on the way down, were unclear, but what I woke up remembering was a pure, relieving blankness.

Students stopped coming to class. It was a school-wide problem, nationwide. The vice principal's assistant took it upon herself to check up on them individually. She said in an email that many were organizing and attend-ing multi-day protests. *They are putting their education into action,* she wrote. *We should be proud.* It gave me pause that our political future rested on young people who bought *Animal Farm* essays from the internet to avoid reading a 125-page book. I wanted to send every student a copy of *Ethan Frome.* The world might have been bad, they might indeed have gotten a raw deal, but yelling at the sky wouldn't get them a do-over. From birth, we were like sleighs rushing down an ice-slick hill toward our destinies. Didn't they know the world was ending? The temperatures had already risen too far. This pandemic was a harbinger.

CINDY LUNDY DIED during finals week. I found out because her family turned her page into a memorial. Former class-mates posted long, vague tributes that could have been attached to any middle-aged, middle-class, white mother. Even after the river, I wasn't sure whether I'd liked Cindy. I imagined what her friends would say if I posted that, while we'd never been close, I'd held Cindy's breasts while she went swimming. Probably, they would "heart" it.

The memorial page didn't specify a cause of death. I wondered if it had been cancer or the virus. I remembered how she'd said she missed everything, as if she meant she was going to miss everything. Cindy Lundy was the sole person who knew I wanted to be a man and now she was gone.

My students' final exam essays were better than expected, which did not mean they were good. While subtracting points, my attention drifted to an unfamiliar image file that had been saved to my desktop. It was a screenshotted order from an international wholesaler that advertised suspiciously cheap shipping and unusual products sold in bulk. I would never have bought anything from that site. What casual internet shopper needed one thousand astroturf tiles or a pallet of music boxes that played the theme from *Schindler's List*?

The answer was my mother. She had borrowed my laptop to watch movies and her attention span was hummingbird-length. I could practically see her opening tab after tab while Hollywood cars exploded in the background.

The image file had been screenshotted wrong. All I could see was a product number with "Quantity: 12" below it, and beneath that, an order total for $5,199. My first reaction was that that number couldn't be right, followed by a sinking feeling that it likely was.

In the living room, my mother was snoring on the couch. Her headscarf had slipped, revealing thin gray hairs combed over a mole-spattered scalp, arthritic knuckles cupping her small potbelly, and a stick-leg poking from her robe. In sleep, her brow furrowed as if she were clinging to the threads of an argument.

How had my mother gotten so old? I made a sound through my nose like a laugh. *I* had gotten old. My mother was eighty. I was halfway there myself, yet kept seeing her as I had as a teenager, the supposedly cool mom who bought me condoms I didn't want, teased me for being "buttoned-up," and once invited my friends and I to share her six-pack so we could get drunk our first time with parental supervision. Then, I'd thought she was trying to humiliate me, to punish me for not being the daughter she wanted. Now, her efforts seemed sensible. I had waited to drink until college and ended up, as she must have anticipated, having semiconscious sex with a boy who passed out on top of me. I wished I'd taken her up on the beers. I wished I'd told her that I liked girls. I wished when she called me "buttoned-up" I'd been able to explain the feelings behind my rigid posture and uniform-like dress. My mother had been cool. I could have told her, as it seemed queer kids told their parents so casually these days, that I felt like a boy inside. She would have helped me become one, back when I was young enough for the hormones to really change things, to have a whole, normal adulthood as a man.

I tucked a blanket around my mother and eased the tablet, still flashing *Sugar Crush!,* from under her crepe-y cheek. What could a woman on a fixed income have bought for five thousand dollars?

I carried her tablet into the kitchen. At the top of her email were delighted messages from people whose names I didn't recognize, all subject-lined, "Re: guess what I got you!" I didn't need to guess; the details were in a confirmation email: "Bottomless Hole (Yard & Garden Accessories) >= 12 units. Est. Time (Days) = 15. Made in Sri Lanka." I clicked "Edit/Delete Order." My mother's password auto-filled in the wholesaler's website. Thankfully, the order hadn't shipped and, in a matter of moments, I received a notification of her pending refund. I forwarded the email to myself, deleted it from my mother's inbox, and emptied the trash.

I had anticipated my mother might become senile, but hadn't realized a mind could be lost in drips. Still capable of arguing me into submission, she could no longer be trusted with her bank account or major decisions. Enough was enough. I would get power of attorney. First, though, the hole had to be dealt with. I wouldn't tell her until it was done. As my mother loved to say, forgiveness was easier to get than permission.

"THERE'S A HOOLIGAN in the yard."

I pretended not to hear, turned my back to the window, and dialed up the volume on the AM weather station. "Huh?"

"We're being ROBBED."

"WHAT?"

My mother unplugged the radio and pulled back the curtain on the sliding door. "There."

"That's the meterman." The Craigslist guy had arrived an hour late. I'd told him 7:00 a.m. or not to bother, but people were assholes about free stuff, acting like they were doing you a favor.

"There's no meter over there."

"It's the neighbors' kid then. He probably threw something over the fence."

"Mm. Maybe." She tapped on the glass. "Hey!"

"Mom, that French café is doing curbside. Want to get breakfast?"

She grasped the door handle. "I'm going to check."

I called a feeble "wait," but discovery was a foregone

conclusion. The guy had said he could get the hole unin-stalled and loaded into his truck in twenty minutes, but those minutes were supposed to be while my mother was asleep.

Through the lace curtain behind the sink, I watched them argue. The guy grabbed his tool belt. My mother's terrycloth robe billowed angrily as he marched off.

"Hannah!"

Her tone jerked me back to childhood. She was staring at the kitchen window. She couldn't see me but knew I was there. The back of my neck began to sweat.

"Okay, okay." I descended the concrete steps and crossed the patio, hands raised in surrender.

"How dare you? To your own *mother*?"

"I thought you'd fall in."

Eighty might have been objectively old, but her gaze was ageless. In it, I felt myself unmade. Her body had once contained my own. Now, we were separate. More so in this moment than even when I was still in Florida, avoid-ing her calls.

She sighed and extended an arm. I fell into the half-embrace, the familiar pat on my back, the way she comforted me when I was little.

"Mom?"

"Mm."

"Do you love me?"

She did not hesitate. "Yes."

I exhaled, releasing a tension of years. The hole, a swatch of pure black, lay between us, its edges fringed by a new growth of weeds. It was, if I was honest, impossible to imagine an end to such darkness. Maybe it did go on forever. There were stranger things.

"But I don't love you most. I love you in the middle."

I looked up. "In the—middle?"

She wore a we're-all-adults-here expression. "It's silly that mothers are supposed to love their children most. Of course I love you, but I have a lot of friends. I love some of them more than you, and some less. It's just a fact. You, I love in the middle."

I tried to be objective. I'd been afraid she did not love me and now I knew she did. She even loved me more than, I assumed, half her friends. She loved me enough to be honest.

The thought hurt like a loose tooth when wiggled, a sweet and jagged pain. "I love you too."

She nodded. She knew. With a slippered foot, she nudged a pinecone over the edge of the hole. I wanted to ask if there was a reason for her medium-sized love. I suspected she would have loved a real daughter completely, one who could be a girl like her.

"Was I always different?"

"Different?"

I wanted her to see me as I did. The squareness of my forehead, the subtle cleft in my chin. How my silhouette descended linebacker-ishly from ribs to hips. These secrets of my flesh, as if a small mutiny of cells had been trying to make me male all along. "Not like other kids."

I concentrated, taking in this moment before she spoke, and her words changed me forever. If my mother said that I had always been a man, the genie would have escaped. I would have to become what I ached to be but of which I was petrified. I would have to take action, because this was the power my mother had over me, this goading, prodding, joking, biting ability to say exactly what I didn't want and most needed to hear.

"You have always been," she said, sounding tired, "unable to face reality."

"That's not true!" I felt I'd been slapped.

She inclined her head, as if to say, *See?* It was just like her to take a position where any disagreement would seem to prove her right. The injustice stung. *I* couldn't face reality? She was the one wasting her life savings on "bottomless" holes. I was here, in her yard, *because* I faced reality. I had driven fifteen hours because I faced the fact that distance teaching was the new normal, and that she could die, that the pandemic wasn't going away, and that I was lonely. I had faced those things while all she faced was a pit in her yard that she wanted to believe broke the laws of physics.

IT TOOK NO time to pack. One large duffel: clothes, teaching materials, a toothbrush, my lumbar pillow. I wadded dirty underwear into a grocery bag and squashed my mother's fleece on top. It seemed like I should have more stuff, but the apartment in Tampa had come furnished and there was box of books in my trunk.

My mother stood on the front porch while I wrestled luggage into the car. "Are you meeting up with your friend?"

I hadn't said I was leaving, but I knew she knew. And I was the one who didn't face reality. I slammed the trunk. "My friend's dead."

She looked perplexed, as if trying to understand whether this was slang. "From laughing?"

"From cancer."

She opened her mouth, closed it. "I'm defrosting cutlets. I was going to make a salad in a bit."

"Enjoy." I climbed in the driver's seat, too angry to say anything else. I wanted her to know me well enough to know how to keep me from leaving. I watched her shrink in the rearview mirror before turning out onto the main road.

The town was quiet. I sailed through green lights and waited alone at red ones for the nonexistent cross-traffic. As I drove, I bid goodbye to the fried chicken place that used too much black pepper, the deli where my father had bought me breadsticks, the knitting store where my mother had let me pick wool for each year's Hanukkah sweater. A lot of the businesses had "closed" signs. I wondered if my hometown was going to dry up and blow away, like so many other small towns. I wondered if the whole country was going to blow away, or if it had done so when we elected the last president—or with small-pox blankets and residential schools, or with slave ships and electric chairs—and we were only now catching on. I wondered this abstractly, as if I were not a part of these places, as if I had anywhere else to go.

The person my mother loved best could throw her dead body in the hole.

For a few miles, I believed it was possible to untether myself from her. I fantasized about having been born male to a mother who dusted, who used her yard for growing flowers. This vignette gave way to others: myself in a tux; my mother saying, *What a good son*; a ridiculously large paycheck made out to Darren H. Becher.

Who was I kidding. I might have felt like a man, but my body was a daughter's. I bled like a daughter, stormed out like a daughter, and woke in the mornings full of daughterly resentment. If only I had been a son, I could have loved my mother in the middle too.

I made it as far as the canola farms before killing the engine. I could have driven back to Florida, but I hated Florida. I was going to quit my job; I would actually do it this time. I got out of the car and found myself wading into a field. Ripped out a handful of yellow flowers and held them under my chin. Kids used to say that if your chin shone yellow from the reflection, it meant you liked butter. I'd been certain that when I grew up I'd understand what that meant, but all I could think now was, didn't everyone like butter? Was that the joke?

At my mother's house, salad ingredients were spread across the counter, but my mother was in the yard. I carried my bags upstairs, re-unpacked my clothes into my old dresser, and sat cross-legged on the nubby bedspread. From my closet door, the sitcom idol grinned back. What had happened to him? Drugs, I supposed. In junior high, that boy had been my imaginary sweetheart, kissing me good morning with bow-shaped lips and deflowering me every night. In the largest picture, the actor was an adult, toned, in his early twenties. He'd still been playing a teenager. I looked him up on my phone. He hadn't gotten into drugs after all; when he was twenty, the internet told me, he'd been saved by a Christian radio show while smoking in his red convertible. Now, he ran a megachurch.

I preferred the younger shots where he was sweetfaced and still godless, smiling dorkily as if posing for a school picture. It occurred to me that that smile hadn't been for thirsty, pre-teen girls but for his mother, who must have been coaching him from just outside the shot.

Through the branches of a willow tree that grew

beneath my window, I caught a flash of my mother's violet headwrap. She was by the hole again. Was it that mesmerizing to her, like staring into flames, or was she secretly trying to understand where it went?

With a ladder and a bright light, I might be able to see down. Or, I could get an extra-long measuring tape. It couldn't be deeper than a well. I would get the evidence and show my mother. Once I knew how far it went, I would know what to use it for.

I could throw myself in, I thought. That would be a use. But I knew I wouldn't.

"Is that you?" called my mother from the bottom of the stairs. I did not answer. What was it to be me? I wondered if this was how the actor had felt before he'd found Jesus on the red convertible's radio.

"Hannah?"

The stairs creaked as my mother began to climb. She was not going to believe me about the hole, no matter how much evidence I amassed. It held her interest as I never could. She had said it was "just a hole," and yet was at peace beside it. At peace with its frigidity and devouring hunger, with its refusal to make sense. The hole was chaos. It was a problem forever in wait for a solution. That's why she loved it.

She stood in the doorway. "Didn't you hear me?"

Behind her, the house was dim. Sad. "Yep."

"Why did I have to climb all the way up here?"

"Because you wanted to?"

"Very funny, Miss Yuks." A frail hand went to her bony hip. She would be so light when dead. Even I could carry her body as far as the backyard.

"Mom?"

"Yeah, what?"

"You really want to get put in that hole?"

She grinned, as delighted as a baby who's gotten the sitter to pick up a dropped spoon for the hundred-thousandth time. "Uh-huh."

I pictured her light body tumbling into the abyss. And what if I didn't let go but followed her in? Entwined myself around her as if I were her little girl again and she was carrying me home?

A Full and Accurate Recounting

HOME (YOSVEN)

The name of our village is various names, as the country to which we are subject is sometimes Lietuva, sometimes Rossiya. So it is with each villager. That is why our handsome Yidl, as we village girls call him, is Yehuda at shul, Iudelis to the tax collectors, Lubya when the Russians make him fight their wars. He is Yidl still in my fantasies as I pine for him over yeasty dough, the whelp of stray dogs coughing hay dust, road dust, sawdust. Nine years, the order says, but girlish prayer stronger than orders brings him back whole in three. Yude now, he insists. Leaves turning from gold to red fall behind him like a royal cape.

The morning after Yude comes home, field to wood has frozen, walking outdoors as stunning as waking. Maybe this is why the goose is so shocking. I am half-asleep when I find its gray, broken-necked body in the square, clouded eyes staring at the cloudy sky.

My scream is of surprise. The villagers come running. Women comfort me with speculation.

"A fox."

"A fox interrupted by a noise."

"Someone likely slammed a door and scared it."

"It dropped the goose."

A vagrant interrupts our female chatter. "Him." He points at Yude. "I saw him cross the fields in moonlight. He was covered in feathers."

There is pause swollen with doubt, the beginnings of question, until the miller spits. "Quiet, you alte kocker."

The crowd adds its favorite curses. We laugh the heretic back to his hole. Yude marries the miller's daughter, and the country of which they claim we are subjects changes its name once more.

I remember the goose when the Germans arrive, led by a group of gentiles whose faces I know from the market. On this stunned morning, we villagers are the goose. The mouth of the fox is a truck bed. The goose snow white on white ground. Strangely bloodless. How is it that a murdering fox can be so gentle, and, too, so forgetful?

Yosven was the name of our village. Without us Yosveners, it must be only Josvainiai.

VILNA

They have erected walls to make a small Vilna within the large one. Little Vilna, a pen for animals.

We descend from our trucks and are driven into houses that they have divided into apartments, those apartments cut into smaller apartments. Who will harvest my turnips, the neat rows of green tops flopping open toward the sun? My goat will go unfed.

I slump into a broken-legged chair. The cries of

children burn through the thin walls of this warren. I see us in miniature as from above, mice in a cage, zhukes burrowing in whorls of dark wood. In my mind's eye, we recede until darkness swallows us.

In the single endless day that follows, we villagers clutch arms in the cramped passageways, swearing Hashem soon will restore us to our Yosven, our home. He would not forsake us.

WINTER

The council is a condition of our internment, its representatives, young men chosen for their early ruined skin. We, villagers from many villages, grind their names into the wet streets. "Council member," we address them, but only when necessary. They are homely, these conscripts. I won't look them in the eye or suffer their stuttering.

There is some good in this place. The boys organize a soccer league; we women, an exchange of bread and clothing. Our rebbes and the teachers and playwrights from the city dedicate themselves to the conservation of knowledge. They fold parchment into coat linings and bury books beneath paving stones while we make noise to distract our hidden keepers.

There is some good here, but much evil. Small thefts occur. Fights over food. Girls are fondled in the crowds, unknown by whom.

No one likes a jail yet we resign ourselves to its construction. Man, woman, child lay brick together. This is, Rebbe says, akin to those higher levels of charity wherein the sages throw coins behind them so that they might not know to whom they give their wealth. Likewise, we lay the bricks for the jail, not knowing who we will protect by locking away our fallen ones.

SPRING

We test the walls of our city within a city. Clomp in groups to the dead ends of the streets. Knock on their boards. The outer city bangs, yells, rattles back at us. There are people there, on the other side. I think they are people. If there are people, they must hear us. Hashem will move them to our aid. He must. They must. We will be patient.

WINTER (AGAIN)

We think our walls are mere wood and proclaim our allegiance to match and adze. Some of us burst into flame. Some break heads over the boards. We cough clouds of sawdust. But the walls persist. There is iron inside the wood. Stone inside the iron. The people on the other side, if they exist, have iron for ears. Otherwise, how is it that our pain goes unheard?

WINTER (STILL)

In the baths, dingy water creeps over women's backs, thick shoulders flickering in candlelight. Sweat drips in the pool.

The bitterness of menstruation hints at a whole family line: daughter, mother, grandmother. Our collective memory. The past is falling out of us. Our wombs can't hang on to anything.

Gazes fix on the water, on nothing. We make chitchat as women do, while under the surface, blood becomes shuddering. Some touch each other. This is the rumor. A slick on the tips of the fingers, a fast heat, nothing more

RAIN (SPRING?)

The normal world continues within our walls but shrunken. The real problem is bodies, which is why some of us flatten into paper, learning to fold.

Eight families share a kitchen in what was once called Coat Closet. We eat potatoes and beets and beans and bread. When there isn't bread, when the beans are gone, the beets soft, the potatoes turned to poison, we conjure food. We chew the insides of our cheeks, pinch murashkes from the window frames.

Windows made of stained glass, frames of molded fir. In spite of everything, I admire the artistry of my first city home. It is indeed breathtaking, what man can work.

RAIN (SUMMER?)

I don't remember who built the jail, who commissioned blueprints, who mortared bricks. "Them," we say. In the council's record, it is titled only "That Lamentable Place." The teachers, keepers of memory, say *They* forced us. There was an order, perhaps, a threat, someone shot in the streets? Already we began to lose these simple facts. In the time before we didn't require the past to be fixed, and so were in the habit of inventing our memories from present needs.

There is now time enough for any man to study Talmud. Women can join for secular subjects. We form a group for the study of History. While cooking or scavenging along our walls, we recite our story from the Beginning to the Present. We teach ourselves to remember in this new way until our heads fill with History's sharp divisions. Before and After. This Now and Back Then. Once/Always. A timeline numbered at equidistant points. I had not known time was a line. Objectivity, nod our teachers. It is the difference between the inside and out. It is how we locate ourselves within Hashem's creation.

FALL

Whoever built the jail, I am grateful. It gives us a reason to avoid mistakes, and anyway, someone has to go. In our study group, I remember the story of Isaac and the punishment of Gomorrah, and how, in particular epochs, Hashem has required a sacrifice of blood.

WINTER I

We dream of smoke trailing into the gray skies, sleep in piles like rats. On Pesach, it is rumored a mother tried to hang herself without thought for her infant. I begin to suspect it was true what They say about us. Or, anyway, about the bad apples. We thank God for the jail He created with which to root them out. We memorize History and our recitations improve. We recall how, for centuries, *They,* the false ones, have done this to us, the swindlers, baby killers, horned devils: our imposter-brethren.

I remember snake-tongued Yehuda, the glaze in his eyes when he returned from Ukraine, his breath stinking and skin yellowed, rotten in places. How earth froze beneath his boots. A desperate goose flapping in his grip.

I remember seeing him in the moonlight, all clad in feathers like a heathen of old.

Shande, curse my fellow history pupils upon hearing this story. It is the fault of such a son that we are here.

Among our numbers slither tens of these serpents, then hundreds. We watch for them. We swear to rout out the demons in our midst.

WINTER

In the women's baths, we strip naked and crowd close. The big women have shrunk but the skinnies are the same, all hard angles and stretched laughter. Their long necks wound with tendons, their spines notched like time's measuring tape. When our bones come together, we make a sound like a neighbor knocking on a faraway door.

I recognize the pounding. A door from my dreams. Bronze handle curled against varnished wood. In the night, a fist collides with that door, shaking some of us from our beds, others into the hollow wall. The apartment became clearer after that, more room to cook and I get decent sleep when it isn't too cold. A woman college graduate recites a play about bumbling gods ravenous for the smoke of sacrifice. No one laughs at the Greek jokes; we are fathoming our Lord's appetite.

WINTER I.III

We walk the circumference of our shtetl, measuring its limits, the lengths of its streets. We women rub skirt hems along the bone-white walls, the children drag sticks. Someone tells about the beginning, when God separated water from water and brought solid forms from the void. We profess our love of solid objects. We beat our breasts repeatedly.

A weak-kneed man claims to hear laughter on the other side of the wall. We laugh. From the other side comes only the echo of our merriment. The weak-kneed man slaps his thigh, amused at his own folly. There is no one there, old fool, we laugh. We laugh until the air tastes of salt, until the clouds burst open, releasing bellyfuls of rain.

SUMMER I

In the jail, people multiply then disappear. Weight slides from our shoulders. We float over the streets instead of plodding. A man known for his kindness to the demented is arrested for vagrancy. He fell asleep on the yeshiva court-yard's sun-warmed stones. Fortunately, the Rebbe found him before anyone could trip and hurt themselves. That afternoon, I smell new grass as they drag him by, hands covering his face, perhaps weeping or perhaps asleep. The sky rumbles, and I forget to watch where they take him. Perhaps he folded himself into wings. Later I recall a story about this, how in dire circumstance Hashem calls His chosen home.

SUMMER I.II

Our impression of History is improving, and the teacher praises us. We know the territories of Europe, the dates of the Inquisition, world leaders of 1902. We can't remember if there was a time before we lived together here in our emptying rooms or the names of those who have left, or where they have gone, so the teacher teaches us that too: the number of fires we've suffered, the beatings, the rapes, the deaths of the firstborn.

"Have we always been here?" one of our men asks.

"No," says the teacher, "but everywhere has been identical. The same rules, the familiar spices, the old rituals. Even football is played according to tradition." Out the window, our children, like grounded hawklings, pound the ball with their shoes. Their rising dust draws figures on the glass.

"Will we ever escape?" asks the man.

"God made the universe as a linked passage of rooms," says the teacher. "Leave one and another awaits. But each contains the same furniture."

SUMMER II.I

Our place grows enormous. We stretch our arms, wave our wrists in circles to test the boundaries. They do not give.

In the baths, I pull a woman close, making the chilly water heave. Her hair stinks like gunpowder.

"We've stockpiled arms. We are only waiting for you," she whispers.

"Who's we?"

"Some of us. I can't say."

"To what end?" I ask.

"Freedom," she says. "How it was before."

Beneath us, the earth's wet flesh shakes.

Before, I think and remember Babylon and the chalk outline of Napoleon's conquests.

Before, I think, recalling a hall of furnished rooms.

SUMMER ~~III II~~ I

I dream that in History we learn the future. It is the same.
It is exactly like now. Time is static. The teacher holds
a device. A black glass that cheeps like a bird and flick-
ers dizzyingly at a touch. "Tablet," he calls it, stroking its
surface. We've never seen one before—although, on the
other hand, we might have. On the glass, a map of our
small city appears: its walls, its trampled courtyards, its
three-story buildings, their mazes of flats. The map blinks
with labeled dots.

"Us," says the teacher, tapping a blue dot: *Arklių* 9,
Teacher's House. He spreads his thumb and forefinger
against the glass. Portraits float in the darkness: women
in drab dresses at laundry tubs; a child on a cobbled street;
men and women bent over a slate, *Ghetto History Club*,
captioned beneath.

Photos of our faces float in the glass, fanned backward and forward as in mirrors facing mirrors. We grow
dizzy with the present and our own knowing. "Tablet,"
we murmur, wondering if the Israelites at Sinai felt
such awe.

"Where is History?" asks a student.

The teacher, seeming disappointed, withdraws the
device. "History is always somewhere else."

Again, we have asked the wrong question.

I dream this night after night.

FALL IIII.IIII

I am awake. We wake. We walk. We work. We eat. I sleep.
Seasons stream reliably into seasons. I dream dreams of a

distant year when the earth is dry, scorched by fire, abandoned by life. But when I wake, all is right. It is cold when it should be, hot when the earth leans toward the sun. The rhythms reassure us. We thank God for the calendar of days, one moon passing into another.

SUMMER I.II

I am awake when the traitors ooze to the surface, hard lines showing through their jackets. I recognize her immediately, the woman from the baths.

"That one," I declare, pointing, refusing to turn away. Four councilmen fall upon her, holding her to the stones. Her hair—it looks different in the light, a cyclone of curls—fans under their knees. The other worms bare their rifles. They press the barrels to our ribs, say we deserve the death we have coming.

"Heretics! All time is this one room," I shout, making myself hoarse. "The only future lies behind!"

I think of the woman's moon shoulders strung pink from someone's nails, the taste of salt on someone's tongue, great shockwaves moving upward through the water as a name rang out against the wooden walls, out into the bloodblack sky. She was singing.

SPRING I

I am singing.

"Your friend is gone," say the others.

I've been calling to no one. In fact, I am alone in the kitchen, my hissing breath mimicking steam.

WINTER I

Later, I learn they've taken her to the jail, and even later that I come to understand she never existed. She has no name, no place of birth, no living descendent; in the dream I dream so often now, she does not roam the barren land calling my name. Her title does not appear blinking on the teacher's magic map. If it did, what would it be? *The Woman Who Never Was*? Or simply, *A Ghost*?

THE BEGINNING

I am grateful.

Water will not cleanse us, but History does.

The right question is no question.

History doesn't owe [me? us?] an answer.

I am just grateful the jail has always been there, that we have a soccer team even if no players, a tidy kitchen, a classroom—more space every day. We are rich. Now I've seen us on the map, I know we will live forever.

End of the World Pussy

The world was ending. They announced it on the radio between an ad raising money for children with muscular dystrophy and Duran Duran's "Hungry Like the Wolf." That was the only song Priscilla and her best friend, Toni, danced to at homecoming before exiting the gym to upchuck their rum and cokes. This morning, Priscilla was still part asleep—wouldn't have been listening during the apocalyptic PSA if the DJ hadn't said he'd play "Hungry Like the Wolf" after a short commercial break.

Remain calm, said a voice so chilled out it might have just come out of a 7-11 drink fridge. *Scientists have put out an urgent alert. Planet Earth has left its normal orbit and is on a collision course with the Sun. Exact time of impact, 1:18 p.m. EST.* Priscilla waited for further explanation. In a movie, the voice would say how scientists were going to avert this disaster. A crazy scheme for a crazy problem. Rockets, the voice would say. Or that if everyone ran for Australia, they could tilt the planet upright again. But the only other thing the voice said was, *For the good of the economy, citizens are asked to go about their normal routines. Schools and businesses shall remain open.*

Priscilla sat for a while in her pajamas, holding the radio, thinking, *How predictable, the world ending like a dud firework.* Ever since she got her period, Priscilla had grasped the anticlimactic reality of supposedly pivotal moments. Blood streaking down her chicken thighs while her grimacing mother paused barely long enough to say, "I'm late for work, Tampax under the sink."

Her mother, who'd be getting the news at the call center by now. Chewing a lip while she digested the fact that she and her workplace would soon be space dust. Then: *snap.* Headset on, dialing out to the next lead, relieved she wouldn't have to clean any offices that night.

Priscilla barely noticed Simon Le Bon singing about night being a wire, too busy wondering where she'd heard the announcement's soothing monotone before. Some telethon? A late-night infomercial? Then it hit her. The Time Lady—the sweet mysteriosa who recited the hour on a permanently running loop. Nights her mother worked and Priscilla couldn't reach Toni, she called the Time Lady. She watched countless horror movies on mute, eyeballs stinging with exhaustion, while the Lady comfortingly murmured, *2:33 and 40 seconds. 2:33 and 50 seconds. 2:34 a.m.*

In the made-for-TV version of Priscilla's life, the actress playing her would have wailed *I'm too young to die*, pounding her fists on the ground. Priscilla playing herself probed for worry—fear—any emotion? Nope. But this: a thrilling animal alertness. Her ears felt like tunnels.

I'm disco and rhyme, Simon Le Bon, fading out, sang.

But what did disco have to do with wolves? Through a tear in the window screen, the Sun stood puff-chested, yet small enough to blot out with a finger. "Hungry Like the Wolf" was a stupid song, she realized, if you listened to the lyrics. If you weren't drunk in the sweet haze of Toni Medina.

IT TOOK FOREVER to reach her.

"If the world is ending," said Priscilla, "we're playing hooky."

"We cut all last week and the world wasn't ending then," said Toni.

"So?"

"Sew your hole. Meet me at the parking structure." Bitingly, she added, "You spaz out, I'm gone." Toni was a bitch, but that's what made her cool. Real bitches, you could trust. Nice girls, girls used to being liked—them you had to watch for.

Toni had an ugly face and a hot body, fist of a mouth clenched over a D-battery chin. Beneath that, super boobs, curvy waist, hips like some black-and-white movie. From the roof of the elevator tower, Priscilla watched those hips roll up. Toni, who hated small spaces but didn't mind climbing eight flights, swaggered out from the stairwell into the sunniest morning in human history.

"I'm not going up there." Toni soured a lip and squinted up the padlocked ladder. "Too damn bright." Beefy with fire, the Sun seemed to agree. Priscilla raised a palm to block it. Light leaked through her fingers.

"You've got shades. It's the last time."

Toni tapped the ladder with a nail, making a hollow ding. "Nah." Toni wasn't into the elevator tower. Swore the pigs would show and that she had enough record, didn't need some petty trespass rap, let alone their porcine stares at her cleavage. *Porcine stares*, a line to drop at people who thought she was dumb. Toni did have brains. She knew which drugs famous people were hooked on, could tell when bands lip-synched, and had memorized multiple states' juvenile emancipation laws. There was bored attention under Toni's toughness. Without showing surprise or really interest, Toni caught things before they happened. Hell, she'd probably known a week ago about Earth's defective orbit. Her MO was always to keep quiet, let the suckers decode their own torpedoed fate.

That's how it had gone down with Priscilla and the cops. They turned up once, minutes after Toni split the scene. Four cruisers with a shrink in tow, united to nag her down. Some wig-out about teen suicide that came around like clockwork, an adult fad, no big deal. The sentence: mandatory counseling, which translated to skipping gym each Tuesday so she could chew gum in Dr. Argyle's office and heed her weekly diagnosis. *Attachment disorder*, announced like Argyle had hit oil. *Depressive personality. Alexithymia.* Blow, pop, nod.

"I don't need you up there ogling me either," said Toni. "Come down or I smoke this bowl alone."

"Christ." But Priscilla swung down the ladder. That was how their fights went. Her insisting, Toni resisting, then smoking a bowl. Sometimes when Toni was in the mood, Priscilla could swipe a hand under Toni's shirt. Sometimes in a TV-and-pot-borne fugue, Toni would let Priscilla hug her from behind, and Toni's drowsy pulse would throb against Priscilla's pubic bone. Sometimes Priscilla fantasized stillborn conversations:

P: I want to ...   P: What if we just ...
T: You want to what?   T: What if we just what?
P: I don't know.   P: Nothing.

Even in her imagination she knew people didn't really talk about this stuff, it was supposed to happen on its own. *Lust is a magnet not a manifesto,* she thought, taking a lung-searing hit. Anything she could confess Toni already knew. Better to let Toni win arguments, then slip through any breaks that appeared, grab what she could. Ants survived through the accumulation of grains. That's how they built elaborate civilizations.

Then along came a pair of Topsiders to kick ant civilization to jack diddly.

A couple of yuppie dudes emerged from the stairwell and headed toward a margarine-colored Jeep. Toni dumped the roach and stuck the pipe in Priscilla's back pocket. It didn't matter, the guys weren't interested in a couple of kids. The bigger one—he looked like the boss, mean around the brow, tan hair extra shiny sat down in the driver's seat and fiddled with something on the dash. The other guy opened his door but stayed standing. He kept wiping his palms on his khakis like they were sweating.

"How much time you think is left?" asked Priscilla.

"Dunno," said Toni. "Couple hours."

The rhombus of shade in which Priscilla and Toni leaned was slenderizing. Anorexic shade headed to its demise. Endangered shade. Someone could print it on a decal, bury it in a box of cereal. *Save the shade!* Grave shade posing on the cover of *Time,* "End of an Era." Tragic shade in *People* modeling sunglasses, cigarette, devil-take-me sneer.

"Turn it up," said Sweat Hands. Boss Guy fiddled again and the voice of the Time Lady crackled on.

Two hours, twenty-four minutes, thirty seconds. Two hours, twenty-four minutes, twenty seconds.

"Fucking hell," said Boss Guy. "Fucking hell to goddamn bitch cunt mother of suckmytits."

"Goddamn," repeated Sweat Hands, an unimaginative type. He combed his fingers through his hair, something Priscilla might have done in a mirror, going for rocker-cool, ice-cold Le Bon cool. Sweat Hands did not look cool. He looked pathetic, a grown-up crybaby.

Priscilla waited for Toni to yell, *Hey goober, want your mommy?* Make this poser feel the hurt. Toni chilled though, slouching on the brick. She started a cigarette. Didn't offer.

Two hours, twenty-two minutes, ten seconds. Two hours, twenty-two minutes. Two hours twenty-one minutes, fifty seconds.

Boss Guy drummed on the hood, careful not to let his gut brush the grill.

"That's a clean shirt," observed Toni.

"It's pretty stain-lifted," agreed Priscilla.

If Boss Guy had been in mandatory counseling, Dr. Argyle would have taken him off suicide risk for sure. *Care for self-presentation*, Argyle liked to say while chomping a gummy bear, *is the strongest denoter of wellness in the individual.*

The Time Lady reached two and a quarter hours before the radio went to a commercial for storage units. *You collect it, we save it*, said the ad. Priscilla thought about how many storage units must exist on the planet, garage doors that if lined up could reach from there to the moon. Behind the

doors, cardboard boxes people had packed intending to
retrieve, pots to be cooked in, stools to be sat on, photo
albums to be flipped through. Glass rolled in newspaper,
ceramic buried in Styrofoam peanuts. Some people had
probably used label-makers to organize their objects by
category, had aisles and drawers devoted to specific items
they were saving. Doorknobs, for example. Whole filing
cabinets labeled *doorknobs, crystal*; *doorknobs, brass*, etc.
Doorknobs that would go permanently unturned. Labels
made useless. Storage units floating loose in space, lodg-
ing in the moon's dust like gravel in a scrape. Priscilla
wanted the Lady to come back on again. She was getting
used to the counting of numbers backward. It felt, in a
weird way, like backward made more sense than forward.
Backward had certainty. Time forward actually seemed
wrong, an error in life's accounting. Forward you couldn't
tell when anything would end, or if.

And then she thought about the doorknobs. They
wouldn't float through space. They'd burn.

Two hours, ten minutes.

"Isn't it kind of sad?" said Priscilla, because sad seemed
the correct way to feel.

"*That's* sad." Toni indicated the yuppies. Sweat Hands
trembled and periodically gasped, "Oh god." Boss Guy
paced circles around him and the Jeep. They were sad—
or they were angry, or scared. Priscilla often took quizzes
like this with Dr. Argyle, where she examined a picture
of a face and tried to name the emotion. *More sad?* he'd
ask. *Or more puzzled?* The tests were responsible for her
continued gym class hiatus—she answered wrong as often
as right. Toni figured she was blowing the assessments
on purpose, but the problem was emotions. How could

you tell what showed was the actual thing? Feelings hid beneath feelings. Surface feelings went against deeper feelings and deep feelings appeared at the wrong time and place, so when you were supposed to feel scared you instead became electric or when meant to be sad instead got bored.

She explained this to Toni in her head.

P: This puke feeling in my stomach, for example. What am I supposed to call that?

T: Don't call it anything.

P: I have to call it something.

T: No.

P: What do you mean, no? I'm feeling it. It's something. It's *my* something.

T: I mean, people don't have feelings.

P: Sure we do. Look at Sweat Hands.

T: People are radio antennae. They pick up signals. They send out signals. Other antennae pick up those signals. And on.

P: They are too my fucking feelings.

T: FUCK YOU, YOU PIECE OF SHIT TOILET-BOWL SNIFFER!

P: WHY ARE YOU ALWAYS SUCH A TWAT??

T: See the pattern. You think you're mad, but you're not. You're picking up my signal.

P: Fuck you. Get out of my brain.

T: Does a radio station care if you tune in?

"*Hey*," snapped Toni.

"Huh?"

"Look alive." Toni mashed out the butt of her cigarette. The Sun had fattened to dodgeball size and stationed itself overhead. Sweat Hands was gazing vertically into the light, his sprayed hair shifted backward on his scalp, toupeeish, his pasty self aglow.

"What's with him?" said Priscilla

Toni shrugged, her shoulder soft and round like a tan melon.

"Who cares? Real life is crap," she said. "Let's watch TV."

ONE HOUR, sixteen minutes, forty seconds.

Abandoned cars clogged the road the whole way to Toni's. Like Boss Guy and Sweat Hands, drivers had climbed out with radios blaring. It gave the streets the aura of a parade late in the day when everyone is trashed and fights start breaking out. They got to walk in the middle of the street and could shove adults out the way with zero consequences.

Still, the going was slow. Thousands of people milling cowlike and stunned while others punched inanimate objects and each other. Pure chaos. Toni plowed through with linebacker force, but Priscilla stalled, rubbernecking. The ones going crazy were upstaged by the transfixed, whose features the shining Sun flattened. The palest of them reflected the light like mirrors, their skin too bright to look at. The news that morning had explained that Earth's unexpected lurch from orbit was warping and thickening the atmosphere. Instant cauterization would protect the planet from heat until they were completely engulfed, but the brightness, that was it. The Sun getting huge. Everyone had shades on except the starers. Priscilla tried staring herself, wanted to see the outline, see if she could measure its distance, but even a split second burned left tracers that made her lose Toni in the crowd. People pressed in, crushed out her breath. She was drowning in human beings.

ONE HOUR, THIRTEEN MINUTES, THIRTY SECONDS, the Time Lady boomed simultaneously from hundreds of car radios. Superpowered by her Lady's call, Priscilla kicked in time to its echo, crushing ball sacs and smashing kneecaps until she was free.

She caught up with Toni at the curb by Toni's house, where she had plopped down to smoke. Arrayed on the lawn, starers of various ages and races posed like garden statues, noses pointed up. The identical poses made them look like whatever came after whatever came after whatever came after octuplets.

"You think they've gone blind?" said Priscilla.

"Who?" Toni squinted over her Praybans—cheap shades from a youth group that had a gold Jesus fish in place of the designer logo. Priscilla had chucked hers; the plastic was thick, nearly opaque, you couldn't see shit. But Toni wore her Praybans everywhere. Toni didn't care about seeing; Toni liked to make people know how much she didn't need to look at them. Toni didn't need, for instance, to see women tearing out their hair, men pounding on each other until blood oozed from their squashed noses. Toni didn't need to see the starers either, those fucked-up pillars of salt.

"It's like the End Times." Priscilla tried to keep her tone as blank as the Time Lady's, but she was bugged. Electricity coursed her bloodstream, beamed from her pores. The world was over. How fucked up and perfect, how unholy and horrible, how awesome and rerun-predictable.

"Duh."

"But like, *His Rebuke with flames of fire*. The beast of wherever coming up from below . . ."

"Yeah, I read that book too," shrugged Toni. "The movie was better."

Hell did seem cheesy, like a carnival haunted house, not even scary when you and a friend were screaming to hype each other up. This End Times wasn't cheesy though. It was power to the max. "Think about it. A planet that's been around a trillion years vaporized, like . . ." Her snap was more of a damp sliding of fingers. She tried again, glad Toni couldn't see. The only sound they made was wet skin, soft and sweat-logged. "You and me, we're alive for it. We are. Doesn't that seem important? Maybe it's not god but destiny. Like every breath that every human being has ever taken made us so we could be here, breathing up the last oxygen that exists."

Toni hiked up her skirt a few inches so her naked thigh smooshed across the yellow-painted curb. She gazed over the top of the shades, her sticky stare on Priscilla, holding it until Priscilla had to look away. Priscilla's crotch burned like a burning bush.

"You know who gives a shit about us? No one." Toni glanced up at the sky-large Sun a moment longer than seemed smart. Then, blinders down, stood and picked her way to the back door, jiggled the key and opened, letting them both in.

The familiar stench of must and rot struck as Priscilla followed Toni down the pathway zigzagging around piled newspapers. Maybe that was how Toni didn't need to see, years navigating the labyrinth of her aunt and uncle's crap. Toni ignored the wall switch and the curtain pull, moving by feel through the darkened room. Once seated on the sofa, Toni grabbed the remote. TV light flooded the dimness, illuminating the dusty curtains and Priscilla's sweaty legs.

One hour, three minutes, twenty seconds, crackled the Time Lady through the TV speakers.

Priscilla stepped over a pile of papers and lowered herself onto one of the gritty cushions, in the spot closest to Toni. Onscreen was a drawing of the Earth and the Sun, depicted as two circles: one blue and miniature, one yellow and large. It looked like a solar system poster she'd been given in elementary school with the heading, *The Sun is 109 times the size of Earth!* Priscilla had gotten detention for throwing away the poster in front of her teacher. She hadn't understood what the big deal was. Nothing about the poster had seemed relevant to her life, or anyone's except astronauts'.

"Fucking bullshit," said Toni, jabbing the remote. Every channel showed the same 2-D picture. Sun. Sun. Sun. "How is it not even live?"

But live TV was useless. By the time the event happened they wouldn't see anything, they'd be too busy disintegrating. Priscilla wished she were a TV producer. For Toni, she'd have presented the Earth's annihilation as an America's Most Wanted–style pre-enactment, complete with gravelly narration to make it feel real.

"Like it's that hard to point a camera at the sky," said Toni. "What are we supposed to do now?"

Priscilla reached. Arms and legs acted on their own, hands latching onto Toni's cushy waist and pulling herself after, one knee against Toni's thigh, the other leg extended behind. Her shoe crunched on something in the rug. Stale bread. Or a cockroach.

Priscilla braced, expecting to be pushed away. Contact with Toni had always required imperceptible movements. But Toni only tensed slightly. Then—it could have been the changing gravity, moving had begun to feel weighted, as if the air were made of sand—softened and reclined. Priscilla's hands kneaded that perfectly curved waist. Toni's lips parted. Priscilla's heart buzzed. She sunk a hand inside Toni's underwear.

A smell seeped from Toni. Floral, pungent. Too strong, like mashing her nose into a garden bed. Priscilla understood, suddenly, bees. Why they wobbled drunkenly from flower to flower. Why they worked so hard.

Toni was not the kind of person you kissed. Not even if you were a guy and especially not if you weren't. Priscilla did the next best thing, dragging Toni's skirt with her as she slithered to the ground. She plowed into Toni's furry morass, tonguing without sense of direction, praying that Toni's huffing and minute hip jerks meant she was doing something right. One of them must have leaned on the remote, because the volume on the Sun broadcast went way up, the Time Lady counting down with thunderous regularity and the broadcast hissing. Outside, a caravan of cops blasted their sirens. The Time Lady counted off the minutes it took for Priscilla's neck to get sore and her tongue to get sore and then for her to stop noticing her own body at all, all of her given over to Toni.

Toni murmured. Toni groaned. Toni squeezed her legs against Priscilla's ears, deafening her. Priscilla moaned into Toni. Toni's hips jerked so hard Priscilla lost her balance, banged her front teeth against Toni's knee. When she tried to stick her head back in, Toni pushed it away.

Everywhere around them, the destroyed smell of flowers.

Priscilla straightened and wiped her chin on her T-shirt. On TV, the Sun-Earth picture remained unchanged, but the Time Lady was into the low double digits. A quarter of an hour left. Toni rustled a baggie, repacking the bowl. The longer Priscilla studied the carpet, the longer she could pretend Toni was about to ask for a kiss.

Thirteen minutes, thirty seconds.

"Light," ordered Toni. Priscilla struck a match. Her hand was shaking. It took two tries. Toni inhaled, passed. Priscilla sucked too much and choked. Her lips buzzed on the glass. Toni pushed her Praybans back into place, lips clenched over her mouthful of smoke. Toni was a wall again. It filled Priscilla with meanness. What would Dr. Argyle have labeled this feeling? She wanted to swallow Toni and be swallowed.

The sirens sounded strange, distorted, uneven. Another effect of the nearing Sun? Could sound waves gain weight? Fatten, slow, drag into the ground?

"Those guys back there," said Toni.

"Guys?" Priscilla felt fuzzy. The noise was messing with her head. And Toni, half-naked, thighs apart. The lingering taste on her tongue. The overripe stink emanating from them both.

"On the parking structure," said Toni. "Which one?"

Which would she screw, Toni meant. They'd played this game before. Partly dumb, partly hot, it could be exciting, talking about sex together even if they weren't talking about having it with each other. *I'd let that one do me doggie-style*, Toni'd say, and Priscilla would imagine herself as the hard-dick man banging a moaning Toni. Right now, though, she wasn't in the mood.

"Who cares?" She reached for the pipe. Toni held it away. "Fine. The tall one."

"I'd do the shrimp." Meaning, Sweat Hands.

"The *cryer*?"

"Yeah," said Toni. "He could even stay on the ground. I'd ride him right there, sitting on top. He'd cry, but for me." She paused. "I bet he'd get all sappy too, swear he loved me or some shit." Toni's cheeks stretched freakishly under the Praybans. Smiling? Like that she looked quasi-pretty. Like someone who'd have spent homecoming dancing with her boyfriend instead of knocking back Castillo Gold until she couldn't walk straight. Priscilla had the airhead thought, *It's Toni's true face*, as if the girl she'd known since fifth grade had been a mask. If it was a mask, Priscilla needed Toni to put it back on. Like, *now*.

"And then?"

Toni's head snapped up. The smile, whatever it had been, shriveled to a frown. "I do him, he cries. BOOM. Earth hits Sun. Everybody dead."

What the fuck did it mean, a smile for that yuppie? Priscilla kept reordering the events of the last minutes, wanting the math to work out so the smile had been for her. Because she'd made Toni cum. Because Toni wanted her the way she wanted Toni. All the ingredients were there, but the facts didn't agree. Sweat Hands blocked the way, changed what the smile meant. With enough time, she could force the pieces to come together and mean what they should. But time was rushing from them like ants running from a stream of water. And the sirens. Blaring, howling. There was no room left to think.

Eight minutes, ten seconds.

"Fucking pigs," said Priscilla, rage-filled. "What are they going to do? Arrest the Sun? We get it already. It's an emergency."

Toni snorted. "That's not sirens, Pris-stupid. That's people."

"People?"

"Duh, dope. Listen."

Priscilla sat back. It was people, not sirens. The sharp bursts of sound were screams. The rising and falling sounds, wails.

Light pulsed through the drapes.

Toni took off the Praybans.

"Tone." Priscilla sank down on the end of the sofa, a safe distance.

"Yeah?"

She tried not to look at Toni's lap, her hanging open knees. "You want to me to . . . do it again? I could go faster if you wanted."

Toni's stubby lashes parted, examining her.

People said time could stretch. There weren't enough minutes to get drunk or filch more of her mom's Virginia Slims, but there could be enough for them to change. There was a reason they were here together at the final stretch of human existence. Not Napoleon, not one of the apostles. Her and Toni.

"Nah," said Toni but didn't look away.

Priscilla didn't look away either. Toni's normal face wasn't really ugly so much as pissed, like a squinched expression that had gotten stuck that way. Except if Toni knew how to smile, then the stuckness was only a temporary phase. She could have grown up to be a nice girl. Married a banker who called her bunny rabbit.

Uh-huh. Sure.

Nice Toni was as hard to take seriously as Hell. Whatever Priscilla had thought she'd seen, it didn't shine through that bulldog mug. Ugly, brutal, tough was the Toni Priscilla liked. Toni shaped like a hammer who could be counted on to pound till every nail smashed in.

Four minutes, forty seconds.

Sun flared through the heavy brown drapes. The wailers had switched to quiet moans. Speech was harder. Breathing too. Silhouetted people crouched, outlined in gold. Priscilla regretted the afternoon. If she'd convinced Toni to climb to the very top of the parking structure, they'd have been flattened to the Sun too, their hands coming together out of fear. Indoors, reality was too filtered. The whole scene felt had at a distance.

Toni'd gone back to staring at the TV screen, where the cutout Sun stayed regular large beside a tiny blot of Earth. "If I owned a camera, I'd be filming it. It wouldn't even be hard." Toni scratched the inside part of her leg, flashing musky bush. Priscilla wanted her animal instincts to take over again, to make her do things so Toni would grin like a tough girl instead of smiling like a nice one. If Priscilla got good enough, touched her exactly right, Toni might shout, *Keep going, you fucking goober.* The world couldn't end while you were eating pussy.

One minute, twenty seconds.

"S'heavy," she uttered, speech itself taking effort. The weight of the world, all its garbage, pulled her deeper into the couch. She thought about pop cans, how many of them there were, how mad teachers had gotten when she tossed them on the ground. There were soggy plastic bags in the gutter and Styrofoam not decomposing in the bellies of seals. There was the landfill of this living room and layers of ancient garbage turned to treasure, like the lost scrolls they talked about at Sunday school. Quotes from Jesus that hadn't made it into the Bible, leftover by accident, nobody knew why—because some apostle got caught in a flash flood, because of a rockslide, because the savior's pal dozed off in a burning hut. They were holy outtakes, like the salt-tang of Toni's vag. Stuff that only meant something if you'd been there, inside her, overwhelmed with desire too large to know precisely what it wanted. Hungry like the wolf.

In a minute, there would be no more Priscillas, nor Tonis, nor vags belonging to anyone. Toni was her first and final taste of that wild flavor.

Priscilla's hand weighed too much to reach for Toni's, even if she'd had the balls.

Forty seconds.

She could barely raise her head but did.

Toni seemed to nod.

Thirty seconds.

If Priscilla could have gathered a deep enough breath, forced sound through the pressured air, she might have said:

I want to do you one last time.

Or even something stupid, a dumb name, to make it small, this ending, as small as the dot of their disappearing planet. As small as their dwindling seconds to remain alive, sorting between options. *Loser, carpet-muncher, numbnuts.* And Toni would have punched her shoulder. Left a bruise.

Ten seconds.

Toni was right. They weren't going to change. Even if the Time Lady added another million hours to the clock, they would only grow into future versions of the selves they were already. Wasn't that the same as dying?

Priscilla wanted to sniff her fingers. If she had a camera she would have filmed Toni's pussy, even if the film was doomed to burn. She couldn't move her hand, but in the heat of those last seconds, she heard a moan, or made one. It could have been Toni's. It smelled like sweet ruin.

Bad Things That Happen to Girls

Birdie worked at the Rite Aid, and then she didn't, as easy as snow clouds coming apart. All she had to say was, "I quit," and it didn't matter that her blue smock trembled as she laid it on Guy's desk, or how he bellowed in the bewildering, sports-related dialect to which she'd grown accustomed over the years.

"Fourteen seasons, Bee. I wouldn't say this if I didn't mean it: You are the MVP of Store #165. Player of the decade. Without you, it's all strikes and balls." A space heater in the background on too high, and Guy, incredulous, swabbing his neck with a handkerchief. She knew she was letting him down. The other employees called him unkind names while smoking in the parking lot, but Birdie, who didn't smoke, had always found his bluster endearing. She even liked the work. The repetitive motion of matching each item to its twin on the shelf, the round chill of coins. The American expressions, too, pleased her mouth with their formulaic poetry that promised resolution to every problem. *How can I help you? Cash or credit? Did you find what you were looking for?*

Watching Guy frown and shake his head, she felt terrible guilt, almost wished to take the words back. Guy had "drafted" her fresh out of English classes at the community college, back when she could only find middle-of-the-night work vacuuming offices. She'd been pregnant then, sharing a bed with her teenage sister, Olga, in the drafty alcove at the back of their cousins' house. The cousins, who already resented the time and expense of sponsoring their immigration from Romania, had not been pleased when a pregnant belly appeared on thirty-one-year-old spinster Birdie. Amid their scowlings and mutterings, Birdie had begun to fear her unborn child would grow up like Cinderella, ash-covered and invisible. The Rite Aid job had rewritten their futures. It made Birdie independent and American, made her daughter American. All thanks to Guy.

"Trish turns thirteen tomorrow," Birdie said. The magic word of her daughter's name fortified Birdie's resolve in the shining future she'd imagined: The RV they'd buy, the silver ribbon of road uncurling before them. They two alone at the edges of the country, leaping over the Martian stones of Utah, toeing the Pacific's ferocious surf, loading their shirts with fresh orchard peaches in Georgia, nectar soaking the fabric to infuse their skin with sugar. They'd take turns picking spots on the map and live on the road like vagabonds. At night they'd bed down on the RV's sofas, at home in the great world, whispering stories back and forth as the stars flickered on outside and the wind rocked them to sleep. She had to quit. For Trish.

"Well shoot, Bee, happy goddamned birthday from Uncle Guy, but I'm not sure what a crapping thing that has to do with you leaving me all bases loaded. The girls haven't got you into their union business, have they? That's the kind of thinking that ruined baseball, and I won't have it in my clubhouse. You want to negotiate? Fine. Door's thataway. That's my counter offor, take it or leave it."

Guy threw himself back in his chair as if expecting Birdie to retrieve her smock and shuffle back to her post. Until the record spring blizzard, Birdie herself hadn't believed she'd ever quit the Rite Aid. Not she, who showed up fifteen minutes before each shift, who never argued, who did not drink or do drugs, who uncomplainingly worked Christmas Eve and Thanksgiving Day. But during the two long and perfect snow days last April, Trish had confessed she was losing herself, said, "Please don't make me go back to regular life." How could Birdie explain to Guy, who had no children, what happened to girls? Over the last two years, she'd watched sparkling Trish become a turtle. Middle school had curved her shoulders, caused her to hide in bulky clothes and hoodies and disguise her golden princess hair in a plain ponytail. Birdie read the magazines by her register. She knew about anorexia, bulimia, wrist-cutting, low self-esteem, binge drinking, and the potent marijuana that opened gateways to heroin, turning little girls into victims of drug dealers and pimps. An American child shouldn't suffer so, and yet danger shadowed Trish.

"I'm sorry."

"Christ, Bee. You been drinking the magic Kool-Aid? Because the Russian Bird *I* know would not split with zero notice. She'd get her butt back to the floor and write a nice apology note to Mr. Guy. You listening? Bee?"

But Birdie was not listening. Chin down, heart pounding, *Trish-Trish, Trish-Trish,* she was walking out.

THE IDEA HAD come to her in April, two days after a spring blizzard fell over the streets and parks, reshaping the town into seamless mounds. The changed landscape, the substitution of bright, blank quiet for human noise, made any hope seem within reach. Birdie expected that her vision of the RV would dissolve the way dreams and stories did. A week after the blizzard, the temperatures rose to eighty. Beer bottles and potholed cement reappeared, and joggers led by their nipping dogs filled the sidewalk. But the image remained. For as long as Birdie could remember, she had done what she was supposed to. As a girl, she followed her mother; as a young woman, her hawk-nosed younger sister. She got jobs and kept them, earning to support first Olga and then Trish. She had been born to care for and protect, and until the snowstorm it seemed simple: food, shelter, and love. Trish's confession flipped this on its head. You could do everything right and still fail your child.

She didn't tell Trish about the plan. She didn't know why. She had always told Trish her every thought, but this dream felt different. It jittered inside her, jolting her awake at night, causing her to put three price tags on one Tylenol bottle and none on the next, making her lose the plot of an episode of *Sweet Valley High* so many times that Trish switched off the set in exasperation, saying, "You're not even watching!"

Birdie did and did not like the feeling of keeping a secret. The gap it put between her and Trish, she didn't like. But she liked the jitters. Like that rare and silent mountain cat, the yellow-eyed râs, was padding around the house, spying down at her bus from the treetops, purring from behind boxes in the Rite Aid storeroom, waiting to be found.

She almost told Trish at least once a day. Each time Mindy Jacobson called and Trish's expression went hard and false, Birdie imagined jerking the cord from the wall, cradling Trish in her arms, coming clean. Somehow, though, she hadn't. After a while, it seemed better, waiting until the money was all there. It would be a surprise.

The money turned out to be harder than expected. Trish had a three-thousand-dollar college fund—a US treasury bond gifted by Olga—but when Birdie tried to cash it, the bank manager said smugly, "Not without the minor present." Birdie did have savings, though, $2,592.70 to be exact. Then, there was their Disney World fund, the cracked, five-gallon container where she and Trish dropped their spare change. When Trish noticed the jug missing, Birdie said she'd needed it to pay bills. "That's okay," said Trish, lids lowered in a disappointment more heartrending than if she had yelled, *I HATE YOU, MOM*, like a television teen. Had Trish known so little good, Birdie wondered, that even this small thing she hadn't dared hope for? She wanted badly then to follow Trish to her bedroom door, wave the little bankbook before her so she could see, as Birdie did, the quiver of motion within the growing numbers. She got as far as calling Trish's name, but when Trish turned, her face was full of unfamiliar distance. Birdie only managed a whisper. "I'm sorry." Trish, monotone, replied, "I know."

Finally, Birdie sold things. Beatles albums brought from Romania. A kayak left in the yard by their landlord. A pair of real pearl earrings. A hand-me-down bicycle Trish rarely rode and thankfully hadn't noticed missing. Even Trish's Happy Meal toys found a buyer in the Sunday Bargains section of the classifieds.

All of these objects held meaning and caused pain

when parted with. The pain brought Birdie back to other separations—her mother's long sadness and sudden death, her father's absence, the departure from Bucharest—and as then, the leaving created a space of melancholy and poignant yearning. That pain, like the stretch and weight of pregnancy, made the plan real.

In December, the bank account still held only five thousand dollars. Enough for a cheap RV, plus a year of food if they bought only lentils and the soft vegetables bagged up beside the grocery store entrance. By then, they'd surely figure out a way to make money—maybe the handwoven potholders Trish's scout troop had once sold door-to-door?—but they'd still need to pay for gas. So last week came the hardest parting: a Yiddish edition of the Brothers Grimm that Birdie's mother had managed to smuggle through the Holocaust. Kept sealed in cellophane on a shelf in their Bucharest apartment with the dictate to never so much as breathe upon it, the book had been presented to Birdie on her own thirteenth birthday. The script on the front page was faint but legible, and the lettering smelled of dust. *To Faige, From Mama.*

"No shit," said the rare books buyer, peeling it out of its plastic, "This is real?" Birdie had not been able to watch him cart it away. But when the bank teller stamped the new account balance, $6,043.03, even that precious object crumbled into departure's dust, gusted away.

WALKING HOME FROM the scene with Guy, Birdie's guilt melted into giddiness. She hummed fragments of half-remembered songs while hopping over slush puddles. At long last she could tell Trish everything. The crooked tree fingers scraping at the gray sky made her think of witch fingers, of curse-bound princesses and the spells that freed them. She pictured Trish's slow smile as the meaning of Birdie's news penetrated. They would spin, hands clasped, around the kitchen. Trish would whisper breathlessly to the ceiling, *Thank-you-thank-you-thank-you*, happier than she'd been last birthday when Olga gave her a Discman.

But Birdie had forgotten Trish would not be expecting her until evening. A note on the kitchen table in Trish's careful, square penmanship said she was at the mall with Mindy and friends, and Mrs. Jacobson had invited her for homemade fried chicken afterward. *Not calling cuz I don't want to get you in trouble with Guy. Mindy says I'm being a worrywart anyway and that you're "decidedly non-neurotic for a mom" so you won't mind.* ☺ ☺ ☺ *P.S. Mrs. J will drive me back by bedtime. xoxo, T.*

That was fine, of course. It was only one dinner. No reason for fuss. Still, a part of Birdie couldn't help noticing that this was happening more lately, these disappearances of Trish's and what if . . .

What if, Birdie didn't know, but underneath the clattering refrigerator motor, the silent râs slunk.

BIRDIE SLEPT THROUGH Trish's arrival and woke, trembling with anticipation, early in the morning. Several hours later, she tottered into Trish's room, balancing a crookedly frosted cake. Trish's hair snaked across the pillowcase, her scrubbed skin glowing as she stirred to the perfume of chocolate. She looked brand new. A thirteen-year miracle, this girl.

Birdie fingered the hair's silk tips, kissed the slightly damp forehead.

Trish cracked an eye. "Cake for breakfast?" she said,

voice too sleep-groggy for Birdie to tell if Trish was
pleased. Trish's hand curled from under the sheet, pulled
a sweet morsel loose. She was pleased. "Cake for breakfast, cake for lunch, cake for dinner," she sing-songed
and reached for another bite. Future dawns lined up on
the horizon, linking yellow arms: Trish chewing cake on
the RV's steps, against a dusty desert sunrise. How she'd
pause to murmur, *You saved my life, Mom.* If Birdie got
the RV tomorrow, they could be in hot, sunny Arizona by
midweek.

"I have an idea," said Birdie. "The snow is so pretty.
Let's skip Big Boy. We'll go for a walk, us two only."

Trish pushed upright. "But Mindy and Auntie Olga are
already invited."

"So?" Nervousness gripped Birdie. She pinched cake
into her mouth. It had baked too long. Dry crumbs stuck
in her throat. "We'll say you came down with a cold."

"You want me to lie to my best friend?" Trish stared
like Birdie was crazy. It stung.

Birdie stretched a wide smile. "No, angel. I'd never ask
you to do that."

BRUNCH WAS A tight-throated mistake. Birdie knew from
the moment Mindy Jacobson breezed into the restaurant, drawing Trish's anxious attention and making Olga
stiffen, irritated. Mindy ordered foods children weren't
supposed to like—egg-white omelets and café au lait—and
questioned the waitress about ingredients and artificial
colorings with a poise that made Birdie guard her own
speech for errors.

"And for the birthday lady?" said the waitress.

Trish always ordered the short stack with a side of

sausage and extra whipped cream. She and Birdie liked to drag the pink meat through the syrup then lick it off, sweet mixing with greasy salt.

With a glance to Mindy, Trish cucked in and folded the menu closed. "Omelet sounds good. I'm going to have one of those too."

"No pork link?" said Birdie, but Olga was already back to the financial lecture she'd begun on the drive to the restaurant.

"*Stocks*," said Olga. "That's not an investment. That's gambling. 'Gambling,' he says, 'is putting money in a failing industrial economy.' To which I say, 'Whose money, sweetheart?' What's Danny going to do? Sell off a few collector's items? Wait for his father to keel?"

"Over," said Mindy.

"Excuse me?" said Olga, elongating her spine in the way Birdie knew so well.

"It's—the expression is 'keel over.' I was just . . ." Mindy smiled and shrugged.

Olga glared. "You were *what*."

"Sorry if I offended you, Ms. Harrison," said Mindy, sounding not sorry at all.

Trish glanced worriedly from her aunt to Mindy to Birdie. Birdie knew how Trish felt. Alone or together, Olga and Mindy were the same theatrics, the same selfish pulling everybody else into a fight they didn't want.

"Angel," murmured Birdie, reaching across the table for her daughter's cool palm. She wished yet again that she'd insisted that morning, made a scene as her sister had no difficulty doing. She wanted Trish to understand. After tomorrow, they'd neither of them have to endure these two or anyone else like them. Not the mean girls at

Trish's school, not the bickering cashiers at the Rite Aid. They were so, so close to gone.

Trish squeezed Birdie's hand quickly before letting go. "Guys, can we please talk about something else?"

"Poor 'Sha. We're *ruining* her birthday."

Trish didn't seem to mind Mindy's baby talk. Instead, she gave Mindy a pleased, clammish smile and leaned her head on Mindy's shoulder.

"I'm having a decidedly non-ruined birthday," said Trish, returning the baby voice. Mindy, in her dyed-pink hoodlum hair, grinned.

Inside Birdie's chest, the râs shifted, its paws treading her heart. "I want to give Trish her present now."

Everyone turned, Olga and Mindy aimed like twin rifles, Trish nodding her encouragement, looking relieved.

"Sure, Mom."

"Who's stopping you," said Olga.

Trish gazed up, patient. Despite the overlarge sweatshirt and bent posture, she glowed, a seed of goodness at her center that the Mindys of the world could only covet. A true princess.

"It's a special story," said Birdie, "for a special, special girl."

A little, rude twitch of communication passed from Mindy to Trish.

"A story?" said Trish, her voice a bit high.

Birdie nodded. "Once upon a time—"

Mindy snickered.

"Oh please," said Olga. "You think a teenage girl wants a bedtime story?"

"Mom," said Trish. "Do you think maybe we could do this later?" Trish raised her eyebrows. Olga and Mindy would mock, she meant. They would not understand Birdie and Trish's private language. Birdie wanted to laugh at how much that didn't matter. Let them make fun. Too late they'd see all along they'd been outsiders.

"Now is right," said Birdie, and it was. It felt like she'd been waiting since Trish's birth to tell her. Or longer, since Birdie was Trish's age, lost and terrified, a girl shut in a stone tower. "Once upon a time, there was a beautiful princess." Trish blushed. Birdie smiled back. "Named Trisha, born with such long, beautiful golden hair that a jealous sorceress made a curse—"

"'Long golden hair!'" interrupted Mindy. Birdie tried to continue, but the girl spoke over her. "Wait, wait, wait. This is too crazy, Ms. Iancu. 'Sha, tell her."

Trish looked upset. "Not right now."

"Girl, it's the perfect moment," said Mindy. "It's serendipity."

"I don't think it is," mumbled Trish.

Frustrated and confused, Birdie shook her head. "Angel, you don't have to do anything."

"Trust me, Ms. Iancu," said Mindy. "You're going to want to hear this."

Birdie took a breath. "The sorceress made a curse—"

"*Fine,*" said Trish to Mindy. Trish's long lashes lifted, revealing her honey-brown eyes. "I want a haircut."

Birdie looked involuntarily to Mindy. She didn't understand if "haircut" meant something other than what she was used to it meaning. "A haircut? But we trimmed last month. It grew so, so fast?"

"Ms. Iancu, you don't understand. She's going to cut off *all* her hair. A buzz cut." Mindy passed two hands over her own scalp.

"Buzz?" echoed Birdie.

"Like a little longer than bald," said Mindy.

"Bald!" Olga hooted. "Like that—the Irish singer, what-shername. That sad lesbian you like, Feygele."

Trish flushed. "Not bald," she said gruffly. "Just, shorter." She hunched back into the booth, pulling the sides of her hood so only a red wedge of face showed. This was some ugly joke Mindy had pushed her into. Trish had Rapunzel hair, a golden light wrung from Birdie's own near-black frizz. Even Trish's birth father, a one-night accident, had been a dark-headed Turk. The blond, a fairy's blessing, came from nowhere.

"A little trim is no big thing," said Birdie. "We can do it this afternoon, if you want." Trish did not want to be bald. In tales, villains cut beautiful hair as punishment, the shorn heroine exiled in brambles and rags. Trish loved to have her hair braided, Birdie's fingertips imprinted with that silk weight, dense as water winding around itself. This was some slippery confusion, that was all. Trish wanted it shorter? They'd take off a few inches, bring it up to mid-back. Once on the road, Trish could grow a whole cape of hair, fly it like a yellow flag into the wind.

"With no hair," said Olga, "people will think she has cancer. Put her outside your store with a donation bucket and beanie—you could earn the big bucks."

"Ha!" Mindy cried. "You should, 'Sha. Like when we sold Girl Scout cookies, except this time you'd have leukemia. It'd be hi-larious."

Trish made a sound that could have been a laugh but which Birdie recognized as hurt's veil. "Ahem." Birdie raised herself awkwardly inside the booth, one knee on the seat for balance. The saucer-shaped light fixture beamed down upon her, its heat drawing a blush to her cheeks. Across the parking lot, a plow heaved snow into cliffs of white. "Once upon a time, the evil sorceress locked Princess Trisha up in a tower. She made a curse and the beautiful princess fell into enchanted sleep. Only great sacrifice—great love—could break this enchantment."

"Mom . . ." Trish put her hands over her forehead. "This is a really cool present, but can you please save it till we get home?"

"Shh," reassured Birdie. She needed to say this now, for Trish's own good. "But the sorceress did not understand the power of true beauty. The princess's mother saw her light from the other side of the kingdom and vowed she would rescue her daughter, no matter how many obstacles lay in her path. The mother walked a long time and had many difficult adventures. Finally, on the princess's thirteenth birthday, the day the curse would become permanent, she climbed the girl's braid into her tower and opened a magic door in the wall."

Olga made a face of mild amusement. "Happily ever after."

"Good story," said Trish, but she looked glum.

"I am getting to the best part," said Birdie. And then she did. In a few giddy breaths, she unraveled the months of secrets, the RV plan, Guy's skepticism, the funny names on the roadmap, Lickskillet and Goosepimple, Pie Town and Why. "Think of it. Everybody there curious, asking, Why. Why? Now we can be the explorers, go and find out."

They made so much noise, Olga and Mindy especially. It was to be expected, but Birdie only cared about Trish, who kept repeating "You quit your job?" as if she'd heard nothing else.

"Everything is okay, my darling. Everything is wonderful. Don't worry. Remember when you were little, I used to wake you up in the night and we'd walk together through the streets, pretend we were the last human beings?"

Trish's voice came out strained. "But we're not the last human beings. We have to pay bills—and *rent*—"

"But it will be like we are! I saved money, so much, and we won't have rent. With the RV, it's better. You don't pay to a landlord. You live *everywhere*." Birdie wished she could make her understand. Their lives would be languid, a sweep of unguided motion under full, fat blue skies along the endless journey. They would call Olga only briefly, from pay phones, hanging up when their quarter ran out. Birdie would leave behind Mindy's address and soon Trish would forget about her and the rest of middle school. Pretty soon, she would be too happy to look backward.

"You are insane," Olga was saying. "Danny always said it. Foolish me for defending you. I'd tell him, talking kooky is different than acting crazy. It's a no-brain job, I said, but at least she works. She raises her child, which is more than some mothers. But now, Faige, what do I tell him? What do I believe?"

Trish clutched Birdie's hand and Birdie clutched back, smiling. She wanted Trish to see: they were done with fear.

"If you say you're sorry," whispered Trish, "Guy would hire you back. I know he's a jerk, but he likes you and you've been there forever."

"What am I saying?" said Olga, leaning between them. "How terrible of me, making such assumptions. You've probably been setting aside for this *lifestyle choice* since she was born, yes? That's how Uncle Danny financed that ridiculous boat. Socked away his bonuses, liquidated his

401(k)." Olga tapped a pink nail on the edge of her plate. "Except that's not smart investing, is it?" Olga stared around the table, daring someone to answer. Mindy had gone quiet and Trisha, pale. But Birdie, for once, did not care what her little sister thought. Her opinion, good or bad, no longer bore weight. "Smart investing views long-term returns instead of short-term gain. Thinks twenty years ahead." Olga pinched Birdie's arm, hard. "Twenty years, Feygele. You understand? Not when Trisha turns fifteen. Not when she turns twenty-one. She'll be thirty-three, mother of your grandchildren. Did you consider that? How it will be for them, their granny toothless on the street? Or, like Trisha's grandmother. Dead."

The râs curled its lip, rejecting this prod. It padded to the door and glanced back.

"You don't need to worry," Birdie said and stood. "Come, angel. We'll take the bus."

ON THE BUS, though, Trish was strange. She didn't talk, and when she looked up, she seemed translucent, face large and empty. At home, Birdie tried to interest her in board games. Then she spread the table with road maps and national-park maps and municipal maps from West Virginia, North Dakota, Oregon, but Trish only nodded dully and stood, saying, "I think I'm going to lie down." Through the closed door came the sound of quiet talking. When Birdie eased the kitchen phone from its hook, she heard Mindy.

"Maybe manic-depressive? There was kid at my old school who used to draw with marker on his stomach during class. People laughed, but he wasn't doing it to be funny."

"This is worse than that. I mean, she basically wants to kidnap me. And that story—that was weird, right? I mean, what's wrong with her?"

"You can call her a b-word, you know. It's not illegal."

"No, I can't."

"Why not? Just do it."

"B-word."

"You have to really say it."

"But she's *not*, though, Min. She doesn't mean it. She's just—I think she could be crazy."

Birdie held the receiver away from her ear, straight out. *That awful Mindy*, she thought, though it was the second voice that seared. A voice that doubled over Trish's, eclipsed it.

Birdie's mother had loved peasant-devil stories. At bedtime, she told possession stories that mixed with real-life tales of soldiers who pressed pistols to children's heads, ordered them to stop crying, then shot them anyway. *The soldiers laughed*, her mother said. *That's how we knew they were possessed.* Birdie hated the violent demons. She would beg instead for enchanted combs, ball gowns, magical beasts. She thought she'd left the devil stories back in whispering Bucharest. To dispel them now, she focused on her râs. The forest cat with its bright, knowing eyes and feathery ears was the best of creatures from her mother's tales. A silent forest-dweller hidden in the remote mountains, but which, if found, would grant one's dearest wish.

The tiny, dim voices murmured from the receiver. Birdie hadn't heard what she thought she'd heard, she told herself. It hadn't been Trish, not *her* Trish, not really. The râs held her in its placid gaze. Turning from the cat, Birdie gentled the phone into its cradle. Animal breath wrapped around her and filled the kitchen. It smelled like meat. She pushed open the window, let the brittle air scrape her clean.

IF BIRDIE THOUGHT about it, the last good time had been that April blizzard.

They called it global warming, for that amount to come down after two solid months of spring, but when Trish woke up, she said it looked like magic.

Mindy Jacobson lived down a long dirt road that would be obstructed for days after the rest of town had been cleared. All the same, Birdie was surprised and pleased when Trish, so serious since the beginning of sixth grade, said yes to sledding. They walked to the golf course, imagining themselves as Antarctic explorers, pointing out mysterious shapes in the blowing snow. Penguins, polar bears, UFOs.

Trish indicated a bundled man walking his poodle. "Look at that. He's trying to disguise himself."

"Three scarves," agreed Birdie. "He must be Martian."

That winter, Trish had grown tall and heavy. She weighed down the front of the sled and together they zipped over the hills, gained air with a shriek before thumping into the loose drifts.

Toward sunset, they lay in the snow, passing back and forth a thermos of hot cocoa.

"You're really fun, Mom," Trish had said. Birdie's knee ached, but she didn't care. Trish's words evoked a mixture of pleasure and embarrassment, as if she were a younger child her daughter had offered to befriend.

As fun as Mindy? she wanted to ask but said only, "You don't wish a friend your age came?"

Trish rolled sideways to sip from the thermos lid. "Not really. Kids always want you to be a certain way. Like, you have to be *cool* but not weird. You have to be unique and, like, talented at something, but if you stand out they tease you. Even if they're your friends. It gets tiring." Trish pressed the thermos into the snow and lay back again. Overhead, rag-like clouds drifted down the river of sky. "Sometimes I feel like I'm forgetting who I am."

Birdie sucked cold air, restraining tears of compassion. Usually Trish related good things about school, nice stories about a math test or a funny mix-up in the cafeteria, but these last months she'd seemed so closed, Birdie had wondered if some darkness was being concealed. To hear it broke her heart.

"Snow angels?" proposed Trish. Birdie obediently swished her arms and legs. Hers looked like a moth and Trish's, a circle cracked by a wedge. Trish wasn't laughing anymore. She sat up and turned away, hugging her knees. Ahead of her, night, collapsing toward the earth.

Oh, my Trisha, Birdie thought.

From behind, Trish looked like a picture of Birdie taken around the same age, the sole photographic remnant of her childhood. Birdie could never think of who might have held the camera, what adult stood behind her to capture that sad portrait, observing her as closely as she now observed Trish. Birdie knew from her long, gawky limbs and primary schooler's white hat that the photo must have been taken shortly after Olga's birth, after their mother's fresh corpse washed up on the stone bank of the Dâmbovița. "This river used to run through a great forest," Birdie's mother would tell her every morning on the walk to school. After she was gone, Birdie recited those words to Olga, the metal-gray river quivering below as if wanting to speak. In the photo, young Birdie-Faige wore a dark wool coat; against the spring evening's falling dusk, Trish's snowsuit looked dipped in shadow. They were the same, Faige and Trish. Two girl-shaped smears against winter, two ghosts.

A CANDY-BAR STRIPE wound around the RV, black on gray in the smeared Xerox. *$3400*, it said. *As Is*. But Birdie didn't need to read the handwritten list of ailments. She could already feel the vehicle expanding around her, roomy like a diner on wheels and smelling of warm vinyl.

Birdie punched the digits into a pay phone, listened to it ring.

Last night, she and Trish had eaten mac and cheese in front of a depressing cartoon where a father chased a son around the living room, threatening to beat him. Trisha had laughed at every joke, a harsh, false laugh that lasted too long, and when Birdie tried to bring up the topic of departure date—Wednesday would be good, but if Trish was antsy, they could leave Tuesday—Trish said she had a book report to write and could they talk later? "You don't need to do any more reports," Birdie had protested to Trisha's retreating back.

"If you're looking for a Spaniard, you got the wrong number."

For a second, Birdie forgot the purpose of her call. She stumbled, vowels compressing on her tongue. "Do you sell—are you selling RV?"

"Oh hell, a Ruskie."

"Romanian," she corrected.

The man found this funny. She didn't know why, but then she did not often know why people thought things humorous. The man, whose name might have been Dylan or Daemon, lived past the edge of town. Birdie didn't want to tell him she didn't have a car. She was afraid he wouldn't sell her the RV without a car. She needed it today. When Trish's school got out at 3:00 p.m., she wanted to be parked on the curb, the RV shimmering among the boring normal cars the other parents drove. She needed to break through to Trish, to make her hear.

The problem was distrust. Something, somewhere had cracked, made a rift that went on expanding. Birdie had blamed it on Trish's friends, on Mindy especially, but after last night, she wondered. During the blizzard, Trish had said she was forgetting herself. Now, she called Birdie crazy. That was the sound of a hurt girl, a girl whose mother had let her down.

When Birdie was still learning English, they'd read a book together about a baby bunny who wanted to run away from his mother. The bunny piloted out into a stormy sea, but his mother turned herself to a rabbit-shaped cloud. No matter how mad the bunny got, the mother rabbit floated above, filling his sail. He never had to be alone.

DAEMON'S ADDRESS WAS farther than she thought. Several times on the long walk, Birdie turned around, as if she might glimpse the last lonely bus stop miles back. It felt wrong out there, the sky swollen a deep purple, no houses, fields of untouched snow as tall as she was. She longed for the company of her râs, but, as if even an imagined lynx shrank from wide, open spaces, the wild cat refused her call.

Periodically, Birdie reached into her pocket to warm her fingers between the soft bills in the bank envelope.

Hundreds felt different. They must have printed them on more valuable paper. It was just after she took the envelope out to smell it, it smelled like oil and like Trish's toddler scalp, that the black mailbox appeared, a plowed driveway behind.

Diamond was his name, short, talkative, and with egg in his mustache, and when he asked where she'd parked, Birdie found herself lying. "My husband, he dropped me." She waved behind her.

Diamond didn't like that but, he said, Ruskie or not, Birdie looked most of the way to frostbite and ought to come in for coffee. She wanted to see the RV—only cars and a small van scattered the snowy yard—but Diamond insisted. She followed him over a porch erupting with frost-fringed clothing into a brightly decorated living room. Doilies and porcelain knickknacks and embroidered cushions lined shelves, draped over chair backs. The house looked how she had imagined America, pre-immigration. In her mind, such a home had seemed sweet and cozy, but, perching on the edge of the sofa while Diamond poured cream into a pink teacup, she felt afraid.

"Like 'em?" Diamond said. Birdie realized she was staring at one of the knickknack shelves. Ceramic children with enormous eyes posed kneeling for prayer, watering a potted flower, extinguishing birthday candles.

"Yes," she lied.

"My wife called 'em 'the kids.' I said if her children planned to come out ugly as all that, might as well not bother." Diamond grabbed a girl figurine wearing a bunny suit and squinted at its pastel face. "One of these days, going to use 'em for skeet."

Birdie nodded. Skeet sounded like *sleet*. She'd always

liked the sound of *sleet*. Quick, wet, alive—a jackrabbit bounding across the surface of winter. Diamond tossed the doll in his palm. His gaze drifted to the window, the blank sky hanging over the graveyard of cars. She wondered where his wife had gone and why she didn't take her dolls.

Birdie balanced her teacup beside a squirrel figurine. "We go see the vehicle now?"

Diamond was still looking outside. "When'd you say your man was coming back?"

She hesitated. Any answer could be dangerous. If she claimed someone was coming to get her, it would soon be clear that wasn't so. But if no one was coming, that would be worse. It would mean no one cared enough to see that she was safe. "He said it's for me," Birdie said evasively. "I decide what I want." She pinched bills from the packet, careful to conceal the rest. The smell of the bills rose between them and she saw Diamond's face change, calculating.

He cleared his throat. "Can't wait much longer anyhow."

The wind was at them as soon as Diamond opened the door. It whipped Birdie's cheeks and stiffened her lungs. She started walking toward the barn at the end of the driveway, but Diamond waved her in the other direction. He led her through a network of ripped-open cars so rusted and patched with snow they looked like part of the landscape, until they reached the windowless white van she'd seen when she arrived.

"I want the RV," she corrected. "The camper. From the advertisement."

Diamond's mustache bushed over his mouth. "Sold it already. This is what I got left."

"No." Her voice climbed. "On the phone, I said RV. I

said I wanted RV, and you said, yes, come, I have it." Truthfully, she didn't remember him saying much of anything, other than those jokes about her accent. Was it possible he hadn't mentioned the vehicle? She could not remember. She felt suddenly disoriented, like the Birdie who walked here in the snow had been someone else entirely and she'd ended up here by witchcraft.

"This one's more up your alley," Diamond was saying, holding a lighter to the rear lock. He tugged the handles, and the doors burst open in a spray of ice. Birdie swallowed a gasp. The plain body of the van concealed a smaller version of the living room, only with a propane tank and metal sink and figurines masking-taped to the countertops. Above a flowered couch, a sampler swung from fishing line: *Home Sweet Home.*

"Go on, test her out."

Because there seemed no other choice, Birdie climbed in the back. It looked like a living room but felt like a dollhouse, a box that would suffocate you once closed.

"Like it?" Diamond leaned on one of the doors, blocking the light. Snow had begun to fall, and thick flakes landed on his shoulders. She couldn't see his face. "Wife hated DIY, but you've got sensibility. I know. Seen you inside my house, looking around. Two of a kind, you and me." In silhouette, Diamond put a finger to his temple, made a cocked pistol.

Birdie had begun to shake in earnest, her teeth gnashing together. Horror movie clips floated in her head, masked men with chainsaws, men with faces melted off. She could feel Diamond watching her. What did he mean, *two of a kind*?

Time slowed to sticky nothing. The sofa dug into her

calves. Behind Diamond, the gray daylight dialed down as
if on a dimmer switch. She saw the white and orange blur
of the râs a breath before she felt it leap. It landed in her,
electric. She stood. "I am getting out now."

"Huh?" The dark shape of Diamond leaned into the
opening. Without thinking, Birdie lunged, knocking past
his outstretched arm. "Hey—watch it!" His hand clamped
around her shoulder, turning her ankle and sending a cold
rush into her boot. It hurt. She twisted away. Inside the
frame of beard and mustache, Diamond flushed. "Calm
down there, Missy. No one's making you buy anything."

"I want it," she said. Fiercely, angrily, she did want it,
more even than she'd wanted the RV.

"What?"

With numb fingers, she pulled the folded thirty-four
bills from the envelope. Held them toward him.

"Take it," she said, like a cowboy in a Wild West movie.
"It's your last chance."

THE CAB OF the van glowed like the inside of an ice castle.
Birdie hadn't driven in years, but her body remembered,
cleaved to the shape of gearshift and pedals. At the end of
Diamond's drive she threw it into park, marched around
the back, tore the ceramic children free from their masking
tape and hurled them, *poom-poom-poom,* into a drift. The
pale sampler she saved for last. She did not know what had
happened to Diamond's wife and did not want to know. It
frisbeed from the driver's side window as she skidded off.

Olga would have called her insane for driving an
unpaved road at the onset of a snowstorm, but Birdie
giggled the whole blinded way. She glided through stop
signs and more than once raised her foot from the brakes

to let the van swim its way out of a swerve. Vibrations siphoned up her arm, the road leaping under her.

Emergency signals bleated from the van's radio speakers and, back in town, storm sirens screamed, but rumbling down the orange-lit streets Birdie felt the world had been wiped clean for her alone. Only visible through the falling snow were the few low cars that pulled up beneath her window at stoplights. Sleepy arms pressed to the glass, while debris like misplaced histories littered the backseat—sheets of paper, cassette tapes, fast-food cups separated from their lids. The vulnerability of these people and their small lives awoke a new sensation of tenderness and pity. But this was mainly a feeling in the background; the rhythm of driving demanded she scan for ice, relax into a turn, press or let go of the gas, press or lift from the brakes. She understood, finally, the obsession with cars. They erased everything: past, present, one's own self-awareness. To drive was to become pure movement.

LABOR. PAIN AND push, the sensation of being torn apart from the inside, overwhelmed by impossible expansion of skin, joints, finally, heart. The sensation of her former self in shreds in a metal hospital pan, while she swelled, bruised, around her the newborn, its skin raw, its expression of betrayal and desperate need. Her daughter.

At the sight of their pitch-black house, that birth-blow hit Birdie for a second time. But this time, the pressure of love and irrevocable change was matched by panicked guilt. Since before getting into the van, she'd barely thought about Trish. She'd been gone hours, she knew that much. It must have been near bedtime. Normally Trish got home around four. Birdie would find her blasting music or sprawled reading in front of the television. In the winter, Trish turned on every lamp in the house, including the bathroom. Birdie didn't mind. It made her happy to see Trish at the center of so much light.

Inside was chilly, layered in shadow, eerily quiet.

"Angel?" No answer, not even the trickle of the fish tank that Trish thought sounded like a man peeing in their toilet. That image recalled itself to Birdie with disturbing force, as did the sensation of Diamond looming over her. Only now she felt Trish instead of herself, trapped and alone. Someone could have walked right in, if Trish had left the door unlocked. Trish could have been kidnapped, or killed, or—worse.

What if Diamond had followed Birdie home?

"Come out, come out wherever you are," she called. The refrain petered into the darkness. Birdie tried the kitchen switch, then the living room lamp. Nothing. The storm had knocked out the power. If Diamond had followed her home, she reminded herself, he would have gotten there after her, not before. But what about an accident? If some streetlights were out too, if Trish had stayed late at school, perhaps intuiting that Birdie planned to meet her, she could have been hit by a car on the icy streets. She should call the hospital. She lifted the receiver. The phone's petulant dial tone blared through the kitchen. Outside, trees whipped the sky. She put down the phone. The only numbers she knew were the Jacobsons', Rite Aid, and Olga's, and she could not bear to confess to any of them that she'd lost her daughter. Trish had gone missing once when she was three. Birdie had called Olga, frantic, sure she'd been kidnapped. Before her sister could arrive,

Trish had crawled yawning out of a laundry hamper. She'd been napping.

Birdie stumbled down the hall and flung open the door to Trish's bedroom.

Purplish light fell across Trish's rumpled bedclothes and band posters. Mindy had gotten her into this loud, mean rock. Screaming girls who wore too much lipstick and didn't brush their hair, the kind who smuggled pregnancy tests from Rite Aid under their safety-pinned shirts. Riot music, Trish called it, and that was what it sounded like. Glass breaking. Fear. Rage. When Birdie was a little girl, her mother had taken her to a parade. Something official, with speeches and children reciting in unison. What had stuck with her, though, what she remembered, was the line of rifle barrels nosing over the crowd. She hadn't known the shots were celebratory noise. How could she? The sound tore her eardrums like they were made of paper. It was the world that seized anything beautiful, anything beloved or pure, and squashed out the hope. Mindy was the worst kind of friend, because she instigated without getting caught and used vulnerable girls like Trish as experiments, discarding them once they failed to excite. Like how Mindy taunted Trish over the phone. What if she had said suggested Trish run away in this violent cold, said, *You have to . . . ?*

Susan Jacobson answered on the first ring. In the background, the noise of kids being herded to bed. "Min says she saw her leave school at the usual time," said Susan. "I wouldn't worry. Trisha's a sensible girl. She's probably just conked out somewhere. Have you checked her bedroom?"

Fear pressing against Birdie's insides, she thanked unhelpful Susan and hung up. She knew it was senseless but couldn't help thinking of Diamond, how he'd seemed at first normal, then piece by piece became a monster. Had he guessed from something in Birdie's demeanor that she had a daughter waiting at home? Could he have divined her address, arrived before her in a smaller, faster car, taking a roundabout route? Couldn't someone like that do anything?

BESET BY FLOOD or rats depending on the season, the basement evoked feelings of biblical plague and trans-atlantic passage. Only the landlord went down there. As a little girl, Trisha believed a devil inhabited the hot water boiler and could not be convinced to so much as peek down the stairs. She would never have gone down voluntarily.

Descending, Birdie felt the shadows shudder. It was dark, so dark, and then, from a corner, frail light stuttered across the cement from a slender gap at floor level. The unfinished bathroom.

"Angel?" she breathed.

Through the door, the *shish-shish* of sharpening knives.

She gripped and turned the knob.

A flashlight leaned against the mirror, illuminating in jagged slices. At first, she saw two girls, two Trishas, grab-bing at their heads, pointing twin blades at their pitted, misshapen scalps.

The metal wings flashed. Scissors.

She meant to cry out, *No!* but her throat was blocked. At the moment, Trish turned, Birdie's flailing hand caught the scissors blade-first. With an odd relief, she felt her palm split and bloom.

TRISH'S HAIR WAS gone, all gone. Not *all* gone. Chunks of blond stuck out from a scalp like raw meat, pink blood shining from little nicks. She had been butchered.

"Let go, Mom! Please, I promise, it'll look better when I'm done."

Trish's pulse inside Birdie's grip as she dragged her up the creaking stairs, to the front door.

"Now," she was saying. "Now. I want you to see."

They stood side by side in the cold, their breaths making shapes that flew up and broke apart. The van shimmered whiter than the snow. She felt herself calming. "We leave tonight."

"I don't understand." Trish was crying. "What did I do?"

Yesterday, Birdie would have surrendered to the tear-tracks freezing on Trish's cheeks, but now, finally, she grasped what her mother had tried to tell her. How the devil seeped into people. Soldiers, strangers, but the beloved too. Even daughters.

"It's okay," said Birdie. "We will fix it."

"But I don't *want* to be fixed. I just want you to " Trish fell quiet as the rear doors swung open. Bits of masking tape and fishing line stuck to the walls, and a fresh gouge from one of the figurines ran the length of the counter, but already Birdie saw how it would go. They'd get a foldout couch, paint the walls a pale blue. Pencil in clouds. Soon they'd forget they'd lived anywhere else.

"What is it?" said Trish in a tiny voice. She sounded how she had on the first day of kindergarten. Uncertain, and needing her mother.

"This is home now." She said it gently, but she was telling, not asking.

Trish took a step back.

"Angel. My love."

Trish raised her scalped head, her round face. Somewhere, a sap-frozen tree went off like a gunshot. "No," Trish said, petal-soft. Then: "Bitch."

Something exploded inside Birdie. She reached to grab Trish, hold her to her. She needed to feel her heart. But Trish took another step and turned. Birdie's fingertips grazed the back of Trish's coat as she broke into a run.

Birdie ran after, sliding on the ice. She fell once and rose. Trish a blur in the snow, zigzagging past the other houses. Birdie's boots refused to grip. Her knee burned. She fell, and fell again. The last time, something crunched. She pushed up, ice grinding into her palms, but the pain in her knee dropped her back down.

Cold seeped under her coat and the blue air bit her cheeks. She felt odd, as if a part of her were floating out there, accompanying Trish from above. A mother cloud. Below, Trish, ink on snow. Below that, a muted thunder like echoing gunshots. They did that, she remembered. They echoed in the place they'd hurt, the invisible hole they'd ripped in you, in the sky. They ripped through the sky. But the sky was made of bleached rags. It didn't matter. *You couldn't tear what was not whole*, thought Birdie. If you tore a cloud that was your mother, it would reshape around the wound.

Dogs of America

In the back of the video store, Sly and I peer at our forgery: *AMERIPASS – 15 DAY* on flimsy paper in Greyhound's telltale font. *Travel restricted to US routes only.* The new expiration date wobbles on its cut-and-paste marks, but what bothers me is my legal name printed in bold block letters, official as a decree: *ANNA*, when in San Francisco I've always been Avi. Two years xeroxed out of existence.

You think I can still pass as a girl? I ask, though it's not what I mean.

Sure, says Sly. If you want to. She snips the pass into a ticket-shaped rectangle and smooths it onto the lamination sheet. She's behind the register in case a rare customer shows up, one of the few not bothered by dust-coated shelves and a new release section that's all made-for-TV movies. I wish someone, anyone, would barge in, and rip the pass from Sly's hands. Her boss. An FBI agent. Or Marion, Sly's girlfriend, come to apologize, saying I can keep crashing on their sofa, that I should be their houseboy. I offered to do it. Clean and cook, fix leaky things. Kill ants. And hell freezes, Marion laughed. Sly said, Aren't there more jobs in Michigan? I said, Sure, Michigan's famous for jobs. That's why everyone in California is always moving to Flint. Besides, it's January. Ice cream places must be hiring. Sly thinks I'm not putting myself out there, but she exists in an employment bracket reserved for nice blond girls. No matter how broke she gets, she'll always have a random job offer, a friend to crash with. No one would tell Sly to move back in with her mom.

I pull random videos from the shelf and stick them back in the wrong places. *Sleepless in Seattle* under horror. *Dumb and Dumber* into documentary. I try *Benji* in cult classics, suspense, and local interest. He pants back agreeably from each slot, wet-nosed heart on his sleeve.

It's five o'clock. The express bus leaves at seven. I hope I miss it.

Ta-da, says Sly, holding up the pass. It's as clean as machine-printed, if you ignore the crooked text and the ragged edges. I push my video across the counter.

How many do you think they used?

How many? she asks, puzzled.

Benjis, I say. Like, for *Milo & Otis* they offed a ton of kittens.

My mom sobbed so hard during the waterfall scene we had to leave the theater. She could tell Milo—many Milos—were drowning because the kitten's eyes changed color between shots. Imagine if that was you, she said out in the lobby, wiping her nose on a napkin.

Oh well, Sly shrugs. She's hardly seen any movies because her Pentecostal family considers Hollywood an abomination. She ran away from them on the legitimate Ameripass that we copied mine from, and which is about to ship me back to my mother and stepfather, freshly minted Jesus freaks themselves.

Ironic. Also: her idea.

Come on, Avi, she says. Presbyterians are minor league. Your parents love you.

We've been having this fight since I found out about them turning Christian. She thinks I'm a hypocrite because isn't female-to-male a kind of conversion? It's not, but I can't articulate how. For once, though, I resist the urge to argue.

You told them you're coming, right? says Sly.

Yeah, I lie. They're geeked.

She sticks the pass into my pocket, inspects me like I'm a kid on the first day of kindergarten. I almost expect her to ruffle my hair.

Call the second you get there, says Sly. If anything bad happens, call collect. She hesitates. Call even if it seems like nothing. Even in the middle of the night.

The fluorescent light quivers. I fail to suck back tears.

Snot-nosed, I say, What's minor league about Jews converting to a hegemonic religion?

Sly's hand drops. You'll be late, she says, handing me my duffel and backpack. She's tired of this fight, tired of my anger, my excuses. She's tired of how I move in circles, of my sleeping bag snail-curled on her living room floor, my empty bank account, the dumpstered bagels that are the only food I ever bring home. She's tired of me in general. We have that in common.

I don't want to go, I say.

Yeah, she says, which is not *stay*. She must feel guilty because she adds, Save up quick. When you come back, Marion and me will help you find a place.

Yeah, I say. I'll scoop ice cream like a demon.

That's the spirit.

The ocean wind smacks me as I cross the threshold. Sly steps out hugging herself. Here, she says. For food. Crushes cash into my glove.

The wind shears my cheeks. San Francisco purples.

Exit me, stage right.

THE GREYHOUND STATION is not actually gray but blue, minus a silver logo looking as banged up as the people waiting inside. I'm supposed to show my Ameripass and photo ID to a ticket agent, tell them East Lansing, Michigan, and request the route that goes through Portland. They'll input the serial numbers and hand me a ribbon of tickets.

Give them a *fake* serial number? I asked Sly. I pictured security guards billyclubbing my kidneys. Or, the ticket agent matching my cracking boy voice to the F, for Fucking Dead Tranny, on my license and calling the real cops.

You're charming, said Sly. Flirt. They'll believe you. I did it a bunch of times and never got caught.

I promised to follow her instructions, but Sly has Shirley Temple ringlets and still wears Lip Smackers. The cops would sooner sing her "Happy Birthday" than put handcuffs on her wrists. Marion is the one who told me I could show the pass to a bus driver directly. No tickets that way but it's safer, Marion said. Avi will get confused without tickets, snapped Sly, like I wasn't in the room. He'll miss his connections.

People push toward the bulletproof window, trade cash for tickets, and fan out toward numbered doors. Sly is probably right about me getting confused, but Marion is butch and Native and knows about cops. I clutch my Ameripass, turning like a weather vane from the ticket windows to the departing buses, not sure which orders to follow. Door 20 lines up and boards, then doors 9 and 14. Who knows where they're all going.

The ticket agents have identical pink manicures. Next! they call in an uncanny unison that makes my internal alarm system beep. I can't show my ticket to an agent. I'll pee my pants.

Door 6 Portland, fuzzes over the PA. Luggage-laden people flood toward door 6. I move into their stream. Marion's right. It's not that complicated. I'll show my ticket to the driver and sleep until Portland. After that it's only three days and two buses to Michigan. What is there to get confused about?

There's a delay at the doors, people grumbling. I see the obstacle: a shouldery terminal guard passing a plastic wand over the Portland passengers' arms and legs. A metal detector. Not intended for hitting but I bet it gets used that way. The guard looks up, gaze creeping over my baggy polo shirt and shapeless Carhartts. I pull the brim of my hat lower. At the opposite bank of doors, a driver last-calls Santa Fe. There's no guard for the Santa Fe bus. The handful passengers are being waved right through.

Hey you, says a voice behind me. Yeah, *you*. Threatening. My private alarm system wails and beeps. My sweat smells like wet dog. I turn slowly. A dreadlocked punk wrinkles his pierced brow, says, Can you please move forward?

IDs please, bellows the guard. He glances at me. At or toward. His skin paste-pale. Why do sun-deprived people all look like murderers?

The Santa Fe driver goes out door 3 and walks to her bus. I tear across the terminal, backpack banging, and hurl myself after. Santa Fe! I say, brandishing the Ameripass. The driver frowns. *Womp-womp-womp*, goes my alarm. Brain cells fling themselves off gray matter cliffs. Mayday, Captain, we've hit an iceberg!

You're supposed to have a ticket.

They said I could just show you the pass.

The driver cranes around to glare at the settling passengers, then back at the lit-up terminal. She grunts, If these fools don't care, why should I?

WHATEVER YOU DO, Sly said, go north, then east, not the other way around. Those desert buses take forever.

THE SANTA FE bus turns out to be headed south more than east. Away from Michigan. Fine by me. We stop in Modesto, Merced, Fresno, and at a gas station in the sun-abandoned desert. A new driver gets on and the passengers buy chicken McNuggets, even though it's midnight. Sly said the express route would take two and a half days. I calculate accordingly that *forever* will take at least four.

SLY HAS WRAPPED herself around me and we are rolling down a hill. She is trying to tell me something but I can't breathe. On every rotation, the ground slams us together.

I wake under the dimmed safety lights to the slam of the bus running over a fleet of armadillos, or another rock-like desert animal. Turtles. Engorged sand clams. Hunching, ossified coyotes. The ACE bandage binding my boobs has cut off my circulation and there's seat grit under my nails. I tell my body to sleep, but my alarm is going off again. *Womp-womp-womp-womp*. Sprinkler system and bail buckets, and ropes prematurely cut. Lifeboats bang into the ship. Fleeing women and children are dismembered by the ropes, bleed out in untimely death.

Everything in my life is fucked. And I still haven't called my parents.

WHO CARES IF it makes them happy? Sly once said about my parents' conversion.

YOU'RE HAPPY? I asked my mom.

You're oversimplifying, she said, the phone line crackling.

THE AIR-CONDITIONER blasts on in the night, even though it's desert-cold outside. One grandma keeps heading up front to complain, and the driver keeps saying, I guarantee, ma'am, the air is off.

I don't mind the cold; it gives me focus. I wrap a pair of sweatpants around my Carhartts and write in my journal, *This is a very cold bus,* which sounds good but leads nowhere. I wake up in Los Angeles to a runny nose and my gorilla-sized seatmate politely climbing over my legs. He says something in Spanish. In English he says, Breakfast break.

The rest of the bus unloads, except for a jittery guy in a plaid button-up who is talking to himself. If I get off, I'll have to show my pass to a new driver. My joints feel glued stiff from sitting but I stay put. Without bodies, the bus smells like a mudroom. Galoshes and crinkled up sport socks.

If the KO-reans and JEWS get inside my house, the guy in plaid mutters, we won't be having just a conversation, we'll be TALKING.

The new driver wants to see my pass anyway.

IN PHOENIX, WE lay over at a station with a food stand. The OPEN sign blinks seductively. I float inside before my brain's safety monitors can opinionate. I haven't eaten an actual meal since lunch at Sly's. We had homemade mac and cheese, my specialty, Sly's favorite. She said it was the best I'd made. We took turns sucking hot noodles and giggling. She sproinged my curls. I smelled her neck. I waited for her to say, *Screw Marion. You stay as long as you want, mister man.* She smelled like lavender.

I buy four pieces of pizza and a small Coke with free refills, jamming the change into my jeans. The refills turn out to be a bad idea. I do the pee-pee dance between the men's and women's rooms. Stocky guys stride into the men's in Wranglers and jackets. The women have fluffy heads and cleavage. I try to picture which side I most resemble. Flattened uniboob chest, hoodie, Chucks, and squeaky T-voice could go either way. The tricky part is my face. The silky quasi-mustache puts me solidly in the boy column, but my skin has this sickening glow, evidence that estrogen is winning. My kegel muscles pulse madly like if they can't make pee they'll make me cum instead. I choose the women's room and immediately wish I hadn't. Waiting ladies stare. A baby fluff-head tugs her mother's sleeve, says, That's a *boy*. I unzip my hoodie and thrust my uniboob out like a prize. In the toilet I pee until my vulva aches. Not you too, I tell it. Someone around here has to keep it together.

MOM AND GEORGE have a new number. I lose most of my change getting it wrong.

Hello? says a high voice. Brodie, George's son.

Tell my mom she was right, I could say. *I'm so broke and clueless my only friend kicked me out. I'm so pathetic I had to steal a bus ticket to get home.*

Hello? says Brodie. Is this a prank?

I could say, *Hey kid, this is your fuckup gender failure of a step-sibling, who by the way is still Jewish. Please put my clinically depressed, Second Coming–awaiting mother on the phone so she can express her lack of surprise.*

I hear you breathing, says Brodie. I'm going to hang up now. He sounds younger than he did last spring, which makes zero sense.

Misery is contagious, I could say.

MY BODY IS changing. It is undergoing a Greyhound-specific transition, molding itself to the shape of seats, retreating automatically from other passengers who pursue by way of flesh and spilling diaper bags and Discman cords. I am the troll of Greyhound Lines, Inc.

Correction: I am one Greyhound troll among multitudes. Exhausted people trickle out at local stops, yet the bus always feels the same amount full. Everyone onboard is greasy-haired and thick-tongued. Except the kids. Middle school–aged to a few years younger than me, they sit in the back and namedrop other teenagers, which makes them seem like classmates on an unchaperoned school trip. Then one gets off and another gets on and the newbie jumps in on the namedropping like every kid knows every other kid now. Like high school finished sucking and now you can have friends even if you're zitty and snaggletoothed. Except they aren't nice. Like all kids, they're brutal and barely contained.

At twenty-one, I look their age. Like a their-age freak, ripe for devouring. But I'm safe up front. I'm miles away, camouflaged by my seatmate, a gnome asleep with her chin on the bag of cotton balls she is hugging.

THE KIDS TROOP out at a gas station for Mountain Dew and candy bars. They troop back in, unpeeling Baby Ruths, talking with full mouths. A white, Black, and Asian trio— edgy, muscly, and plain big—stop at my row. Close enough to smell nougat. They look like a brochure for diverse Camp Kick-Your-Ass, enrollment status: open.

What's your name? says the Black kid, staring at a space next to my head. I glance where he's looking. Technicolor seat fuzz. He continues staring. Suicide bombers never make eye contact with their victims. Friendly dogs avoid other dogs' gazes, going for the butt-sniff instead. So, is he friendly dog or child soldier? *Womp-womp-womp.* Captain doesn't know, sir.

Avi, I whisper, chickenshit.

Sit down, yells the bus driver. Hilarious shrieks from the back. The boys swivel.

Suck it, sluts, calls the white boy. Girl laughter. The boys stomp joyfully down the aisle. The Asian boy, fast eater, tosses his empty wrapper over his shoulder. It lands on the gnome's shoe like a chocolate-smeared bow.

IN SANTA FE, I debark on quaky sailor legs into sunrise. A pink street where soft-cornered buildings drowse. *Adobe,* a word I must already know, runs down to my mouth and does a hip-wiggling dance there.

Adobe, adobe, adobe, adobe, oh do be. Oh don't be.

It's cold but I don't care. I rode a thousand or something miles for free. I'm a fucking champion.

AT A TAQUERIA decorated with paper circus girls and acrobatic poodles, I eat a breakfast burrito standing. Someone elbows in, body mashing mine with familiar heat and pressure. *Sly*, I almost say and catch myself. For a hopeful second I wonder who I know in Santa Fe.

Sheri G., says this girl, offering a sticky hand. But people call me Cherry Cheese. It's better for remembering.

Avi, I say automatically.

Like Chevy, she says. You know they went bankrupt.

Sheri G. wears a patch over her left eye. She flips it to the right. Talking to her feels like water going down a drain, fast and slow at once.

I've got this brain condition, she says. My eyes can't combine their pictures so if they're open together it makes me barf. Like with you. She bugs out her naked eye. Are you a he or a she or both?

The usual heat slinks up. Sheri G. cocks her head, flips her pirate patch. Her maraschino cherry bob is growing in black at the roots. Her brown skin is riddled with spray drops of white. She reminds me of dessert, or a cartoon character. Or a person in a dream.

I'm a wolverine, I tell her.

A mutant? she laughs, displaying sharp rodent teeth. That's funny. You're funny.

Wolverines are weasels, I say gravely. Rare ones.

Oh yeah, she smiles. Going extinct, I bet.

Habitat fragmentation. They keep getting kicked out.

Sheri G. twists her mouth, chewing avocado. Want to know why I can tell you're a girl? She stops chewing to smile. Her teeth line up in a pointy row. You're ugly.

I must have heard wrong.

Yeah, she says, happy, like she solved a tough equation. Only girls can look ugly. For guys, ugly is normal.

My reflection ripples in agreement from the salsa-smudged metal counter. Thirty-six hours of yuck coats my skin. I wish for a hole to hide in. And to punch Sheri's discolored face.

Got a bus to catch, I say.

Don't worry. She tails me to the door. My sister's a total dog. Guys go nuts for that. You know what I mean, she says. Humpety hump.

A COWBOY MISSING a thumb sells me a postcard featuring the different New Mexico flora. Unlike the roadside cactuses, these ones are festooned with blossoms so pink I can practically hear my mother call them tacky.

Dear Mom and George,
Good news! Left California. Due in to Michigan Sunday
morning. Can't wait to see you.
Love,
A.

At every word, ask myself, Is this what a normal person would write? Is this what Sly would say?

THIS IS *YOU*? asks the driver of the Oklahoma City bus, scrutinizing my license photo.

This is you? he says again, pointing to the line on the pass where Sly pasted my old name. The *A* in *Anna*, I realize, is lowercase. When he hands my license back, his thumbprint is outlined over my neck.

The bus is near-empty. I take the back row, the teen row. It's mine now. I am the teen.

DEAR SLY,

Bus roulette

(instructions for a game)

Object: *To reach Home**

Obstacles: *Uniboob, silkworm mustache, Greyhound cops, anxiety disorder*

Contents:

—1 fraudulent bus pass

—1 government-issued ID

—1 fifth grade US geography education

—Unlimited: senseless excuse about why you didn't visit the ticket counter to get a real ticket

—Natural charm (purchase separately)

Gameplay: *Play begins at any major Transfer Point ("Greyhound Station"). Using fifth grade US geography education, player must select a bus headed in the general direction of Home. Should player choose wrong bus, s/he must go back a corresponding number of spaces on the board. Player may opt to skip a turn and remain at the Transfer Point.*

Play ends when one of the following occurs: *player is arrested, player reaches Home, player forfeits the game*

*Home = a malleable destination, potentially non-geographic in nature, ref: "Home, where the heart is," home plate, homestyle, and "my home is in God"**

Embroidered on this lady's baseball cap. She's reading a pamphlet called 52 Uses for the White Space at the Back of Your Bible*

***Not really. But she should be.

Love,
Avi

MILITARY GUYS FILL up the back, boxing me into the corner. They talk about beer pong and a video game where you can tear off a bad guy's balls and feed them to a Doberman pinscher.

You need an unlock code, explains the kid beside me, mano a mano, conspiratorially. He leaks his thigh across my seat's frontier. In my peripheral vision, his Adam's apple bobs. My pulse too loud in my ears to hear whether he's breathing fast too. Buzzed hair and tucked camo, a code signaling claustrophobic male spaces where bodies grab bodies to the music of grunts and hard breaths like those now emerging from my mouth.

Our respective testosterones are smoke signaling each other, I'm sure. I'm pretty sure.

I say, Can you figure out the code by playing?

He chews loose a sickle of thumbnail. The Doberman stands out but in other respects the level's normal. He rubs the bitten nail across his own knee and I feel it along mine. He's tall and wide like a buffalo. He could crush me. Trans guys trade stories about this shit. Sucking cock in bus station bathrooms, flipping bio guys before they see your hard-on is pure silicone. They say no one notices, no one gets hurt. Those silicone dicks cost a hundred bucks, but I can do the first part. Push him against the wall, unzip him with my teeth.

I've never seen an erection up close before. How tricky
can it be? Guys are easy is what Sly says. She used to screw
for money. Sly also says: Steer clear of men. They're all
psycho.

The outside of the Clovis truck stop is painted to look
like a US flag.

Gonna take a whiz, says my army kid. Then, low, a
thrum that might not be words, might be my own hunger,
Coming? He marches ahead.

Dizzying racks of trucker products. King-size candy
bars, footlong subs preserved in plastic wrap, sunglasses
with polarized lenses. Bulk packs of ribbed condoms. Christian audiobooks. The men's room is on the left. Private
shower rooms on the right. For *showers*. Sure. My army guy
passes the subs, the king-size bars, the sunglasses. Nods to
me across the condoms. A super-alarm in my brain, boss
of all alarms. Throbbing white noise that blots out sound.
Sly is always telling me to want something. Choose, Avi,
she says. Quit hiding. My sneakers land where his boots
vacated. I'm the *Titanic* awaiting the iceberg. So horny I
could crack my own damn hull. Go right, I will him.

My army kid goes right.

FROM ACROSS THE rows of shelves, the military guys look
identical, baby faced and muscular, like brand-new guns.
They buy creme-filled snack cakes and tromp out through
the automatic doors. My army guy, having realized he
was stood up, has long since returned to the bus. The
other passengers have also migrated back to their sleep-
encrusted seats. Not me. If anyone sees me, they'll think
I'm praying, kneeling in front of an audiobook display
featuring angelic, airbrushed children whose ginormous
eyes are at risk for poke-out accidents. I'm ordering my

body to stand up, but my backpack weighs a million pounds and my knees stay stuck to the linoleum. Right pose, wrong place.

The PA system howls for remaining Oklahoma City passengers to reboard.

My duffel is under the bus, I tell my body.

There's no clean underwear in this backpack, I tell my body.

It's over, okay? I tell my body. *We're not having sex with anyone. I promise.*

The PA message repeats twice and then not again.

I drink Pepsi refills, mostly foam, in front of a grease-streaked window overlooking the diesel tanks and urinate in a porta potty. Single flakes of snow melt midair.

THE NEXT EASTBOUND Greyhound to arrive at the truck stop is full, but a lady says her toddler can sit on her lap. She's light as a feather, says the lady. Eats like a whale grows like a tadpole. Not an inkling where she gets *that* from. Traveling alone, hon? says the lady.

Yeah.

What do your parents think of that?

Don't know.

She shakes her head. The baby sways in time. No matter how bad things seem, running off isn't worth all *this.* She gestures around randomly—people slouched across their seats, the pencil-smear highway, the blue sky. You look like a smart young man, she says. Go back. Finish school. The world will be here.

You're right, I say. A high school diploma will open many doors.

Too cute for sarcasm, the lady smiles. She is living

proof that people figure this stuff out. They take their diplomas to cities and sign leases, earn paychecks, make friends. They get naked with fellow adults and enjoy it. They commit themselves to people who commit back. They stay instead of always leaving.

Sly says it's because I'm trans, but I know it's not. Trans guys figure out those things too. Everyone does.

Sandwich? Without waiting for an answer, the lady passes me American cheese on pillowy white bread. The cheese is melted into the mayo and the dairy mass is mushed into the bread. It's soft and good. My tired teeth barely press before it slides into me, cushioning my stomach with its chemical flavor. Outside is turning pink again, desert and stone. I guess we're nearly to Texas.

The baby sticks pinches of sandwich into its mouth. Kicks me with an inquisitive Nike. Weird they even make sneakers that small.

Getting out in Amarillo? I ask it.

Amarillo? says the lady, That's east, sugar pie. We're headed west. To Santa Fe.

RATON IS HUNGRY for a shootout: low roofs, red paint jobs, moon-glow hills climbing up around the city. Every place is a saloon.

Raton, New Mexico, or Raton, Colorado? I ask a man outside the transit center.

How you get so beautiful, beautiful? he says listing off his bench.

I pace outside the empty men's room until my bladder aches, then go pee in the dust behind a movie theater. The marquee advertises a double feature: *Osmosis Jones* and *Red Planet*. Cold stings my nether regions. It's Saturday evening. If I'd taken the Portland bus, I'd be in Illinois by now. I bet I'm only a day's drive from San Francisco. I bet anywhere is closer than Michigan. It seems possible I could travel indefinitely, living on peanut M&Ms and Pepsi and local fast foods, turning the same pair of underwear inside out every morning, injecting my biweekly testosterone in the rear bus potty.

Are you a complete idiot? says Sly, angrier than I've heard her.

I pump more quarters into the phone, whispering so she can't tell I'm crying. The wind gusts my face-holes dry. I tell her I'm having an awesome time. She rattles off names of dead transsexuals. Asphyxiated. Dismembered. Dragged behind a truck.

Sly says, That woman last year in Idaho. She didn't even look like a human being afterward. The EMTs left her corpse in the street! She says, Are you hearing me?

I say, I met this girl named Cherry Cheese. We're going to get married and move to Seattle. She told me I look like Dick Van Dyke. I think we'll be happy.

Call me back in ten, Sly orders. She hangs up before I can protest.

A woman shuffles over to the pay phone and asks for a cigarette. I fish in my bag, pretending. Sly got me to quit last summer when I went on hormones.

Sorry, I say, coming up with MUNI transfers and a lint-covered stick of gum.

I'll take the gum, she says. Pulls out a Diet Pepsi that she splashes over the stick. She wipes the last bits of fuzz off with a finger before popping it in her mouth.

We both like Pepsi, I say. It's something we have in common.

I just use this for cleaning, says the woman.

When I call back, Sly's calmed down. She tells me I can pick up my ticket tomorrow at the customer service desk in Kansas City. She had to put it on Marion's credit card. If I don't use it, she says she'll take the bus here and murder me herself.

Maybe I should feel patronized or ashamed, but I'm numb except for the tiny hope that maybe Sly will come find me. Is that a promise? I say.

There's a midnight bus from Raton to Kansas. You'll have to keep busy until then.

I say, Cherry Cheese, isn't that weird? Who would change their name to that?

Go home, Avi, says Sly. Fucking go home.

IT'S BLUE IN Colorado, a trembling, almost translucent cerulean and I get see-through outside with the smokers. In a ditch where the snow appears shallow but goes halfway up my shins, I pee the white into yellow. An elderly lady squats ten yards away. Her red coat folds around her making her look like a poisonous mushroom. The only reason I can tell she's peeing is her expression. Relief beamed up at the jagged mountains.

I'd rather go out here than in a gas station, she says.

I just use it for cleaning, I say.

I want to ask her if I look like a he or a she with my bare ass brushing on the snow, my labial folds forming ice sculptures. A patchy stubble is starting to show on my jawline. *Your three-day o'clock shadow*, Sly calls it, because that's how long the hairs take to poke out. This bus is rougher. Drunk dudes arguing through the night and more than one loud comment meant to be overheard. *Dog*, I got earlier. *Fag. She-male.* It makes me want to correct them: *Bulldagger. He-female.* They could at least hate me accurately.

I think for a second how if I get killed I won't have to go home.

If I get murdered, I want to be shot. In the back of the skull before I hear them coming. They can do what they want with my body after I'm dead.

WHY DOES MY internal alarm sound like the theft alert system at Tower Records? Down to the blinky orange light? The only thing I've ever stolen is wrong-size men's briefs that hung off my butt like a diaper. And why is my panic *Titanic*-themed?

THE PHONE RINGS a bunch before Brodie answers.

I say, It's, um, Avi. Your step . . . brother.

You sound weird, he says. Are you high on drugs?

I'm in Columbia, I say, Missouri. I don't take drugs.

Oh, he says. I thought you did.

You shouldn't either, I say.

I'm eleven, he says.

All the more reason.

Mom comes on the line sounding scared.

What's happened? she says.

Nothing. Did you get my postcard?

It said you were coming in this morning. Are you okay? Why did you leave California? Why didn't you call? We'd have bought you a plane ticket.

I thought you'd be excited.

And we are excited, Avi. But we want you home *safe*.

I can tell she's really upset because she starts retelling one of my aunt Ruth's knock-knock jokes.

Pineapple who? I ask. She's quiet. Mom, pineapple who?

Brodie has your old bedroom now, says Mom. We packed up the posters and books, we didn't look inside your journals—

You can throw them out. It's all crap.

—because we felt like we deserved a guest room, says Mom. But I was nervous to tell you.

Nervous why? I say. It feels like another knock-knock joke. Knock-knock, nervous. Nervous why? Nervous to see you! Knock-knock. Nervous why? Nervous to still be breathing! Knock-knock. Interrupting nervous! Knock-knock. Aren't you glad I didn't say nervous breakdown?

Is it a Jesus thing, though? I ask.

It's a guest room slash meditation space, says Mom. Meditation is nondenominational.

I bend the phone cable until I feel its links pulling apart.

My ten minutes are up, I say, like I'm in prison.

Believe me, she says. It's peaceful in there.

I BUY A pack of Benadryl, knock myself out until Indianapolis. Locked fences around gray factories and a group of dogs throwing themselves at each other in an alley. My dad used to call Indianapolis the most depressing city in the world. He hung himself in Ypsilanti, though, and he always said that was a sweet little town. Where else can you get cobbled streets and pasties without having to fly to Poland? he liked to say. Detroit, I'd reply, my coached response. He'd shoot back, But then we'd have to find parking!

They turned Brodie's bedroom into a chapel, I tell Sly.

You mean a church? she asks sleepily.

No, like in the airport, a neutral prayer room.

You sound angry, she says, how a therapist would. Nonviolent communication is all the rage in San Fran.

I'm fine, I say.

Good, she says. I want you fine.

Good, I say.

A high-pitched scream pierces our conversation. Stray dog, I explain. I don't mention that the dog is in a fight and that from up close it sounds like it's getting torn to pieces. A bunch of pitiful yips buried under sudden barks, mean low snarls.

Speaking of dogs, says Sly, Marion and I looked at puppies today. You can adopt these ones with disabilities.

What kind of disabilities? I ask. There's a long, miserable howl. The barks fall silent.

Anything that would make a shelter want to put them down. Missing eyes. Missing legs. Epilepsy. One Saint Bernard runs into walls for no reason. He's wicked cute even with the scars. You'd love him.

I try to imagine loving a dog who collided with walls hard enough to draw blood. How on edge you'd be, bracing for impact. Would Sly and Marion pad their furniture in a layer of foam? Would they carry the dog around like an infant? Amputate his legs for his own protection?

You should name him "Avi," I say. The operator is cutting in and Sly doesn't hear.

I love you, she shouts before it goes dead.

I try to imagine loving a dog like me.

FOR CRYING OUT loud, Avi, says my mother. We would have picked you up. She pronounces my name like she's been practicing its two syllables in the mirror and each one makes her separately sad.

Where's your luggage? asks George.

You're wet, says Brodie. I can't believe you walked from the station.

The shower stall shrunk since I left. It is the size of Clark Kent's phone booth and clogged with hair. Mom leads me to the meditation room, her fingers resting gingerly on my neck. It *is* peaceful. The furniture's been cleared out except for a brown bookcase, a Renaissance painting of Jesus crossing his fingers, and a photo of the late family poodle, Kitten. On the floor are three meditation pillows for Mom, George, and Brodie to get peaceful together.

Kinky.

Their energy ghosts vibrate the air with Christian thoughts about fishes from loaves, feet on water, the dead who start breathing again.

Mom hands me a stack of sheets and an air mattress folded into a cube.

Since when do you fold?

She shrugs. This leads to a sort of collapse, her face melting like icing. Does it hurt? she says, pointing at my throat, the megaphone of my proto-male squeak.

You need a crucifix, I say.

That's for Catholics, Anna, says Mom, through bulrushes of tears. She is small when she hugs me, a frail cage of bones. Or I, the son, have grown large. It is largeness now that will be expected.

A-vi, I say, each syllable sad on its own.

Listen to those dogs, I say.

How many do you think there are? asks my mom.

A lot. Maybe hundreds, I say.

Maybe millions, she says.

We think about that.

Outside, the trees look like bone cages lit with electric lights. Every dog on the block takes to howling.

Publication Notes

Certain Disasters. An earlier version of this story was published online under the title "Live Feed" in *Slush Pile Magazine*, issue 17, in July 2014.

A Full and Accurate Recounting. An earlier version of this story appeared online, under the title "The Invention of History," in *Midnight Breakfast*, issue 2, in July 2014.

End of the World Pussy. An earlier version of this story appeared, under the title "Destroyed Flowers Everywhere," in *Fourteen Hills*, issue 21.2, in 2015; and was reprinted online on *Writer's Bloc* in 2015.

Bad Things That Happen to Girls. This story originally appeared in digital and print issues of *Colorado Review* as the Nelligan Prize Winner, in November 2015; was performed by Meghan Pipe and broadcast on the *Colorado Review Podcast* in November 2015; and was published as a stand-alone ebook from Plympton in 2017 in the New York Public Library's SimplyE collection.

Dogs of America. An earlier version of this story appeared in *Crab Orchard Review* as the Jack Dyer Fiction Prize winner, issue 24.01, in 2019; and was excerpted as "Bus Roulette" in *Home Is Where You Queer Your Heart* in 2021, which was edited by Miah Jeffra, Arisa White, and Monique Mero-Williams, and published in San Francisco by Foglifter Press.

Acknowledgments

The writing of this book spanned eleven years. During that period, I finished two degrees, lived in seven cities, belonged to five great writers' groups, was a student in and teacher of countless workshops, got cancer and had it (fingers crossed) cured, experienced the arc of a really huge love, and was buoyed throughout by some pretty awesome human beings I am fortunate to call friends. It would be silly to imagine I—a person of terrible memory—would succeed at naming everyone who made this book happen. Consider this, instead, a highlight reel:

Adam Schear, my dream agent, and his crew at DeFiore.

Lauren Rosemary Hook, an editor in whose hands I am so grateful for my feral little manuscript to have landed, and the inspiring Feminist Press team: Jisu Kim, Drew Stevens, Nadine Santoro, Margot Atwell, copyeditor Veronica Esposito, and everyone else behind the scenes.

Juana Silva Puerta, who fixed my Rulfo translation in about a second.

The institutions, publishers, editors, contest judges, scholarship funders, program directors, and publishing industry professionals who held open the heavy doors: AROHO, SLS - Lithuania, Tin House, 360 Xochi Quetzal, the SFSU CW department, Lance Cleland, India Downes-Le Guin, Molly Howes, Rebecca Rubinstein, Taylor Pavlik, Stephanie G'Schwind, Lauren Groff, Rachel Branwen, Miah Jeffra, Soumeya Roberts, Esther Patterson, Jacob M. Appel, Kirstin Valdez Quade, Jess deCourcy Hinds, and my fellow Binders subgroup members for morale and insider scoops. Authors whose work I turned to often for example and inspiration: Julio Cortázar, David Wojnarowicz, Pedro Lemebel, Virgilio Piñera, Suzan-Lori Parks, Lorrie Moore, Etgar Keret, ZZ Packer, Andrea Long Chu, Nafissa Thompson-Spires, Nick Cave (the *Soundsuits* one), Sara Jaffe, Kayla Rae Whitaker, Salman Rushdie, Taffy Brodesser-Akner, Lisa Locascio, Leslie Pietrzyk, Megan Giddings, Howard Jacobson, Jade Chang, Daniel M. Lavery, Kevin Wilson, Danzy Senna, Jenny Zhang, Miranda July, E.L. Doctorow, George Saunders, Cristina Peri Rossi, Morgan Parker, the Coen Bros, Lynda Barry, Donald Barthelme, Pablo Neruda, Michelle Tea, Patrick Nathan, Nafkote Tamirat, Percival Everett, Tony Kushner, Jonathan Lethem, Hannah Tinti, Jeanette Winterson, Jean Kyoung Frazier, Jen Silverman, Elvia Wilk, Patricia Lockwood, Nona Caspers, and, obvs, Juan Rulfo. Also, Migueltzinta Solís, whose style, ideas, editorial input, artwork, essays, and stories are embedded in this collection's DNA and my own.

The teachers who supported my development as a writer, reader, and person: Matthew Kelly, Alice Nelson, Marilyn Frasca, Leticia Nieto, Janet Fitch, Marian Palaia, Jenn Berney, Alice B. Fogel, Cristina Rivera Garza, Michelle Carter, ZZ Packer, Matthew Clark Davison, and

Toni Mirosevich; above all, Nona Caspers, craft sage and fiction priestess.

The peers who pored over drafts of these stories, some at the eleventh hour, with as much care as if the project was their own: Julián Delgado Lopera, Stephanie Doeing-Nicoletti, Randall Jong, Nancy Au, Carson Ash Beker, Marco Antonio Huerta, Majo Delgadillo, Temim Fruchter, Laura Laing, Jenn Audette, Molly Gallentine, Mary Greenshields and Rebecca Novack. Special thanks to Steve Wilson for helping me with legalese, Maia Ipp for Yiddish help and Ashkenazi history gut-checking, Reena Shah for line editing me off the edge during final revisions, Helen Connolly who is truly a typo bloodhound and an eleventh-hour hero, and Lauren O'Neal—as good a friend as she is a skillful copyeditor which is saying a lot.

More friends: J, LJ, Brittany and Pati, Julia F, Laurel S, Kim M, Harley, Helen O, Jona, Devon, Heather Graham (the one and only), Nicole H and Joanne P (martyrs and heroes), the rest of my LPLW peeps, Queer Cancer Happy Hour (esp. Leah M for the invitation!), and many I am forgetting at this moment but who are surely in my heart.

Queer fam: Jac, Kate S (plus Walnutte, Igor, and several late birds), Tara R, Ducky, and Ezra.

The outlaws: Norma Alicia for inspiration, wisdom, and trouble-making; Nuwati, mostly for the latter.

The family fam, who never doubted there would be a book, esp.: Jesse and Kat and Sheryl, Leah and Ben and Elliot, Rick and Lisa, Dee and Sharon and Matt, Cynthia, Leah G.

Judy F, who got me through the final edits—my one and only wacky aunt.

Marcia, who got the subtext.

Pickle and Bacon, who are dogs, and perfect.

My students, who remind me again and again why to write and how to love fiction.

My astrology clients who enlarge my perspective by sharing theirs.

The brilliant and compassionate doctors who held my life like it mattered: Drs. Glaze, Karpakis, Daley, Saad, Novick, and Haner.

Finally, Tzinta. Without you, to quote Jay-Z: "No book." Not this one anyway. I hope the jokes still make you laugh.

Amethyst Editions
at the Feminist Press

Amethyst Editions is a modern, queer
imprint founded by Michelle Tea

**Against Memoir: Complaints,
Confessions & Criticisms**
by Michelle Tea

Black Wave by Michelle Tea

Fiebre Tropical by Julián Delgado Lopera

Margaret and the Mystery of the Missing Body
by Megan Milks

The Not Wives by Carley Moore

**Original Plumbing: The Best of Ten Years
of Trans Male Culture**
edited by Amos Mac and Rocco Kayiatos

Panpocalypse by Carley Moore

Since I Laid My Burden Down by Brontez Purnell

Skye Papers by Jamika Ajalon

The Summer of Dead Birds by Ali Liebegott

We Were Witches by Ariel Gore

amethyst editions

The Feminist Press publishes books that ignite movements and social transformation. Celebrating our legacy, we lift up insurgent and marginalized voices from around the world to build a more just future.

See our complete list of books at
feministpress.org

THE FEMINIST PRESS
AT THE CITY UNIVERSITY OF NEW YORK
FEMINISTPRESS.ORG